Sins of the Raven

For information, contact: henrygraypub2022@gmail.com

Publisher's Cataloging-in-Publication Data

Names: Kobrin, Steven, 1971—.
Title: Sins of the raven / Steven Kobrin.
Description: Granada Hills, CA : Henry Gray Publishing, 2025. | Series: The man from Belize ; book 2. |
Identifiers: LCCN 2025922691 | ISBN 9781960415592 (pbk.) | ISBN 9781960415608 (hbk) | ISBN 9781960415615 (ebook.)
Subjects: LCSH: Assassins -- Fiction. | Mercenaries -- Fiction. | Spies -- Fiction. | Surgeons -- Fiction. | New Orleans, Louisiana -- Fiction. | Vail, Colorado -- Fiction. | Khangai (Khanghai) Mountains, Central Mongolia -- Fiction. | Barcelona, Spain -- Fiction.
BISAC: FICTION / Action & Adventure. | FICTION / Thrillers / Espionage. | FICTION / Thrillers / Suspense.
Classification: LCC PS3611.O53 S56 2025 | DDC 813/.6—dc23
LC record available at https://lccn.loc.gov/2025922691

Library of Congress Control Number: 2025922691

Cover illustration by Bruce Scivally, © 2025 Bruce Scivally.

Made in the United States of America.

Published by Henry Gray Publishing, 17020 Chatsworth Blvd. #1125, Granada Hills, California 91394.

For more information or to join our mailing list,

visit HenryGrayPublishing.com

Sins of the Raven

Steven Kobrin

HENRY GRAY
HG
PUBLISHING

Granada Hills, CA
"Select books for selective readers"

1

THE NORTH ATLANTIC OCEAN

Approximately 600 miles east of North Carolina, basking in the moonlit night, a gorgeously embellished yacht floated quietly in the tranquil seas. The Blue Princess was adorned on the outside with more gold and platinum than a Tiffany jewelry store. Designed and constructed with the utmost care and polish, this was truly one of the crown emeralds of the sea, garish to the extreme but built with precision care and craftsmanship. She basked peacefully in relative peace fairly adjacent to the principal island of Bermuda.

Inside the yacht, there were elegantly designed bedrooms and play centers to be certain, but this was no ordinary evening— it was pumping with music and adrenaline inside the central living room, almost as if it was the gala opening of a high-end nightclub.

Rhett Palmer, 38, was a trust fund kid like no other. He lived for the moment, and this was certainly one of them. Boyishly charming and handsome, his parents bestowed upon him a 200 million dollar-plus fortune, as his father, Scott, was one of the most successful hoteliers in the U.S. They sadly met with a tragic fate a few years back, victims of an unforeseen plane crash.

Their only child, Rhett, now lived life to the fullest, and he cared only about the present. The future meant nothing because in his eyes he had all the money in the world, far too much to spend in a single lifetime. And this jaunt to the island of Bermuda was no fluke. He was in good company, celebrating a special occasion... the 40th birthday of his best friend, Mitch Bergman.

There were six of them. Three couples. The men and their girlfriends. Scattered and spatially distant from one another in this most ample of rumpus rooms. Only on this occasion it was more of a romping room as the three couples in question were in the throes of some serious bacchanal-type debauchery. It was an orgy of sorts, and they were going at it in every way conceivable.

In one corner of the room, Perry Tyson, 39, was seated in a salmon colored lounge chair as his girlfriend, Tisa Quinnell, 35, ace corporate attorney, was frenetically going down on him. They were both workout fanatics, graced with lithe, elegant bodies which were currently in the midst of a level 10 workout. Perry and Tisa were no strangers to heated encounters, and they loved the idea of going at it wherever and whenever possible.

Mitch, the birthday boy, was nude and kneeling at the center of the room. Proudly erect and positioned in the middle of a beige shag carpet the size of a small swimming pool, he was performing some impassioned cunnilingus on Jami Gibb, 37, owner of a chain of high-end clothing stores. She was seated on a plush, U-shaped lime green sofa. It was a mystery what Mitch did for a living. He had swarthy, dark good looks and the type of penetrating green eyes one could swim in for days. He was always at Rhett's beck and call, and they had been friends since childhood. That seemed to be his way of keeping in good stead with the so-called elitists—being a hanger-on. Jami was a whip-smart half Latina bombshell, who simply lived for the moment, and this was undoubtedly one of them.

And then there was the owner of this sexually charged floating fuckhouse... Rhett. He and his girlfriend, Cynthia Tommani, were engaged to be married. She was 40 and coming off the heels of a failed first marriage. Passionately in love, they were delighted to be hosting this special occasion with some of their closest friends. They were at the opposite end of the rumpus room, completely nude, fucking each other feverishly by the bar. Rhett had her firmly against the mirrored wall, her tanned legs wrapped tightly around his buttocks, which were pulsating ardently.

The smell of tawdry sex wafted in the air like an ocean-caressed mist. All six of them were going at it with their partners at full swing, and the moans were perpetual, low and guttural. These pleasure seekers were at the heights of ecstasy, the Mount Everest of carnal bliss when suddenly...

A hard pounding slammed against the side of the Blue Princess, adjacent to the walkway by the rumpus room. Just outside the windows. It was as if someone had landed on the yacht. Trampling feet began to scurry along the outside, and it snapped Mitch out of his state of sexual frenzy.

"What the fuck is going on?" he asked.

Looking over at Rhett, who was firmly entrenched with Cynthia, he was swiftly concerned that no one else seemed to be reacting at the sudden interruption outside the watercraft. "Rhett!" Mitch said louder.

Mitch quickly paused his thrusting to address his friend and the slowly accelerating pace of the strange sounds, which were now emanating from above them.

"I know. I just heard it," responded Rhett.

Rhett and Mitch looked over at one another. Cynthia and Jami quickly pulled away from their lovers and put on their scanty beach wear. The sounds from above were now like firm footsteps on the deck above them. The quartet now pivoted their attention to Tisa and Perry. Ironically, they were the first to react to the disruption and were both completely distressed.

"Is there an incoming storm we didn't know about?" asked Tisa.

"I don't hear any winds," said Perry.

"No, there's nothing in the forecast. It's supposed to be smooth sailing for the next three days," responded Rhett.

The upward facing footsteps were now more spaced out. Deliberate and marked. This was no weather anomaly, and they all knew it. The group looked visibly distraught.

"We might have an unexpected guest," said Jami.

They all looked at one another, acknowledging that very distinct possibility. Rhett exchanged glances with Mitch, who nodded in the affirmative, saying, "I'll check it out. Give me a piece."

Rhett reached beneath the bar, pulling out a 9MM Beretta 92SB. He checked the magazine. Registered a full clip. Loaded and cocked it, then handed it over to Mitch.

"Watch your six," said Rhett, looking ruefully at his best friend.

"Always," responded Mitch.

The other five moved close to one another, gathering as a group at the center of the rumpus room, seating themselves across the entire sofa. As Mitch approached the door to step outside, he took one last look over at his lovely companion, Jami. He winked at her and managed a slightly nervous smile. Jami closed her eyes and nodded. The quintet of friends stayed close, holding one another, as Mitch stepped outside, his own footsteps making their way across the side deck.

Mitch clearly handled the pistol as if he had familiarity with guns, the 9MM aimed and positioned in front of him. He came from a military family so the likelihood that weaponry and shooting were a staple of the Bergman household was highly likely. He noticed that the winds were picking up. A slight drizzle began to fall like warm summer rain. Checking all corners carefully as he kept the Beretta closely pointed out, he approached the ladder leading up to the sky cabin, or top level of the yacht. There was an incessant creaking following each and every footstep he took as he ascended the stairs. Once at the peak of the vessel, he quickly jumped with a catlike stealth to the ground of the highest floor and whipped all the way around, gun pointed, looking for the glimmer of a presence of some sort. It seemed like someone had to have been there because the steps everyone heard were undeniably human in their pronouncement.

And yet, carefully surveying the entire perimeter, what struck Mitch as being the most peculiar element of it all was what he actually found... nothing. There was no one and absolutely nothing out of the ordinary on or around the surrounding area of the upper deck, simply the swaying sounds of the deck ornaments, arranged with various flags and aquatic gear for diving and exploring. The proverbial coast was clear. And so it stood to reason that Mitch could exhale a well-deserved sigh of relief. He lowered the gun, swaying it by his side and turned all the way around only to be greeted by something unexpectedly savage.

Too fast to even release a cry of distress or an anguished scream, the whooshing sound of the blade of a hand-held ax descended with blunt power right into the base of Mitch's skull, cleaving it completely in two. The hand behind the ax was strong. Rubber, form-fitting black gloves adorned the hands of this unseen killer as he reached for the ax, pulling it out of Mitch's mangled skull. The glistening pulp of flesh and bone scattered across the deck as the finishing death stroke came down as fast as it was undeniably furious.

Below the scene of carnage, in the rumpus room, the five friends nervously awaited the return of Mitch Bergman. Rhett looked over at the other four, posing a question informed by sheer nerves and unrestrained anxiety.

"Anyone want a drink?"

And in that moment, the sliding door behind them was thrust open. They turned around, looking at first into a void of sheer blackness. The night sky was unforgivably dark that evening, and then the piercing sound of Cynthia's scream echoed across the room and the evening skies when she noticed something that terrified her to her very core.

The unseen killer tossed Mitch's severed head into the rumpus room, bloodied and lifeless. It rolled across the polished wood floor like a soccer ball reaching the goal post as it clinked against one of the platinum poles standing at the center of the spacious area. In that instant, the five remaining passengers scattered. Cynthia and Jami rose from the sofa screaming. As quickly as they stood up, the life was taken from them as the masked killer responded with yet another finishing deathblow. This was no ordinary assailant. Clearly, this was a professional. Wearing beneath a tight mask what appeared to be something resembling ski goggles, the killer unsheathed two curved blades and threw them with a swiftness and accuracy that was unforgivably lethal. Finding their marks instantly, each knife penetrated the bodies of Cynthia and Jami. Cynthia's blade penetrated the base of her skull as it shot into the socket of her eye. Jami's blade went right into her forehead, killing her instantly. Both women struggled momentarily and gradually hit the floor, exhaling their final breaths as they landed. Rhett pulled another gun out from behind the bar. He began to fire, but this assassin moved with the speed of a panther and the stealth of a phantom—all he did was shatter the surrounding furniture and mirrors aligning the entire rumpus room.

Panting and flustered, Tisa tried to unlock the central door connecting the rumpus room to the main cabins, to no avail. The shining edge of a compact scythe connected with the edge of her throat, slitting it from one end to the other. She bled out quickly as her body slumped and crashed lifelessly to the ground.

Rhett, Perry, and the unidentified killer were all who remained. Rhett walked cautiously around the massive room, his pistol cocked and drawn, while Perry anxiously tried to get a signal on his cell phone to make an outbound call. Then, like an unforeseen bolt of lightning crackling through the sky, it happened... A whizzing arrow flew through the air, fired from a deadly crossbow pistol at the hand of the mysterious assassin. With its unforgiving spiked tip, it pierced Perry's throat, pinning him against the wall like a human statue. His eyes widened, terrified, until they slowly but inevitably closed forever. Now all that remained were the killer and Rhett, who heard the shuffling of a few catlike footsteps to the side of him near the sliding door. He fired six more shots from the fully-loaded 15 round magazine, merely tearing his inner sanctum to even greater shreds. The detritus of glass, wood, and metal rained throughout the once glorious rumpus room. His efforts were finally stifled with the resounding echo of the clicking of the empty Beretta. Throwing it across the room, he could only scream in desperate resignation.

"Who are you?" he yelled at the top of his lungs.

And the moment he turned, the iron grip of the black-gloved hand braced the curve of his throat. The unseen killer had hands of steel as the bones cracked. With the final remnants of strength at his disposal, Rhett attempted to unmask the killer, which was met with the finishing blow—the killer pushed away his feeble grip and with both of his hands snapped Rhett's neck like a dangling twig.

Rhett's body was thrown across the length of the room like a heaping rag doll. This mysterious death dealer had immense physical strength and the skills of a high-end professional. Killing was this person's business, and the Blue Princess had something very valuable hiding somewhere within the confines of its wide berth. The killer looked all around the room surveying the carnage of the corpses who had fallen prey to the lethal touch of an unseen assailant. And then the predator went to work, tearing out drawers and throwing the papers and personal effects of each and every cabinet all over the floor. The rumpus room turned into an absolute mess within seconds. There was soft rock emanating throughout the room, creating an even more ironic sense of fate for these doomed travelers. The killer unfolded a curved blade with a serrated edge, sheathed in the knee brace of the pants. Swiftly, pillows and cushions were ripped to shreds as feathers flew throughout the room like Mardi Gras confetti. And then, as if frozen into submission by some sudden revelation, the assassin stopped. He was clearly a very powerful man, standing well over six feet tall with a lean, muscular build. The sinew of his legs and arms could be seen shaping the outline of his form-fitting black suit. The face was still covered by the mask and the flyer's goggles. Slowly, he began to approach the wall that was adjacent to the bar. There was a gold rimmed clock hanging at the center of it just behind the bar. The killer laid his hands on the clock and lifted it very gently. It clicked itself off the wall revealing a short lever to the right of the nail which held the clock in place, protruding ever so slightly from the wall. The assassin turned the handle of the lever and then it happened...

A small square-shaped portion of the wall, just beneath where the clock was hanging, began to extend and move forward. There was a small incision-sized space between the piece of wall that came out. The killer opened it. The safe, as it were, was embedded within the space in the wall. And then he saw what he was looking for...

There were jewels inside this seemingly invisible wall safe, and stacks of foreign currency. But the real prize was a leather satchel containing legal documents. He removed them and began to examine the papers closely. The stack of sheets had a title page at the beginning. And as the killer looked at it, he nodded affirmatively, confirming that he had what he was looking for. This was his reason for being there. And the people on board, including Rhett, were unfortunate casualties of a mission that had absolutely nothing to do with them. The title page of the documents said, "OPERATION: BEECH GROVE."

Rhett Palmer was the current owner of the Blue Princess. But this exceptionally well-endowed sea craft was gifted to him by his father, Wade Palmer. Wade had been a covert operative for the global organization known as The Sandbox. Tied to corporate affairs as much as they were involved with international assassination plots, they operated on the right side of the law... most of the time. Palmer was in possession of trade secrets. Secrets that he knew were better left unrevealed. They needed to remain hidden, for they possessed vital information which could threaten the safety and sanctity of the free world. But Wade Palmer's moral compass outweighed the virtues of membership in the Sandbox.

He was willing to die to do the right thing, and that is precisely
what happened. He and his wife, Lorraine, had been suddenly
eliminated in an unforeseeable accident, which turned rather
dubiously into an open and shut case. No questions asked.

After they died, Rhett Palmer, their only son, became the
sole heir and recipient of an enormous family fortune. So the
circumstances of Rhett's death at the hands of this nameless,
faceless hitman were layered with as much irrefutable tragedy
as they were with indisputable irony. The satchel containing the
documents for OPERATION: BEECH GROVE represented the
leavings and the detritus of Wade Palmer's former life. And now,
his only son, Rhett, along with five of his closest friends, were all
dead because of it.

The killer strode back to the top level of the Blue Princess.
There was a duffel bag on the floor next to him. He unzipped
it and placed the satchel containing the top-secret documents
inside. He zipped it back closed, sealing its safety with a small lock
that fit firmly inside the handle of the zipper. Finally, he removed
the mask and the glasses, setting them down on the chair beside
him. He had long, shoulder length black hair which cascaded
downward to the back of his neck, barely caressing the top of his
back. His face remained unseen. He grabbed his thick, mane of
dark hair creating a ponytail and tied it with a piece of cloth cord,
similar to a shoelace. As the tail fell softly at the back of his neck,
he moved it slightly revealing a most ominous sight...

There was a homing device with a red blinking light grafted
to the back of his neck. He gently pressed an invisible button on it.
This switched the light from a flickering red to a steady shade of
lime green. He appeared to be sending a signal to an unseen party
who would be there to collect him momentarily. His mission was

accomplished. The skies began to crackle with the bellowing sounds of distant thunder. The occasional bolt of lightning shimmered through the clear, night sky. A light summer storm was brewing over the horizon. And sure enough, within minutes, the noise of an incoming aircraft beckoned in the distance, approaching the Blue Princess from the skies above. They had arrived to pick up their precious cargo.

2

TIKAL, GUATEMALA

For centuries, the jungles of Tikal, Guatemala, have housed some of the most magnificent ruins in the entire world, representing one of the largest archaeological sites of the pre-Columbian Maya civilization. These ruins are delicately nestled throughout a lush jungle environment containing everything from temples, pyramids, and public squares to ball courts.

Tikal was always a dominant political, military, and economic center for the Maya. With over 3,000 structures spread across six square miles within a larger national park of 220 square miles, it was also among the largest Maya cities. That the ruins were so firmly entrenched within the tapestry of the rainforest simply added to their overall mystique and sense of discovery. And although modern visitors could most certainly climb some of the most renowned temples such as the Lost World Pyramid and enjoy unparalleled panoramic views of the jungle, there was something vaguely sinister in our modern age about these natural earthbound surroundings. They were more than just regions designed for ripe exploration... These were killing grounds just waiting for the next victim to join its legion of spirits of the dead.

Kent Stirling was dressed in camouflage fatigues. He ran with a grace and stealth instantly denoting his singular athleticism. Making his way across the vast terrain of this tropical paradise, he flinched slightly as a silenced bullet whizzed closely next to his ear, splintering off fragments of the large oak tree just north of him. His run became more of a charged sprint as he headed for the cluster of greenery just ahead. Following several feet behind were half a dozen of the most well-trained assassins money could buy. They were guerilla-equipped mercenaries., soldiers of fortune who lent their services to the highest bidder. Stirling had enemies all across the globe, hired by one of his most sadistic rivals... the Sandbox. This team was playing for keeps, and they had no intentions of leaving this jungle until Stirling was eliminated for good.

Three men and two women. All of them equally lethal and armed with a densely furnished array of weaponry. The first soldier approached the cluster of bushes where Stirling had turned the corner. He communicated to the others with a series of hand signals that they should separate and keep a sharp lookout on all corners. They knew Stirling was no ordinary target. Even at half-speed, he was the best in the business. The leader, the one who gave the other four their marching orders, had his pistol drawn. A 9MM Glock with an extended silencer. As he quickly turned the corner of the bush formation, finding nothing, he grabbed his neck as a dart laced with toxic chemicals penetrated it. Stirling had released it from a carefully designed blowgun. The leader fell to the ground dead. Lowering the blowgun away from his lips, Stirling turned the corner and disappeared once again into the haze of forest green.

One of the women was paired with another of the male assassins. They had their MAC-10 machine pistols fully loaded and ready to be dispersed. Rustling sounds moved the dense foliage just east of their direction. They cut loose with a decimating spray of 9MM gunfire from their MAC-10's. Confident that the sounds of Stirling were their calling card, they both approached the vicinity of their discharged shots only to find... nothing. And then, they both met their maker. Perched like a gallant hunter on the large arm of an oak tree just northwest of their location, Stirling took aim and unleashed two perfectly aimed bullets to their heads from an UZI 9MM with an extended, silenced scope and laser sighting. He moved the weapon swiftly from his eye, strapping it across his shoulder as he made his way down and gracefully escaped into the thicket of forest ahead. The two enemy agents hit the ground like stones. Killed instantly. And then there were two.

The last man standing was tall and lithe, his slender frame topped by a coarse head of dark, glistening hair. The beads of sweat trickled into his eyes as he brushed the dampness from his brow. This was nerves and adrenaline at their absolute apex. Not knowing what could be waiting around every corner was nerve-wracking, but this assassin was prepared and more than a little pompous. His walk began to slow to a crawl as he approached a strangely gnarled-looking tree. Branches were sharp and protruding. The tree just seemed like an anomaly amidst all the lushly imbued, powerful oak trees. This tree was almost barren with shavings of green sprinkled here and there. Now, the lone assassin was entranced, looking at the odd formations of the branches before him. One in particular looked a little smoother, though. Not as brown and not as rough. As he extended his hand to try and pull it off, he didn't even have time to flinch as in the blink of an eye, Stirling had removed the presumed branch from its attachment. This was actually a cleverly disguised garotte, and he pulled it with such speed and precision that it looped over the assassin's neck before he even had time to react. The razor-sharp wiring cut through the soft flesh of his neck, killing him gradually but mercilessly. Stirling dropped the man's body then wrapped the sleek weapon back up and concealed it in one of the pants pockets draped across his leg.

The final female assassin in the group was now the sole survivor, and she was nowhere to be found. Stirling knew there were five from the outset, and was certain she had taken the high ground. Perhaps she had him in her sights, tracking him from a slightly elevated place just as he had done with her two colleagues who fell prey to his silenced bullets. He was a skilled sweeper, and he knew this terrain was treacherous for all of them because they weren't as skilled at topographical analysis as he was. His stealth was born from education and experience. Stirling was simply in a league of his own. His 9MM Beretta 92SB was drawn.

He slowly connected the silencer to the end of the barrel. His eyes were drawn skyward, though he occasionally looked down at the ground before him. Never losing track of his immediate surroundings and constantly maintaining focus of his final target, Stirling stood with his feet planted firmly on a slightly curved bit of earth. Fallen leaves, broken twigs and rainbow-colored flora dressed the ground surrounding his boots. He looked at his boots closely, and the unexpected suddenly took form as a hand-held scythe swiftly emerged from the ground below, stabbing his femoral artery. It was a fatal blow, with the unseen woman's hand slicing upward, insuring the maximum degree of bleeding and damage

She was skilled. Hiding herself in the heaping pile of earth and greenery. Perfectly blended with her surroundings. Stirling grew pale by the second as every breath he took caused blood from the thigh area to spurt like a small fountain. He was finished, and yet, thought the assassin, how could that possibly be?

He lay before her eyes, now resting his head on the sturdy oak tree just behind him. And in that moment, she dealt the finishing blow, slicing with her handheld scythe across Stirling's throat. It was the death stroke, and she was its dealer. He had encountered skilled professionals in the game of death all across the world over the course of decades laying waste to each and every one of them. Yet this was his time, and he'd finally met his maker in the most unexpected of places... the jungles of Tikal, Guatemala.

Or had he? She knew her antagonist was formidable, trained in the art of killing and self-defense. Versatile with edged weapons and firearms. Knowledgeable with the immediate terrain and how to use it to his advantage. But she was also increasingly aware of something else. This was not Stirling.

As she nodded in recognition of her kill, she reached down at the opening where her scythe had cut across his throat and pulled violently upwards, removing a perfectly engineered mask that had the face and features of Dr. Kent Stirling, former operative of the Sandbox. This wasn't him. The face before her was that of Luis Delloplane, a half French, half Latino contract killer, who also trained legions of underworld assassins. He had met his match, and this was his final day on Earth. And in that moment, the Earth beneath Luis and the female assassin suddenly began to move away revealing a much more deceptive sense of surrounding and design. This hadn't actually happened. This was a training film. It was an image on a wall, and it slowly became covered by a sheet-like screen descending from the ceiling above.

This was the conference room / lair of one of the rogue cells representing the global criminal syndicate known as the Sandbox.

They had just finished watching captured footage on the ways of killing. Specifically how to go about eliminating the one mark who continued to pose a threat to the Sandbox and their nefarious schemes just by virtue of his continued existence... Kent Stirling.

The room itself was spacious and sparsely but elegantly adorned with pieces of furniture from all around the world. Very expensive taste was clearly on display, and the sultry, seductive voice of a woman echoed throughout the room as she began to address the surrounding six individuals, one of whom was seated before her desk. The five others stood symmetrically at various points in the room. Tough, ornery looking men from different parts of the world. She was seated in a swiveling chair, looking away from her group, facing the wall where the film had been projecting.

The man seated before her at the opposite end of the glass desk was Damon Chambers, 35, a cold-blooded killer with no remorse. He was also Harvard educated, an intellectual with a propensity for evil because power was his ultimate aphrodisiac. His close-cropped hair accentuated striking features that denoted the potential for having been a male model. He easily could have been. So when this stunning exterior was coupled with keen, calculating intellect, the combination was positively deadly. Thus, he was primed to be one of the movers and shakers ready, willing, and able to take over the world. Or at least, to try...

The five men stationed at various portions of the conference room were Damon's personal quintet of killers, each of them skilled marksmen and expertly trained in martial arts. Damon himself was a Jujitsu master and took his martial arts abilities very seriously. But the woman in the room at the head of the table, the one seated at the end of the glass desk, was the ringleader. She gave the orders and ran the show.

This was Iris Ravenne, owner and proprietor of Ravenne Industries. She had a soothing demeanor and a seductive voice coupled with drop-dead good looks and an effortless European charm. Her slight accent was both odd and indecipherable, as if she had been a woman of the world who grew up everywhere but was raised nowhere. When she spoke, people listened, and she answered a question only when asked directly.

"Iris, the woman who took Stirling out—where is she now?" asked Damon.

"Stirling? No one has taken Stirling out. I'm sure you were watching the film," she responded.

"Of course, I meant... the Stirling surrogate."

"Careful. Be very fucking careful with your choice of words. Luis was more than just a lover and a trusted friend. He was one of my closest personal confidantes who gave his life for the cause."

Damon bowed his head. He knew Iris couldn't see him, but she intuitively sensed his presence and his movements.

"My apologies, Iris. I didn't mean to offend."

"Oh, Damon. My dear Damon." Iris rose from the dark leather-bound chair and walked, or rather slinked, sensually over to the massive window overlooking the city lights below. Although the training film was taken in the jungles of Tikal, Guatemala, this was not where Ravenne Industries was based and headquartered. No, they were actually deeply embedded in the mountains of Barcelona, Spain, overlooking the city. The view was beyond mesmerizing. As she continued to address the entire group, she would not turn to face them. Rather, she was quietly intoxicated at the sights of a moonlit Barcelona.

"The thorn. And not the rose's thorn, mind you. I'm talking about the proverbial thorn sticking each and every fucking one of us right where it hurts. The thorn that is Kent Stirling. It is only once he has truly been eliminated, after the truth has been revealed, that we will all be able to settle firmly into the seats of power awaiting us."

"But it can be done, Iris. The film proves beyond a measure of a doubt that given the right circumstances, Stirling has his Achilles Heel. He is vulnerable."

"One can only hope, Damon. His weakness has always been women. They are his fatal flaw. The simple fact is that you and your men, superbly trained though you may be, have a far better chance of getting killed by Stirling than actually defeating him."

"You underestimate us, Ms. Ravenne... especially me."

Sharply and unexpectedly, she turned from the window, facing Damon, her face enshrouded by shadow and darkness, with streaks of moonlight forming a rapturous silhouette across her perfectly shaped figure.

"No, Damon. I'm perfectly aware of the skills and talents you and your men bring to the party. But I'm afraid that it will take the wiles and yearnings of a woman to bring Kent Stirling to his knees once and for all. The right woman..."

"You... sound as if you speak from experience."

"Yes, I suppose you could say that... we shared our moment."

Damon nodded affirmatively, but with a sense of longing tainted by a slight edge of disapproval.

"I see."

Her face still clouded in darkness and standing calmly by the window, Iris tilted her head slightly, noticing Damon's reaction, but she was not particularly moved or fazed by it.

"Our man in the Yucatan. Has he made contact?"

"Regarding?"

"The mark in Bermuda."

"Everything has been taken care of, Iris."

"Damages?"

"Apparently there were six people on board, but our man was... instructed to handle the situation accordingly. No witnesses were left behind."

"Casualties are inevitable in our game. They were at the wrong place at the wrong time. But our concern was the satchel. OPERATION BEECH GROVE."

"It's in the hands of Mr. Thulin. Iris."

There was an extended moment of silence between them.

"Perfect. Our work is done. Now it's all about zeroing in on the source. Any word as to his current location?"

"We have eyes and ears everywhere. It seems that he's fallen off the grid lately, but we've made a recent sighting. I'm sure we'll have an opportunity sooner than later."

"Yes, Damon."

She smiled and laughed with a coquettish sexiness. "Of that, I'm absolutely certain."

3

KHANGHAI MOUNTAINS, CENTRAL MONGOLIA

Terkhiin Tsagaan Lake was located in the North Central Khangai Mountains in the Arkhangai province of Mongolia, part of the exquisitely picturesque Khorgo-Terkhiin Tsagaan Nuur National Park. The marshes along the west end of the lake were an important breeding and staging area for the numerous species of birds indigenous to the region.

Kent Stirling was there, and he chose the winter season deliberately because he was studying the birds for his own sense of education and pleasure, but the purpose of his refuge was layered. This was an escape from his former life. There were tragedies he was still nursing and healing from emotionally. The further away from reality, the better he would feel and the more likely he would mend those savage wounds. The loss of the woman of his dreams, Irina, was an insurmountable tragedy, one from which he had still not yet fully recovered. But he found serenity here, and peace, especially when in the company of the birds and a very rare breed of Himalayan Snow Leopard.

The ice formed a sheet of cool flooring across the top of the entire lake. Easy enough to skate but quite deceptive in its level of endurance. One could slip and fall through very easily.

Stirling was bundled up for the winter weather. Snowfall was light, but it was leveled out by the middling heat of the sun's rays. It was gray and overcast on this Wednesday afternoon. He was more fit than ever. Possibly in the best physical condition of his life. More adept at his skill set than ever before. He knew that maintaining his sense of stealth and professionalism in all facets of his life were absolutely vital to his existence and his general sense of survival. But there was something more to Stirling, and the closest people in his life knew that this was what made him an extraordinary and singular human being. When everything was said and done, Stirling was first and foremost a man of medicine. A doctor trained in the ways of cardiovascular surgery and recovery. His range of abilities and knowledge in the realm of personal care coincided with several types of medical arenas, and this was why he was world renowned in this particular field. Better this one than the other, because in the world of killing and assassination, his reputation preceded him. He wished he could erase that aspect of his life. But it was impossible. He was simply too good at it.

His excursion to Mongolia was purposeful, and he could now see why. In the distance, just beyond the beckoning horizon, he finally caught a glimpse of the principal reason he chose to be there in the first place. A Himalayan snow leopard loped carefully along the rim of the icebound lake. Stirling was across the lake at the opposite end, hiding behind a sloping hill with a perfect bird's eye of the view of the lake just slightly below. He watched with binoculars, but his attention was captured by what he noticed ailing the beautiful creature. He sharpened the focus of the lenses, catching a detailed glimpse of what appeared to be a wounded leg right around the ankle of the leopard. There was blood, and it was dry and hardening just at the surface of her fur. This was definitely a female; its hair was shorter at the base of the skull. As with the native lions of Africa, these cats tended to have fuller heads of hair when they were the male of the species. Her eyes were like lasers. Magnetic and rich with character. Like yellow-green orbs, they could hypnotize you with a mere glance. She was beyond magnificent, and Stirling knew she was hurting. He rose stealthily, trying to be unnoticed. She limped steadily, clearly in severe pain. But then a very rare species of bird landed on the sheet of ice at the edge of the lake, and it captivated her attention instantly. Stirling froze in his tracks and just watched for a moment. He knew he needed to get close to her and hopefully mend her wound, but something was happening...

A White-naped Crane, one of the most globally threatened birds on the planet and a native of this particular part of the world, was resting on the ice, picking away at a small thicket of leaves on an adjacent tree by the rim of the lake. The leopard was smart and approached the bird very cautiously, looking down and limping while maintaining a fixed gaze on what could've been her much-needed next meal. The crane sat absolutely still, locking eyes with the snow leopard. Then, with effort and a measure of pain she pounced forward. The crane took flight before it could get ravaged by the cat. The leopard fell through the ice.

Now, Stirling acted. He ran with as much speed as he could muster despite the heavy winter clothing. He wasn't going to lose her. She tried desperately to grab hold of the dry patch of land or the protruding tree by the rim of the lake, whatever worked, desperately fighting to keep from drowning in the icy waters below. In the nick of time. Stirling curved his body and fell to the ground. He grabbed her paws and with his total upper body strength, he hoisted her completely out of the lake. She growled in pain as the wound was deepening from the brusqueness of the struggle to swim and survive. and winced and struggled with him as well, too fearful to attack and too exhausted to defend herself. Stirling knew that what she needed to calm down and heal from her wound was right beneath them. Buried in the snow, there was a shrub laced with healing agents including aloe vera. Commonly referred to as ice plants, the Delosperma genus was known for its medicinal properties, including its ability to soothe irritation, pain, and swelling. Stirling had a soft touch, and he knew she would mend quickly as soon as he applied it. She purred softly because she instinctively sensed the kindness and caring within Stirling and realized that he was far from a threat. He was a friend. As he massaged the juices of the ice plant gently into her paw, he noticed the nature of the wound, and it quietly enraged him.

She had fallen into a poacher's snare. These Himalayan snow leopards were slowly but surely being eradicated from the face of the Earth. To call them a steadily rising endangered species was the epitome of understatement. They had reached somewhere in the range of only 800 to 1,000 individual snow leopards remaining in existence throughout their indigenous territories. If Stirling could save just one of them, he would've accomplished something even greater than the reason he was there in the first place. These fucking poachers were the bane of humanity. Without heart or soul, their cruelty knew no bounds, and they lived merely for the thrill of the hunt and the pure adrenaline rush of the kill. Stirling knew of a lodge where these poachers convened to share stories and recent trophies, which is how they referred to their unfortunate victims. He wasn't going to allow them to get away with this. Not even close. But first, he tended to his patient. She was coming around and feeling better. As he caressed her face warmly, she even began to lick his hand affectionately. He looked into her eyes knowing she could understand him when he spoke.

"Don't worry about this. You're going to be alright. I'm going to take care of you."

She licked his face gently, knowing she was in the very best hands.

He exchanged an even deeper glance with her, staring and getting lost in her yellow-green eyes.

"Your eyes remind me of the lilies of the field back home," said Stirling. "How about if I call you Lilia?"

He lifted her and carried her. His gear was strapped across his back. She cradled her head on his powerful chest. Lilia was safe, finally.

Stirling and Lilia arrived at Valencia's Lodge. In the central valley region just beyond the Khanghai Mountains, this was the hangout for the locals and resident poachers. Just outside, there were heavy crates with latch openings connected to them for master locks. He knew she'd be safe here while he tended to the riff-raff inside. He collared her with a safety harness from his backpack. Placed a lock on the unit that could only be opened with his key. Lilia was already looking stronger and feeling better. He petted her softly on the head, and went inside.

Stirling surveyed the joint quickly and without much effort. There were about twenty people inside. Most of them were lodge employees. There was only one table being used by a group of poachers. They were directly responsible for Lilia's injury, and he knew it right down to his core. The group was rough and callous, drinking feverishly and speaking almost incoherently in a variety of indistinct dialects. There were seven of them. Stirling laid down his knapsack at the corner by the front door and approached the table carefully. As he stood there quietly hovering over the group, they paid him no mind, completely immersed in their cups and idiotic joking with one another. Seven men who were going to wish they had never been born...

"Gentlemen," said Stirling.

The group ignored him deliberately, pretending that he wasn't even there.

"Gentlemen," he repeated in a slightly louder tone of voice.

The group stopped conversing momentarily, pivoting their heads in Stirling's direction. They literally looked like a U.N. sector from across the globe who had united with the sole purpose of poaching rare animals wherever they could find them, proof positive that the unfortunate reality of hunters who profited through poaching existed everywhere in all races, creeds and colors. The leader, a heavy-set fellow of seemingly Italian extraction, looked at Stirling coldly and addressed him sternly. His Italian accent was fairly pronounced as he spoke.

"How may I help you, sir? My name is Enzo. Would you like a drink?"

Stirling scanned him from top to bottom. Gave the quick once around to the other six characters as well. They were no great shakes, but looks could be deceptive. Various shapes and sizes, some of them seemed like they had edged weapons sheathed and strapped to their sides.

Enzo's casual delivery and nonchalance sickened Stirling. He wasn't going to waste any time here.

"Let me be clear to you because I'm only going to say this once... No more snares. Leave the animals alone. And take all of your shit with you. Never ply your trade again in this part of the world or I promise as on the day you were born that you will regret it."

The resulting silence was so deafening. Enzo looked at his six companions, and they all simultaneously erupted into thoughtless laughter. Stirling was far from amused. He managed a very slight, sarcastic grin.

"I'm glad you all think that's so funny because now I'm going to share a little story with you."

Enzo raised his hands, waving them slightly in the air for his friends to be silent and listen to Stirling.

"Go ahead," said Enzo.

"There's a very rare and beautiful breed of Himalayan snow leopard just outside that door. She fell victim, unfortunately, to one of the snares I'm sure you have littered throughout the entire landscape... thankfully, she lived. I nursed her back to good health. But they don't deserve that. They need to thrive and flourish because soon they'll all be gone, and the world will be a much emptier place without them. So what I'm going to do now is teach you all a lesson in what it means to risk becoming extinct. You're not going to enjoy this, but God willing, you may learn from it..."

His words rendered the entire group speechless. Enzo rose from the table and looked straight into Stirling's eyes as he spoke.

"Sir, the one who's going to regret that he had never been born...is you."

And with that said, the other six minions got up from the table, clenched their fists, and a few of them even had the temerity to pull out their knives. The employees began scuttling away and either hid in the kitchen or simply went out the back door. They were a noble, decent people, and they understood the impending threat of violence.

The seven men all began to surround Stirling, forming what ultimately became a perfect circle around him. He spun around slowly and methodically surveying every aspect of his opponents.

"One versus seven. The odds are definitely not even," Enzo smiled malevolently, firmly clutching the handle of his knife.

"At least... not for you," said Stirling.

Enzo's smile quickly transformed into a furious sneer. Then he attacked.

He lunged directly at Stirling with the knife pointed at his torso. But Stirling was simply too fast, disarming him with lightning reflexes and puncturing him through the side of his throat, tossing his body to the side. Enzo now lay there dead in a pulpy, bloody heap. Two of the other men charged him with the blunt weight of a freight train. Stirling, trained in the Japanese art of Aikido, simply turned their forceful aggression against themselves, pivoting one versus the other as the second man's exposed blade stabbed the other in the heart. The flailing third man was now caught in Stirling's iron grip, and as he reached over attempting to grab him from behind, Stirling lifted him by the jaw, snapping his neck and breaking his back simultaneously. Within the space of ten seconds, three of them were already dead. The other four looked at Stirling now with a combined mixture of fear and rage. One grabbed a carving fork from the table where they had been eating and drinking and charged with the force of a steamroller. Stirling once again rapidly and swiftly used his own strength against him by disarming him, placing his arm in a snapping handlock and stabbing him in the eye with the very same carving fork. The blow was so powerful that the sharp end tapped the base of the cranium, killing the fourth man instantly. His body dropped with the weight of a stone. The other three looked at each other, and not wanting to join the ranks of their fallen comrades, they made like bats out of hell, running out the back door into the snowy landscape. Stirling knew when to leave well enough alone, and knew they weren't worth any further effort. Karma was a bitch, and one day, they would most certainly get theirs.

He noticed that the entire staff of workers had cleared out completely. Only he and the four corpses he had created remained inside. Without a moment wasted, he grabbed his backpack and went back outside to see Lilia. Removing his cell phone from his pants, he speed dialed a familiar number. The phone rang three times, and then a voice answered. A friendly and familiar voice to Kent Stirling.

"Bernie," said Stirling. "Good to hear your voice... Listen, I need a favor. I need you to create a simulated habitat with a fully functioning exterior environment... Come again... Yes, focus on the snow."

4

VAIL,COLORADO

Once considered the "shining mountains" by the Ute Indians, who made the area their summer home, Vail, in the intervening centuries, had developed into one of the premiere ski resorts of the world. With the town having been founded in conjunction with the opening of the first ski resort and incorporated in 1966, Vail was now the primary residence of Bernie Llewelyn. Close friend of Kent Stirling, former employee of The Sandbox, and an inventor of nearly Herculean proportions, there was nothing he could not create in the realm of gadgets, disguises, weaponry, or even environments. In many ways, Llewelyn's gifts of creation were weapons in and of themselves. But he was a man of decency and tremendous heart, prepared to drop everything in the blink of an eye to assist his friend Stirling. Their history was as tattered as it was circuitous. The tangled web of international espionage left many open doors and forged many unbreakable alliances in the wake of much death stend destruction. The bond Stirling and Bernie Llewelyn shared was a precious one.

A hybrid Range Rover Sport approached the hilly curvatures of the road leading to Llewelyn's firmly tucked-away estate in the hills of Vail. Nearing the main entrance, the driver's tinted window rolled down. It was Stirling. There was a keypad, and he clearly knew the entry code. Slowly, the wrought iron gated began to slide open. He cruised through and parked along the curved driveway. Taking his personal belongings from the trunk, he walked to the front door and rang the bell. He smiled from ear to ear when the door opened and Llewelyn greeted him. A little grayer and a bit heavier, he was a man in the twilight of his life, approaching his late sixties. His mind, though, was still a thing of beauty. He had the recall and memory of a steel trap. Additionally, he had the mental acuity of an Einstein, with the capacity for problem solving and obtaining a solution to literally anything and everything. The fact was that Bernie Llewelyn was one of the world's greatest minds, and much to Stirling's relief, he was a man with a propensity for goodness, as he knew the world was a place in dire need of repair and restoration.

They hugged one another firmly as close friends do. Stirling, now 43, saw him as a surrogate father, especially in lieu of the mysterious tragedy surrounding the demise of his own parents.

"Great to see you again, kid," said Bernie.

"You too," responded Stirling.

Stirling grabbed his two suitcases and followed Bernie inside the house.

The exterior belied the expanse and enormity of the inside. It was positively palatial. Filled with adornments and furnishings from around the world, the house was perfectly suited to Llewelyn's sensibilities and eccentricities. It was more like a lair than a home, but this was precisely the way he liked it.

Stirling was notably awed but not the least bit surprised. "I love what you've done with the place," he remarked.

"Yeah, I tried to go more minimalist this time," responded Bernie.

They looked at one another, desperately trying to contain themselves, until they both burst out in simultaneous laughter.

Bernie pointed at the immense sofa at the center of the ornately designed living room. A fireplace was quietly burning in the background, keeping the place pleasantly warm.

"Grab some plush."

Stirling took a seat on the soft cushioned leather sofa. Bernie walked over behind the bar.

"Drink?"

"Yeah, ginger ale would be nice."

"Big spender. Rocks?"

"No other way."

Bernie dropped a couple of ice cubes into the glass. Cracked open a can of ginger ale and poured it inside. He grabbed a cold bottle of Corona for himself, pulling the bottle cap off with his bare hand. With both drinks in hand, he walked over to the sofa and sat in front of Stirling. They held their gaze with one another for a few seconds, raised their glasses in salute, and each took a sip of their drinks.

"I'm glad you're back," said Bernie.

"It was time. I hadn't expected it to be this soon, but you know how it goes. Things happen."

"Actually, I know exactly what you mean."

Stirling looked at Bernie closely as he took a swig. Bernie closed his eyes. Stirling could tell that he was holding something back.

"What's going on?"

Bernie focused back on Stirling. The look of concern became readily apparent.

"I know that look," said Stirling. "I hope this isn't company business." He knew Bernie was having a hard time coming clean with the truth. "Bernie, come on. Let's not fuck around. How many times have I got to tell you? I'm out of the game."

Bernie looked at Stirling now with a laser-focused intensity. "It's not company business."

Stirling could sense the gravity and burden of something serious in Bernie's tone. "Alright, then. What is it?"

Bernie exhaled. Took another sip of his beer and leaned back in the sofa. "Angie Miller."

Stirling's eyes widened. The name was clearly very significant to him.

"I thought she was..."

"Dead?" said Bernie. "She thought the very same thing about you."

Stirling rose from the sofa, nodding his head in stunned disbelief as he approached the window seat and sat, looking out at the snowcapped mountains. "The agency hasn't found her? I find that hard to believe. With her... gift, she must be one of their prime targets."

Bernie stepped back over to the bar. Took out a bottle of water from the freezer, opened it, and began to drink. He was nervous. "Look," he said, "I'm not sure where they are in proximity to her. She has a whole other string of issues she's dealing with now. We've been in conversations for about four months now, but her problems aren't going anyway... She needs you, Kent."

Stirling nodded, not able to process that Angie Miller was still around, especially considering their past. He deflected with, "How's Lilia doing? How is she adapting to her new home?"

Bernie exhaled, realizing that Stirling was concerned but couldn't face the past. "Lilia's fine," he grunted. "She loves her new home. But do me a favor and don't change the subject."

Stirling rose from the window seat and turned to address his close friend directly. "That part of my life, Bernie... I buried it. I fucking burned it... a long time ago. She was..."

"Never mind. You know that she's out there. She's never forgotten you, but I'm telling you now... she is in trouble."

Stirling nodded affirmatively.

"Alright... where is she?"

Nikon

5

NEW ORLEANS, LOUISIANA

Audubon Park was a mesmerizing green space, hypnotic in its scenery and splendor. It was completely run through with live oak trees, walking and cycling paths, and picturesque waterways. All of it was framed by some of the city's grandest residences. Students from Tulane University would lounge on the grass, whiling away the hours beneath the billowing Spanish moss, while joggers would lope by getting in their round of daily exercise. Dog owners would play with their pets, and groups of friends would convene for a casual outdoor sundowner. In the best possible way, you could get completely lost here as it was basically an emerald urban idyll.

Of even greater value and interest, the Audubon Zoo was inside the park. It was a lovely riverside spot with almost two miles of multi-use paved trail unfurling beneath a shady canopy of live oaks. Long considered one of the most impressive and visually resplendent zoos in the United States, it was divided into numerous different sections, including African, Asian and South American landscapes and fauna, each populated by indigenous animals, with popular animals including leopards, tigers, crocodiles, elephants, and giraffes that children always loved to see.

The sections of the zoo were divided into very precise, specific categories. There was the Louisiana Swamp, a Cajun wonderland of bald cypresses and Spanish moss, natural wonders of southern Louisiana bayou country. Here, one could always count on finding bobcats, lynx, alligators, bears, and otters. On occasion, it was even possible to find a red fox relaxing on a log in the swamp scrub.

There were other memorable sections including the South American Pampas with its raised walkway. Equally impressive was the Reptile Encounter, displaying some of the largest snakes in the world, from the king cobra, which grew to be more than 18 feet in length, to the green anaconda which extended as far as 38 feet. Indeed, this was the prime ground for students and lovers of animal life around the world. But on this warm, summer afternoon, Angie Miller was relaxing in a part of the zoo known as the Jaguar Jungle. It was a Mayan-style habitat for various felines from around the world. Watching them in their natural surroundings gave Angie a soothing sense of calm and repose. She needed that now more than ever because she was currently in the midst of a very difficult time.

Angela Renee Miller, Angie to her friends, was a sight to behold in every way, shape and form. A native of Bismarck, North Dakota, she was loyal to a fault to both lovers and friends. In her 42 years of life, she had only been in love once... with Kent Stirling. She had a look that was positively hypnotic and deceptive. Her beauty was infinitely beguiling, looking still like a woman 10 years younger than her actual age. Her eyes were dark brown, almost black. Shoulder length dirty blonde hair cascaded over her neck. Her body was to die for, and she was proportioned like a model. Modest about everything, Angie was Yale educated, as she came from privilege. But she possessed a gift that few could ascertain or decipher. She was able to see into the near future by simply looking into someone's eyes. This was not telepathy or anything of the sort. It had more to do with understanding the fate and destiny of a given individual and connecting it to the future surrounding that person and the people closest to them. It had become her burden. Both a blessing and a curse, she discovered it gradually as she developed into adolescence. Eventually, her senses and awareness of this dilemma became so heightened that she began to share it with the wrong people.

The Sandbox, a covert organization always operating under the guise of governmental intelligence and maneuvers, was actually a very duplicitous criminal syndicate bent on something that vaguely resembled world domination. They had their hands in everything... science, politics, entertainment, industries, global corporate affairs. Whatever could be converted into information and power was of keen interest to the Sandbox... even the world of education. Since the turn of the twentieth century, they consolidated their stronghold on world affairs through very subtle means of charitable affairs, medical advancements, and societal improvements. By subverting their intentions and creating the illusion that they were the shepherds and benefactors of all noble causes, they could connive and seduce people from around the world to acquiesce to their every whim and desire. Placing the most brilliant minds in the world into seats of power in the country's most prestigious learning institutions was simply a matter of time. And so it went that all the Ivy League schools across the nation were solicited and invariably staffed with Sandbox affiliates. Princeton, Northwestern, Harvard, Yale. All of them.

Angie connected with the wrong people, and in the years that followed, she had several close scrapes with the Sandbox. But her training was fierce and unparalleled. She fought her way through, but not before they had gotten their hands on her and performed several experiments, which involved examination and penetration of her cerebral cortex. Of course, they wanted to weaponize Angie. This was their intention the moment they realized she was gifted in ways that others weren't. This didn't compromise her stealth or her skills. But the last couple of years, she periodically would see visions of another her. A doppelganger, who clearly was designed to distract her sense of self and, more importantly, weaken her intellectual resolve. Whether she was actually seeing her double or not was not as important as determining what the Sandbox did to her all those years ago that contributed to her instability and her power being affected and impeded.

She took in the crisp breeze coming from the North, studying the family of black panthers sprawled across the layer of the zoo called the Jaguar Jungle. This was Angie's solace and escape from reality. It soothed her nerves and warmed her heart because she truly loved these animals and connected with them deeply. Seated at a bench and snapping some photographs from her vintage Nikon F3 camera, she sensed a presence behind her. It made her shudder as she inhaled ever so slightly and closed her eyes.

"Thought I might find you here," said a familiar man's voice a few feet behind her.

She smiled from ear to ear, relieved like never before to hear a voice which clearly moved her heart. It was a voice from the past, and it was exactly who she wanted to be there at that very moment.

"You still talk to the animals?" she asked in her lilting, feminine voice.

"Every chance I get," the man responded.

Angie turned, and she almost burst into tears when she saw the man standing behind her, real as the sky above and larger than life.

It was Stirling, and he couldn't contain the barely suppressed ecstasy and joy he felt just being in Angie's presence. They embraced and held one another for what felt to them like an eternity. As they pulled back to gaze into each other's eyes, the old passions began to simmer. Softly and warmly, their lips met and they kissed with a fullness and passion that only consumed former lovers. Stirling held her face, almost unable to believe that she was really there. But indeed she was, and Angie couldn't hold back her tears, releasing a wellspring of heartfelt emotion.

Hand-in-hand, they strolled across the manicured campus of Tulane University, an attractive tableau of live oaks, red-brick buildings and green quads spread across 110 acres just north of Audubon Park.

Eventually, they found themselves inside the Howard-Tilton Memorial Library, a sight to behold both inside and out. A haven and a refuge from the world outside, it was accessible to the public and Tulane students alike. What mattered most was that it was where Stirling and Angie first met, and it was a memory they both cherished dearly. Arriving at the research section on the main floor, they tucked themselves away so that they could remain hidden and anonymous. There were a few scattered students seated along the aisles and across the tables, but there wasn't anyone there within earshot of them. Stirling knew something was wrong, and he needed information to determine how to go about helping the former love of his life.

"Why are we here?" asked Angie.

"I want us to talk, and I don't want either of us to be looking over our shoulder every ten seconds," said Stirling.

There was one thing about their relationship which was very distinctive. They had met as college students, and once they got together and became a firm couple, they began to refer to one another by last name only. Not an uncommon thing, but they never deviated, and as they soon discovered, some things never changed.

"Stirling, the situation's fucked. Bernie never should've gotten you involved. Besides... I thought you were dead."

"I seem to hear that a lot nowadays."

She looked around the library. As she glanced over Stirling's shoulder at one of the aisles, she caught a glimpse of her doppelganger yet again. She flinched and grabbed her head,caressing her temple almost as if she was nursing a headache. The doctor in Stirling reacted. He instantly gave her a look of concern.

"It's nothing," she said. "I just thought I saw someone I recognized."

He immediately turned to look in the direction her eyes were fixed, but no one was there. The aisle was empty. A slight look of puzzlement formed across his face. He raised his eyebrows and focused his attention back on Angie. "Miller, there's nobody over there."

Angie flinched, as if she'd snapped out of a daze.

"I know... So what did Bernie tell you?"

"He said you were in trouble. Big trouble. And that you probably needed my help."

Not simply because they were in a library, but because they really didn't want to be noticed or heard, they deliberately spoke to one another in hushed tones.

"Fuck!"

"Just calm down," said Stirling.

"I swear I never wanted to get you involved in all of this. It's coming at me from all corners, Stirling."

"What is?"

Angie looked away and nodded negatively.

"Miller, come on..."

She pivoted her dark eyes back to Stirling. She still carried a torch for him and loved him deeply. The feeling between them was clearly mutual.

"I'm here to help... and because I care about you."

Angie held his hand in hers. Looked him in the eye, trying to penetrate his soul with her stark gaze. "What happened to you, Stirling? Why did you disappear?"

He exhaled, closed his eyes, and gathered his thoughts. "Do you remember when we convened in Houston for that medical conference?"

"How could I forget...? It's the last time I saw you. Even though it was ten years ago, I still remember like it was yesterday."

"Well, things didn't go well. On the surface they did... Where my medical career was concerned, I was appointed head of Cardiovascular Surgery at the Karl Heusner Memorial Hospital in Belize. I had a secondary facility I oversaw called Star Medica in Merida, Yucatan. Things were good for a while, but then, inevitably, the past followed."

"Sandbox?" asked Angie.

Stirling nodded affirmatively.

"Was there... a woman in your life?"

At first, Stirling was reluctant to answer. He closed his eyes, and the image of the former love of his life, Irina, flashed through his mind.

"Stirling?"

He shook off the memory of his now deceased former flame and refocused his attention on Angie.

"Her name was Irina. And we, uh... we were engaged to be married."

Angie heard the visible pain in Stirling's voice, especially conscious of the way it cracked somewhat as he remembered Irina. She caressed the side of his face gently. "I'm so sorry."

A pained smile formed across Stirling's face. "It's alright. It was... it was a long time ago."

She nodded with great empathy for his loss, holding back tears of her own.

"Now...," he said, "Tell me what's going on. And don't leave anything out. Details matter, as I'm sure you know."

Angie clutched the side of her head again, rubbing her temples with her elegantly manicured fingertips.

"You still have the headaches?"

"It isn't what you think... I see things now. People who I know... aren't there."

Stirling looked at her suspiciously. "That's not all."

"No, Stirling... It isn't."

Stirling leaned forward. "Tell me everything."

6

The undeniable clang and swoosh of the St. Charles Avenue Streetcar were as essential to Uptown and the Garden District as live oaks and mansions. New Orleanians were and always have been justifiably proud of their moving monument, which began life as the nation's second horse-drawn streetcar line, the New Orleans & Carrollton Railroad, in 1835. In many ways, the streetcar was the quintessential vehicle for New Orleans public transportation. It was slow, pretty, and if not entirely efficient, always extremely atmospheric. It may have been slightly hyperbolic to claim St. Charles Ave as the most beautiful street in the USA. But the truth was that once you entered the Garden District and later, Uptown, the entire street was shaded under a tunnel of live oak trees that looked like they were forged from the earth of an alternate universe with their ominously arranged branches and overwhelming bursts of green. Basically, they were very old and very big.

Angie and Stirling were seated at the center of a streetcar en route to Julia Street in the Warehouse District, where Stirling had made arrangements via Bernie Llewelyn to pick up his car during his stay in New Orleans. The streetcar was filled to capacity, with no less than fifty-two passengers seated or standing throughout the trolley. Stirling held Angie's hand as the car moved carefully across the tracks. It was just after 5pm, slightly overcast, with the ever-present rumble of rolling thunder crackling on the horizon.

Stirling always made it a point to survey his surroundings, especially when in public, among crowds. There were locals and tourists alike on this particular ride, but he was cautiously mindful about four passengers in particular. There was a young girl around 25 with auburn hair, clean scrubbed face, olive skin and a very natural beauty. She also happened to be extremely pregnant. Probably already nine months. Her boyfriend, or perhaps her husband, was with her, looking after her lovingly as he whispered in her ear and kissed her softly on the cheek. He was Creole and approximately 30 years old. Stirling smiled warmly as he connected and made direct eye contact with both of them.

The other two passengers who captured Stirling's immediate attention were slightly more sinister.—two pale-looking men standing well over six feet tall, both oddly garbed for the humid weather, adorned in long duster-style trench coats, dark glasses, and distressed black leather boots. These were unconventional passengers to say the least, and they were up to no good. Stirling knew it. Catching a quick snapshot of these two with his hawk-like vision, he confirmed his suspicions.

"Stirling," said Angie, "I'm sorry about this. But living and working in the Walnut District, it's just not practical to even own a car."

The pregnant girl was having major contractions. Clutching her stomach closely, she seemed at the razor's edge of having her child right then and there. Stirling noticed it and became instantly concerned after surveying the entire scene in the streetcar.

"No need to explain. It makes perfect sense. Listen... I need you to do me a favor."

"What is it?"

"You still carry Bernie's hand toys from our days at the agency wherever you go?"

A wicked smile formed across Angie's face.

"You kidding? I never leave home without them."

With that said, Angie revealed a couple of openings beneath her bracelets which slid open when she turned her wrists, releasing a pair of clutch-sized hat pins with button-sized handles. Easy to conceal and lethal when injected.

The pregnant girl was moaning slightly from the pain. She held her boyfriend's hand.

"Morris, I think I'm going to have this baby," said the pregnant girl.

A few of the surrounding passengers gasped in astonishment.

"We're almost there, darling. Just hold on," replied Morris, holding her hand.

The two trench-coated fellows felt awkward as they held their arms upward and remained completely still and silent.

Speaking in a low voice, Stirling said, "Miller, listen to me. I need you to be careful about this. That woman is going to have a child. Her water just broke. And you see those two suspicious looking characters over there with the dusters and the sunglasses?"

Angie quickly checked out everything and was completely on point with Stirling.

"Got it."

"Okay, I need you to hatpin those two quietly while I help the pregnant girl."

Angie panicked momentarily, quietly grabbing Stirling by the arm as he rose from his seat. "Wait a minute! What are you going to do?"

"I'm going to help deliver a baby."

"Holy shit," Angie muttered underneath her breath. And without missing a beat, she quickly transformed into character. "Honey, wait!" She grabbed Stirling's leg as she bolted to her feet. "I'm not sure, but we night have just passed our stop. Let me just move to the front and see exactly where we are."

Excusing herself, she gracefully slid across and between the passengers, including the two men in trench coats. As she swept past them, she noticed they were each clutching a silenced pistol inside and beneath their long coat sleeves. She'd have to be swift and catlike with her movements.

In the meantime, Stirling pushed through the passengers to get to the couple who were expecting their child. "Please get out of the way. I need to help this woman. I'm a doctor."

Morris looked relieved, while his girlfriend cried tears of happiness through her labor pains.

Stirling knelt directly in front of them. "Sir, what is your wife's name?"

"Heidi," said Morris.

"And you are?" asked Stirling.

"Morris."

The two trench-coated hooligans seemed to have their pistols primed and pointed. Whether they were there to steal or kill was irrelevant. They needed to be put out of order immediately, and Angie was just the girl for the job. She moved right behind them, unseen and unheard as she held a pin in the palm of each hand. With a quick prick and a delicate touch, she pinned both of them in one fell swoop. This was a Bernie Llewelyn special. One of his deadliest inventions, once used by Stirling in Miami, when he eliminated Gavin Weller, one of the former heads of the Sandbox, at the Sheraton Hotel. All it took was a light tap at the side of each one's throat. The hooligans didn't even have time to breathe; the toxins laced around the pin stopped their hearts instantly. Angie smiled as they both fell back into her arms.

"Whoops! These boys must have had a little too much to drink," she said, smiling with another one of the passengers as she gently seated them on the chairs located right behind them.

Stirling was in full comforting mode with Morris and Heidi. For better or worse, he was about to deliver their baby.

"Heidi and Morris. My name is Kent Stirling. No need to worry. I am a doctor, and I'm going to help you guys deliver this baby."

"You're a doctor! Hold on! Have you ever delivered a baby like this before??" asked Morris.

Stirling, ever so cool and composed, said, "You mean a human baby? Yes, Morris. Trust me. You're in good hands."

"Human baby," Morris couldn't help but to begin laughing.

"Please, doctor, please!!" screamed Heidi.

The passengers surrounding them formed a semi-circle of sorts around Stirling, Heidi, and Morris. Soon, Angie was right at the center, watching everything. She caught Stirling's eye for a split second and winked at him, the indicator that everything was taken care of on her end.

Stirling took the initiative without fear or hesitation. Although he was a cardiovascular surgeon by training and design, his medical knowledge and training was so complete that if need be, he could deliver a child during unforeseen circumstances. It happened a few times in the Yucatan. And it was about to happen here, on the St. Charles Avenue Trolley.

First things first, Stirling knew that for this child to come into the world cleanly and safely, he had to make the most of what limited resources were readily available. He pivoted his focus to Morris and the crowd in general.

"Ladies and gentlemen, if you please, I'd like your attention. Heidi is about to have a baby, and I need as many warm garments as you can spare that I can use for both covering and blanketing as she brings her child into the world."

Without missing a beat, a few of the passengers removed their scarves, sweatshirts and light jackets. Stirling placed them around and underneath Heidi, ensuring that the trolley floor was covered, layered and provided her with the maximum degree of comfort.

"Doctor, please! It's happening!," screamed Heidi.

Stirling refrained from overt displays of emotion, there to be a beacon of security and reassurance.

"Heidi, I'm going to take care of you and your baby. Morris is here, and it's going to be fine. I just need you to push as hard as you can and breathe out. Just stay focused. We'll get through this together."

Hearing the confidence and authority in his voice, Heidi immediately felt safer. To one side, she had Morris, holding his hand tightly as the contractions amplified. Sweating, she pushed with all of her might and emitted a low, bellowing scream.

"Almost, baby. Almost!" said Morris.

One of the passengers took the initiative of calling paramedics to arrive at the next stop, which was the final destination on this particular route.

A tear gradually formed in Angie's lovely dark eye. She looked at Stirling with a combined sense of awe and affection. Ever the prototype of absolute calm and composure, he could hear the baby coming as its crying echoed throughout the cable car.

The head was gradually coming through followed by a little pair of shoulders. With his powerful hands and gentle touch, Stirling pulled the baby free as she took her first breath of life in the outside world.

"She's here, Heidi... You have a beautiful baby daughter."

Morris and Heidi kissed warmly. The entire crowd began to cheer and applaud. Angie smiled as she wiped away her tears and stared at Stirling with a longing she had never felt before. Without missing a beat, Stirling wrapped the little girl in a large, oversized sweatshirt as a makeshift blanket. He then delicately wrapped a small scarf around her head as he wiped her clean and carefully placed her in the warm and loving embrace of her mother's awaiting arms. Heidi kissed her on the forehead, and Morris gently held them both in his arms. He extended his hand to Stirling, and they shook firmly.

"Doctor, how can I ever thank you?"

Stirling saw the kindness and sincerity in Morris's eyes. He knew just by gazing at him that he was a truly decent man, grateful that the ladies of his life were healthy and in good hands.

"Your look says it all, Morris. I'm happy to have been of service. Take care of them. You're A lucky man with a beautiful family."

The siren of the approaching ambulance was arriving from the distance as the trolley reached its final destination at the Garden District.

7

The mansions aligned along both sides of the Walnut Street mansion district represented some of the most stunning and elegantly designed historic dwellings in the entire city of New Orleans. The most impressive, located at the southernmost tip of Walnut Street, was the Rhodesia En Rouge. It wasn't just that it was an immense, prime piece of real estate, ideally and centrally located with close proximity to St. Charles Avenue, the Garden District, and the French Quarter; it was also a thriving business that happened to be the private residence of Angie Miller. The front of the building was a hotel that comprised half of the town block. Behind it, at the back of the estate grounds, was her home.

The hotel complex included shops, restaurants, two nightclubs, a full fitness center, a spa, and two Olympic Size swimming pools. Truth be told, this was vaguely akin to a Las Vegas resort, and it was essentially the only one of its kind in New Orleans. What made it even more desirable is that if one looked along the vast stretch of residences and businesses nestled symmetrically along the tree-lined street, they all had signs in front of them saying "Property of Ravenne Industries." The hotel was literally the only business on this stretch of the Walnut district that hadn't been acquired by Ravenne Industries.

Iris Ravenne was claiming her stakes here, and it was her ultimate calling because she had large caliber plans, and they didn't all involve large caliber real estate acquisitions. There was an ulterior motive behind all of this, and it was inevitably going to reveal something that dealt with Angie Miller and Kent Stirling.

The Rhodesia En Rouge was the brainchild of Angie Miller. Her parents were both heavily entrenched in the world of real estate. She followed in their footsteps and applied her natural skills in the professional, corporate world. That is, until she realized she had a gift, and the Sandbox eventually came calling.

When she left the dark world of espionage and returned to her former life, she applied the new techniques and skills she'd acquired, along with an enormous 250 million dollar inheritance from her doting parents, into her dream project, which through time, effort and innovation blossomed into one of the premiere getaway spots in all of Louisiana, the Rhodesia En Rouge.

Angie and Stirling walked across an immense lobby, adjacent to some of the shops, restaurants, and front desk where guests would check in.

"Why don't we just have a seat over here?" asked Angie. She pointed to the lounge area by The Awakening, the central restaurant bar of the entire resort, with an adjoining night club at the third floor. They took a booth below, and she was the type of working owner who was on a friendly, informal basis with all of her 200-plus person staff. She waved at Tony, a veteran server of about 65, who worked both the bar and the restaurant area. His smile was warm and inviting as he approached them. Dressed to the nines, there was an effortless grace, charm and elegance to his demeanor which spoke of impeccable southern manners and dignity.

Stirling basked in the singular atmosphere of a place that clearly represented the manifestation of a fully realized dream for Angie Miller. In his lifetime, Stirling had traveled and stayed at many hotels throughout the world, but the design of this one was truly unlike anything he had ever seen before. He prided himself as being something of an authority on styles of global architecture, but this place spoke to him in a way that was uncannily familiar and personal...

For starters, the New Orleans interior design reflected a blend of French, Spanish, and Caribbean influences, which invariably adapted to the city's hot, humid climate. Key features adorning each and every physical element of the Rhodesia En Rouge were accented by the Creole styles of furniture, carpeting and cross-ventilation which highlighted nearly every room in the city-like structure. There was wrought iron and arched doorways throughout the interior which contributed to the city's unique aesthetic. There were even rows of galleries, projecting from the walls of the building supported by salmon and russet colored posts and columns.

"Do you like our humble abode, Mr..." asked Tony very politely.

Stirling snapped out of his awed state of observation and kindly introduced himself. He always greeted by shaking hands. "Stirling. Kent Stirling."

Angie observed them, smiling as she flirtatiously placed her index finger at the edge of her lips.

"Tony Moreau, sir. I'm the resident jack-of-all-trades. Whatever you need, just ask."

"Thank you, Tony. Yes, I couldn't help but to be a little bit dazzled by all of this. Someone has a very fertile imagination where the design of this place was concerned, that's for sure."

"Indeed, it's Miss Angie's brainchild. The old world fused with the contemporary. We're currently the most popular resort in New Orleans."

"I'm not the least bit surprised," responded Stirling.

"What can I get the two of you?"

Angie chimed in, "Yes, Tony, I'll have a Mint Julep with a twist and Mr. Stirling will have a Seven and Seven."

Tony gave her a curt nod. "Done. I'll have them out shortly. Lovely to see you again, Miss Angie."

"You too, Tony. Great seeing you."

Tony walked away with dignity and grace, denoting that this was clearly a gentleman who took pride in his work and was very happy to be there.

"Where'd you find him?"

"Tony? He actually frequented a coffee house I used to go to in the Quarter called Intrepid. We got to talking one day while I was in the process of staffing key positions for this place. Things just took off from there. He's been with me now for almost three years."

"And speaking of this place... Angie, first and foremost, congratulations. If ever there was a southern equivalent of what could accurately be described as Heaven on Earth, this would undoubtedly be it."

Smooth jazz music wafted throughout the entire hotel. It was classic Miles Davis, and it embraced the atmosphere in a manner that could only be described as soothing and flawless. Angie and Stirling simply gazed at each other, with an unspoken understanding that there was something of greater concern that hadn't quite been addressed.

Tony returned with their drinks and placed them on the small, circular marble table in front of them.

"Thank you, Tony."

"Of course, Mademoiselle."

Stirling sipped his Seven and Seven, savoring the flavor.

"Mmmm. That is perfect."

Angie smiled as she took a sip of her Mint Julep. "So," said Angie.

"What do you mean?" asked Stirling.

"Well, I see you definitely haven't lost your delicate touch."

"How's that?"

"To be honest, I don't know too many heart surgeons whocould deliver a baby with the tact and precision that you did. And on a fucking trolley car?"

Stirling almost choked on his drink as he suppressed his laughter.

"I know, right? And the St. Charles Trolley no less."

They both shared a momentary laugh with one another. Stirling looked at her with concerned affection. "Miller, what's going on?"

Angie looked up and a puzzled expression formed across her face as her doppelganger walked across the lobby yet again. She made eye contact with her and tried to point her out to Stirling.

"Look... look, over there."

Stirling turned around and looked precisely in the direction Angie was looking only to find a woman of about 40 with her two children arriving at the front desk and preparing to check in. There was a passing resemblance to Angie, but it clearly was not her. Stirling turned back to face her.

"You know that woman with the two kids?"

Angie grabbed her temple, shook her head slightly and looked again, only to realize, as Stirling observed, that the doppelganger clearly was not there. "Stirling, that wasn't who I saw…"

Now Stirling was completely aware that something was seriously wrong. She was hallucinating. Seeing people who weren't there. It wasn't a question of believing her. Seeing was believing. It was now a question of getting to the bottom of it.

"What's happening to you? This is sounding like experimental Sandbox bullshit. How did they find you?"

"It isn't that simple, Stirling. There's much more to it than what you're thinking."

"What I know is that Gavin Weller and Max Thulin were the dual heads of the Sandbox. Now that Weller is gone, and it's all Thulin, he's probably placing greater effort on the science sector of the organization, since that was always his specialty, his… obsession. And the Sandbox got their hands on you. Made you another one of their token guinea pigs because of your particular… gift. When you disappeared, you became top priority for them as far as renegade targets were concerned, because you were seen as representing a form of… unfinished business… How am I doing?"

He wasn't entirely wrong, and Angie knew it. She also realized it was time to come clean about everything. "Well," she began, "those plans have taken a very strange turn, and it actually has nothing to do with Thulin."

Stirling finished his drink and sat back in his chair, expecting her to lay down her cards with a complete explanation. "Go on."

Angie exhaled, folding her hands, leaned forward and looked straight into Stirling's eyes. "Have you ever heard of Ravenne Industries?"

Stirling thought for a moment. "Doesn't ring a bell."

"Okay, well, they have their hands all over some of the most prime real estate in the southern U.S. Especially here in New Orleans."

Stirling realized something and raised his hand, interrupting Angie momentarily.

"Hold on, as we were driving up the street to get to your place, I noticed the signs in front of every single house, restaurant, place of business..."

Angie cut him off mid-sentence. "Exactly. Every single place on Walnut except mine has been acquired and bought out. The signs all say Property of Ravenne Industries."

"Why here? Why now?"

"The name Iris Ravenne doesn't mean anything to you?"

"No. Should it?"

"I figured on one of your special... assignments, you might have crossed paths with her."

"How so?"

"Iris Ravenne, along with you and I, was another one of Thulin's top five."

Stirling leaned forward. Now his curiosity was completely piqued. "I'm stunned... Stunned that I never crossed paths with her and more perplexed that I've never even heard of her."

"Can't say I'm entirely surprised," said Angie.

"Why's that?"

"Because, like you, Thulin and his little legion of minions abducted her at a fairly young age. They groomed her, transformed her into this sort of chameleon. She could slip into any alias, succeed on any covert assignment, mark any target and make any man in the world fall in love with her. But I think she got high on her own rising power."

"I don't understand," replied Stirling.

"The rumor was that she orchestrated the accidental deaths of her parents. A bomb detonated in their house while she was conveniently away for a weekend. She was sole heir to what was apparently a massive family fortune."

"Sounds vaguely familiar, Miller."

"No, Stirling. Not like me... I used my money to fulfill goals. To realize dreams. To create jobs."

"I wasn't trying to offend. I just meant the whole... sole heiress coincidence the two of you seem to share."

"I get it... But whereas I went out of my way to achieve something good, this woman..."

Stirling knew this was going south in the worst way.

"What...?"

"Well, for starters, she severed all ties to the Sandbox. Formed and funded her own little private army. Her right hand is this GQ-looking model-type with the eyes of Valentino and the heart of a serpent. Damon Chambers."

"And?" asked Stirling.

"And they take no prisoners. Apparently she's usurping as much high end real estate as she can in the richest sectors of the Eastern seaboard because I thinks she wants to basically give

Thulin a run for his money where the science experiments are concerned. Instead of being a player, she wants to run the whole fucking show. Sit at the throne, if you like."

"I see... So it's a parallel race for global domination, and the contestants are Ravenne and Thulin."

"Exactly," replied Angie.

He leaned even closer and looked into her eyes.

"But that isn't everything... is it?"

Angie knew he was deeply concerned about her, but she was afraid that if he got in too deep, it would put both their lives at risk. She still loved Stirling deeply, and she didn't want to place her life in his hands yet again. Not when the stakes were this high. Fortunately, she was saved by the bell, without having to divulge the rest at that given moment, when her cell phone rang. She looked at the number, smiled as she recognized it and raised her index finger to Stirling, indicating she needed to take the call.

"Hey there... Yes, we are. Right over here by the front desk lobby lounge. Okay... we'll see you soon."

"Friend of yours?"

"One of my closest friends, actually."

Stirling smiled as he nodded affirmatively.

"But not just a friend..."

He looked at her curiously.

"They're my business partners."

"They?" asked Stirling.

"That's right. Rockne Bail and Diane Bouvier. They're life partners and two of the most beautiful people I've ever known. Local heroes in New Orleans. They put a stop to all of the gentrification in the historic sections to preserve the cities' sense of identity and integrity."

"How did you meet them?"

"At a real estate convention about six years ago. I was looking for a marketing team to promote and publicize this place, and their reputation already preceded them. They had the gift of gab. Hard workers who just exuded free spirit and charm. I knew that if I had them on my side, I could probably make a go of this little dream of mine. Turned out to be the smartest business decision I ever made."

Stirling was notably impressed, pleased that at least this element of her life had worked out well for Angie. He smiled warmly as he looked into her beautiful brown eyes. "I'm happy for you."

Angie leaned forward, and they kissed quickly. As she looked up and over his shoulder, she noticed her friends arriving. "Here they come."

Stirling looked behind him and rose to his feet as one of the most refined, elegant looking couples he had ever seen, dressed to the nines and with a pair of infectious, million dollar smiles. approached them.

Rockne Bail and Diane Bouvier were life partners and business partners as well, just as Angie had described. He was 54. She was 49. They were an unstoppable team, all about community and making things better for those around them. Honest and loyal to a fault, they were also remarkably attractive people. Half-Creole and half-French, they each had very slight accents, olive skin, emerald green eyes, and fit eye-popping figures. And they each had a heart of gold to boot. People like Rockne and Diane did not grow on trees. They were human treasures, and Angie appreciated their friendship and partnership as much as one could imagine.

As they arrived at Stirling and Angie's table, they each hugged Angie and did the customary kissing of each cheeks.

"Rockne, Diane. I'd like you to meet my very close friend, Kent Stirling."

Stirling shook hands with Rockne, a powerful man who stood eye to eye with him, both well over six feet tall. "Rockne, very nice to meet you."

"The pleasure is mine, Kent."

Stirling then shifted his eyes and attention to Diane, a little awestruck by the stunning eyes looking towards him. They kissed and hugged lightly. "Diane, your loveliness is just beyond breathtaking."

Diane and Angie looked at one another, waving their hands at their faces like fans from the heat. "Oh, I like this one, Ang," said Diane.

"I knew you would, Di."

Diane looked over at her partner, Rockne. "Rock, you never say things like that to me."

"No, I just show you things like that!"

They all burst into simultaneous laughter, reveling in the fact that the ice had been broken, and they all took an immediate liking to one another at first sight.

"So, what's new on the horizon?" asked Angie.

Rockne and Diane looked at one another, unable to contain their excitement of the news they had to share. "The brand new conference room and ballroom in the North Wing."

"Something wrong?" asked Angie.

Diane immediately chimed in excitedly. "Girl, we are five days ahead of schedule. With the exception of some last-minute set dressing, she will be ready for the L Street Band premiere even sooner than expected!"

"That's great news!" said Angie.

"Our latest project in the never-ending expansion of Rhodesia En Rouge, Kent. It's going to be the place where people go to be seen in New Orleans. Would you like to check it out?""I'd love to," said Kent.

* * *

The doors swung open, and Angie and Stirling could barely restrain their awe at the sight which lay before them. Still unnamed, this was the latest new construction of the Rhodesia En Rouge. It was a conference room and ballroom combined into one. Banquets, meetings, and celebratory occasions of all sorts would be held here. The setting was incomparable.

Black and gold checkerboard floor made of pure marble. Pillars with Moroccan textures and engravings perfectly aligned, resembling the Roman palaces of Nero's era, but with a touch of French Creole inspiration and design. The dining table was long enough to seat over 100 people, with seats made of the most perfectly sewn fabrics from Africa and Casablanca. The dance floor was an immaculately polished wood floor painted scarlet and black. This was truly a place of architectural beauty, conceived and executed with the type of handmade feel that made it as intimate as it was exquisite. As the four of them entered the deluxe room, they paused at the center of the dance floor, which was symmetrically aligned with the conference room and dining table. There were no additional furnishings yet as they were on the cusp of adding all the finishing touches before their premiere event, which was just a few nights away. Angie nearly had tears in her eyes from the joy and rapture she felt at this latest accomplishment.

"Diane, Rock... You guys have truly outdone yourselves. When you asked me to hand over this project to you, I knew we'd be in good hands. But I never anticipated this... Thank you both, so much."

Diane, Rock and Angie all took turns hugging one another in appreciation and recognition of their latest gem of interior design to add to the slate of treasures that was the Rhodesia En Rouge. Stirling was happy to sit back and let them bask in the moment of personal and artistic triumph. And then the voice. The all-too familiar voice echoed throughout the immense space. Angie cringed as she heard him. Rockne's eyes filled with suppressed rage. Diane closed her eyes and placed her cupped hand over them.

"Isn't that just a poetic thing of beauty," said the man.

Stirling turned to see who it was, but he didn't recognize the elegantly-dressed figure approaching them. It was Damon Chambers.

8

Damon never went anywhere alone. Especially when it pertained to business affairs related to Ravenne Industries. He always was in the company of his entourage. They were a darkly clad group of what he often referred to as his business associates. In actual fact, they were a league of overpaid assassins.

He made his way forward and stopped at the center of the ballroom dance floor. Stirling, Angie, Rockne, and Diane were all seated at the opposite end, just slightly adjacent to the conference room area.

Stirling looked over at Rockne and Diane in anticipation of what could be imminent danger and a potentially violent situation. He had a sense of intuitive understanding that far exceeded normal human beings. Angie looked over at him and nodded affirmatively, confirming that Damon undoubtedly posed a threat.

"Rock, Diane. Please wait here. We'll take care of this," said Stirling.

"Both of you, please be careful," said Diane. "This kind of trouble isn't worth it."

"That's right. We have other things to concern ourselves with that are far more important than this," echoed Rockne.

"We're fine, Rock," said Angie.

Stirling simply waved his hand, acknowledging them both politely but carefully. He and Angie rose and walked over to the dance floor, stopping approximately ten feet from where Damon stood. They were all very symmetrically posed, as if preparing for a standoff. There was stillness and quiet between the three of them, like a trio of samurai sizing one another up before swords began slashing.

Damon, standing with his arms crossed in his dark suit, looking rakishly sinister, remarked, "You know, Miss Miller, your friends, colleagues, whoever they may be sound very reasonable given the circumstances. If you and your... friend here had a modicum of sense between the two of you, you would realize that it's in your best interests to just sign our agreement."

Angie just shook her head in disbelief.

"Do you believe this shit, Stirling? They don't seem to understand that no means no. No isn't a figure of speech," said Angie.

"Stirling? Not the infamous Dr. Kent Stirling, the world renowned cardiologist?" asked Damon, his interest and enthusiasm clearly aroused.

Stirling remained poker faced and absolutely still as he simply stared at Damon and said nothing, the faint hint of a smile forming ever so slightly across his lips.

"The one and only," remarked Angie.

Now, Damon was notably intrigued as he took three more steps forward. He leaned in slightly wanting to take a closer look at Stirling's face.

"You're much better looking than I imagined, Doctor."

Rockne and Diane raised their eyebrows at Damon's comment, not entirely certain where all of this was going.

"Damon, you have exactly ten seconds to turn around and get the fuck out of my hotel," said Angie.

Damon completely ignored Angie's statement, instead focusing his relentless gaze entirely on Stirling. "I must say, Doctor, your reputation has preceded you for quite some time. But I ask myself... Is it with good reason?"

Rockne and Diane looked at one another curiously, not understanding the implicit nature of Damon's remark.

Angie arched her eyebrows and looked carefully over at Stirling, almost in anticipation of something that was about to happen.

"Is it real... or just a smokescreen?" continued Damon.

Stirling smiled now, knowing that with Damon, there was clearly no turning back. "Maybe you should find out for yourself," he said.

Upon hearing Stirling's words, which vaguely resembled an invitation, Damon grinned from ear to ear, enthralled by the prospect. "In due time, Doctor... But for now... I'd like to determine if that future date you so kindly proposed would frankly even be worth my own time. So on that note, I'd like to introduce both of you to some associates of mine." He pivoted his head back towards the open door he'd entered through and called out, "Gentlemen!"

Stirling, Angie, Rockne, and Diane all looked towards the door and were curiously baffled by the group who entered. They were five men of various shapes and sizes. All of them looked to be in their thirties, dressed in black clothing. Wearing silk shirts and flowing dress pants tailored to their length and height, they were an odd lot to be certain, with just a dose of heightened threat about them. One of them looked over at the billiards table by the corner of the bar and grabbed a pool cue. He casually began spinning it in his hands rather expertly. Stirling sized them all up rather quickly. They were hitters. Each of them probably trained in some form of street fighting or martial arts. They began to form a circle around Angie and Stirling.

The one with the pool cue looked at the other four and with an implicit nod of his head, he seemed to be indicating a signal. As they all exchanged looks with their leader, they each began to pull out their weapon of choice. The first man slid his hands into his pants pockets and when he pulled them out, they were adorned with brass knuckles. He crushed his palms to form fists.

Angie pursed her lips, blowing him a sarcastic kiss.

The second man reached behind his pants, revealing a pair of nunchucks. These were quite lovely, made of platinum and connected by a chain about an inch long. This one was clearly gifted as he begin twirling them quite intensely, showing off his expertise. Damon smirked and placed his hand momentarily over his mouth to suppress his barely contained laughter. Stirling wasn't remotely fazed by any of this.

The third one extended his leg up rather high, almost in the form of a side posed karate kick. As the outstretched limb reached a perfectly poised position, a glistening blade snapped out of the toe of his shoe. Diane looked over at Rockne, stunned by the array of sights which lay before her. Rockne just waved it off, indicating she should just stay calm. Angie shot a quick glance over at Stirling. They knew this was going to erupt at any moment.

"Now, I must say to both of you that I think this last one will truly impress in that it took ingenuity and skill to create something so... novel," said Damon.

With that said, Damon and the fourth man exchanged a quick look and Damon nodded affirmatively.

The fourth man then unleashed a snapping motion with both arms revealing what looked at first sight like a pair of unopened fans. But then he flicked a switch at the bottom of each device, and the real weapon was revealed... These were spinning propeller blades, about the size of a large donut, designed to slice and dice the unfortunate victim who fell into its whirring path.

Now the assailants had revealed their tricks. Angie and Stirling were prepared. He was casually dressed in a V- Neck sweater and khakis with flat leather shoes. She wore a purple form-fitting velvet blouse with brown jeans and Western boots. Adequate for the occasion. They clenched their fists as they stood side by side.

"So... let the game begin," said Damon.

And with those words spoken, it was like a starting gun at the Olympics. The combatants were now off to the races.

Angie jumped straight into high gear in full combat mode. Stirling caught lightning quick glimpses of her in action, and he was beyond impressed. She hadn't lost a step or missed a beat. Her stealth and speed were just as good as they had ever been. She was a trained martial artist, a skilled sniper and fairly capable at rigging explosives. All this, plus she was an uncannily savvy businesswoman.

The nunchuck man came at her full speed. She dodged his whizzing blows accordingly, bobbing and weaving. Inevitably he spun too wide, enabling Angie to grab his arms in the air, while the nun chucks missed the presumed target of her skull. In a matter of seconds, she spun them around, allowing her to place the platinum death sticks around his neck and snap it. She let them go, and the first assailant dropped to the floor dead.

At the same time, Stirling was occupied with the brass knuckle man and the shoe blade man. He initially let loose with a dizzying array of fist work, cutting down the brass knuckle man with blows to the midsection, the face and a punishing elbow to the side of the head. Brass knuckle man shook the hits off and charged at Stirling like a raging bull. Using his own fury against him, Stirling grabbed one of the clenched fists and with his opponent's own full throttle force, he punched into his throat, crushing the larynx in the process. This momentarily stunned him and knocked him down to the floor, where he grabbed his throat, trying to catch his breath.

Shoe blade man then lunged at Stirling with a threatening side kick, emitting a crazed scream as he flew through the air with what seemed like the greatest of ease, but alas... His intention of slicing across Stirling's shoulder was to no avail because Stirling's sense of intuition and speed, of knowing exactly where the next blow would be coming from, was incomparable. He caught the man's leg in mid-air and swiftly broke it, causing shoe blade man to emit a piercing scream which emanated throughout the cavernous room.

Brass knuckle man, then fully recovered, launched himself at Stirling, and it was the worst move he could have made. With the singular grace of a panther in flight, Stirling then took the broken leg with the exposed blade and punctured the brass knuckle man right in the jugular. Shoe blade man, still screaming, lunged forward as Stirling held him to try to grab his face and gouge his eyes out. Again, Stirling merely knocked away his arms, grabbed his head and broke his neck with inimitable catlike reflexes. Dropping the shoe blade man's corpse down like a sack of potatoes, there were only three left, including Damon.

Damon simply watched in the corner, standing by one of the coolers seething with a sense of silent rage. In that moment, the pool cue man, presumably the leader of this motley quartet of killers, charged at Angie. She elegantly ducked from his whooshing stick, and as she executed a perfect backflip, the movement allowed her to deliver a powerful spinning back kick, sending her assailant, the pool cue man, backwards, where he hit the floor with a resounding thud. He rose groggily, stunned by the strength of Angie's resonant blow. He shook it off with frustration and broke the cue in half, exposing splintered, sharpened ends. When he attacked, she stealthily delivered kicks to his cock and balls. Falling like a crumpled heap, he had enough energy to try to stab her with one of the broken pool cue halves. Angie caught the stick, reversed the blow, and punctured him right through the eye, killing him instantly. He crashed forward, hitting the ground with maximum impact.

With her back now facing the propeller blade man, she was exposed, and the assassin tried to capitalize on this as his whirring blades hissed threw the air. He jumped off the stage, poised to descend upon the back of Angie's neck, when he swiftly was intercepted by a new opponent, who was not part of Damon's crew.

Omitting loud, penetrating screams, the mystery assailant caught the propeller blade man in mid-flight. One hand around his throat and the other firmly embedded in his torso, the mystery man dropped him to the ground. Damon leaned forward, reaching for something in his coat pocket.

With the fallen propeller blade man on the ground, the other assailant took the initiative by turning the rotating blades towards its owner's throat. Just as the blades were scant millimeters from propeller blade man's throat, a gunshot sounded. It was a 9mm round.

No one was hit, but everyone turned in the direction from which it was discharged. Damon had shot off a round aimed at the gorgeous chandelier, dangling precariously above the center of the ballroom. As it crashed, it separated both struggling opponents from one another.

Propeller blade man merely fled out the door, while the mystery man, who was clearly there in the aid and assistance of Angie and Stirling, tucked and rolled away from the shattering glass as it spread all across the dance floor. Rockne and Diane, their nerves frazzled from the scuffle on the floor, ran to the sides of Angie and Stirling, making sure they were alright. Angie and Stirling were fine, unscathed by a battle which clearly belonged to them. They held one another and embraced momentarily. The mystery man, rising from the floor brushing bits of shattered glass off his arms, locked eyes with Diane. There was a knowing familiarity between them, an unspoken connection. In fact, they were all familiar with him. All except for Stirling.

His name was Tyler Wilkes. He was 35, and he was actually the personal head of security for the Rhodesia En Rouge. A close personal friend of Angie's, he was strikingly attractive with light brown hair, hazel eyes and a dark complexion. The connection ran even deeper, though, for he was also the nephew of Rockne and Diane. When their eyes connected, Diane and Tyler embraced one another. She held his face affectionately and addressed him.

"You had no idea what that was all about. You know you could've been killed?" Diane asked, with thoughtful concern in her voice.

"Don't worry about me, Auntie. I'm here to take care of you. All of you," replied Tyler.

Rockne stepped forward and threw an arm around his shoulder, while Tyler reached back and grabbed his uncle's hand firmly.

A burst of applause began to echo resoundingly throughout the ballroom. Everyone looked over to find Damon, standing in the corner, by one of the marble pillars, a sarcastic smirk painted on his chiseled face as he clapped. When he stopped suddenly, his eyes widened.

"So sorry about the sudden interruption, but I couldn't very well have you decimate all of my team in one fell swoop. That just wouldn't be right," said Damon.

"Try it again, Chambers. Just one more time. I promise you'll regret it," replied Tyler.

Stirling and Angie remained still, standing close to one another, not sure what Damon's next move would be. As far as they could tell, everyone was unarmed, including Tyler. And the general rule of serious combat was one and the same anywhere in the world... Never bring a knife to a gunfight. It was clear that the only one brandishing a pistol was Damon. They needed to remain cool and not give away their complete position.

"Careful, Mr. Wilkes. You may end up learning sooner than later that it would benefit you greatly to have eyes in the back of your head."

Tyler nodded slowly but maintained his calm and composure. Damon walked over to them, stopping first directly in front of Tyler.

"Was there something else you wanted to say?" asked Damon.

"You're the one with the gun," responded Tyler.

"So glad you noticed, Mr. Wilkes."

Tyler looked unusually striking in his wardrobe this particular day. White blazer with aquamarine t-shirt, blue linen pants, beige loafers. As he turned away from him, Damon patted him hard on the shoulder three times, as if to say he was either impressed or taken with him. Tyler was neither moved nor interested in returning the gesture. He was disgusted as Damon walked away and now stood eye to eye with Angie. Stirling was standing a few feet from her right at her side, watching every move Damon made like a hawk.

"Miss Miller... I'm certain you would agree that there has been far too much killing today. This type of violence and bloodshed only exacerbates the situation further, pushing us into the realm of, shall we say, desperate indifference."

Angie closed her eyes, nodding her head, undeniably flustered by Damon's ruthless sarcasm and threats. "Your point being?" she replied.

"This little soiree could've easily been avoided... If not for the fact that you refuse to concur with our more than agreeable arrangement."

"Happy to oblige. When can we do it again?" asked Angie.

Tyler, Diane and Rockne all looked at one another nervously, knowing that Angie was taunting Damon because of her refusal to acquiesce and accept his persistent business offer.

Damon turned and walked away, smiling facetiously as he approached the door. He turned to address them one last time.

"Miss Miller, you've become incredibly brazen as we've tried to assist you with moving forward. Even more so now, since you've enlisted the aid and services of the good doctor."

Stirling kept his gaze firmly on Damon, never losing eye contact even for a split second.

"But, I'll end by saying this..." Damon continued. "This is the third time I've made you this offer, which from a purely business standpoint, is so potentially profitable from where you're standing, that only a fucking fool could refuse. So just bear this in mind... The fourth time around, you won't even see us coming, and it may just be the proverbial straw that finally breaks... the camel's back."

Angie, without missing a beat, raised her hand, pointing at the door with her index finger.

"Out."

Damon nodded, flashing his painted smile at the entire group. "Good afternoon ladies…" He then shifted his eyes to Stirling. "And gentlemen." Then he turned and walked out the door, leaving in his wake only the air of toxic sadism.

Diane and Rockne approached the three protectors, Stirling, Angie, and Tyler, addressing all of them as a group.

"The inaugural ball notwithstanding, I'm assuming we're full speed ahead and business as usual?" asked Rockne.

Angie turned and looked at Tyler who nodded affirmatively.

"100 percent," replied Angie.

"In that case, we'll get a cleaning crew over here to remove the mess of the… chandelier," said Diane.

"Thank you, Di. I'll call you later."

"No problem. Listen, all of you, please, be safe."

Stirling nodded at her.

Tyler waved at his aunt and uncle. "I'll see you both soon."

Diane and Rockne left hand-in-hand, exiting through the back way, into the main lobby of the hotel.

Angie knew a brief introduction was in order between Tyler and Stirling. The two men stood in front of one another, equally impressed by the other's physical presence.

"Tyler Wilkes, meet Dr. Kent Stirling, a longtime confidante and one of my very closest friends in the world."

Tyler extended his hand, and the two shook firmly. "Dr. Stirling, a pleasure watching you… work." An inside joke and an implicit understanding, surely embraced by these two implacable men of steel.

Stirling managed a slight but very sincere smile. "Likewise, Tyler."

"Tyler is my general head of security here at the hotel," said Angie.

Stirling raised an eyebrow. "I see."

"He also happens to be the nephew of Rockne and Diane."

Stirling, both impressed and even somewhat moved at hearing this, nodded in approval. "They're wonderful, people, Tyler. You're very lucky to be able to call them family."

"Yes, I am. To be honest, they're like my parents. I was basically raised by my aunt and uncle."

Stirling patted him on the side of the arm, recognizing the value and importance of family in general. The three of them then refocused their attention to the smattering of corpses littered across the floor.

Stirling addressed them both. "In the meantime, I'm going to call our friend, Mr. Llewelyn, Miller... Seems we need to acquire the local services of a... different type of cleaning crew. I'm sure Bernie knows of someone."

"Good idea, Stirling," replied Angie. She surveyed the four dead bodies one last time.

"Good idea," she repeated.

9

It was an abnormally cool and pleasant evening that night in Barcelona. Mid-seventies with clear skies, a full moon and not a trace of the typically wretched humidity which generally defined the climate condition of the summer months. Ravenne Industries loomed large and ominous with its perched castle-like tower overlooking the city below.

On the third floor of the corporate office building, the fast moving click of heels could be heard down the elegantly furnished hallway. At first sight, this interior could pass for a five-star hotel in Las Vegas with its ostentatious furnishings and garish, neon-tinged lighting arrangements. The clicking grew closer and more pronounced when a most ravishing woman turned the corner and continued her fevered spring towards the main office.

This was Zara Zianne Zimmermann, the half-German, half-Spanish honey trap who was being groomed by none other than Iris Ravenne herself to be her top female operative. This was a woman who could set even the coldest man's pulse racing. She stood about 5 feet 6 inches tall. A mane of dirty blonde hair draped across her sleek shoulders. Hourglass figure, dark, almond-shaped eyes and a face that could truly stop traffic. She had just turned 30, and this was her golden hour. She was being primed for bigger things, and no one was more aware of this than Zara herself.

She arrived at the door to Iris Ravenne's office and knocked

From inside, a woman's voice said, "It's open."

Zara entered. The office was more brightly lit than usual, with emphasis on the Moroccan and Italian furnishings arranged symmetrically and quite deliberately along the office floor. Dressed to the nines, Zara appeared both professional and incredibly seductive all at once. She was a vision in ivory white, all the more mesmerizing as it brought out the radiance of her intoxicating brown eyes.

Iris turned in her swiveling chair. She was in her early forties, but her exact age wasn't known. The care she took of herself was painfully apparent as her appearance belied her actual age. She was curvaceous to the extreme. Painfully aware of the power of her own sexuality, Iris was an absolute stunner in every way conceivable. She was French by background, but she was also completely fluent in Spanish, without the slightest hint of a foreign accent. As Zara approached Iris's desk, she pointed down with an extension of her hand as they spoke in Spanish.

"Please have a seat, my dear."

"Thank you, Miss Ravenne."

"Zara, I've told you a thousand times, we can skip the formalities when we're alone. You can call me Iris."

"My apologies... Iris."

They examined one another as women sometimes do, from head to toe. There was a ripping sexual tension between them. They may have been lovers once upon a time, perhaps they still were...

"So... our contact in Iceland. Were you able to establish the connection?"

"Yes, there was no problem. In fact, we acquired a little bonus in the process."

"Really, how so?"

"Well, it seems that the plans regarding Operation Beech Grove are not exactly in alignment. Not yet anyway. So Professor Thulin is probably trying to extract agents from around the world..."

"Because he doesn't yet realize that Stirling holds the key to unlock the entire formula," interjected Iris.

"Exactly right," said Zara. "So where all that is concerned, it seems we're not only ahead of the schedule, we're taking the lead in the entire race."

Iris smiled and nodded in approval, seducing and hypnotizing Zara with her torrid gaze. "You look lovely, Zara. Better than ever, I might add."

"Thank you, Iris."

The sexual tension between them was palpable, and then, suddenly, the intercom rang. Iris answered in Spanish. "Yes?"

"Miss Ravenne, Damon Chambers and Mr. Zamora are here to see you," said Iris's receptionist.

Iris and Zara raised their eyebrows and smiled with one another wickedly.

"Thank you, please send them both upstairs."

In that moment, Iris stepped up from her chair, walked around the desk, and proceeded to caress the nape of Zara's neck softly and seductively with the back of her hand. Zara closed her eyes, moaning quietly. She reopened them and looked deeply into Iris's hypnotic gaze. "To be continued," said Iris.

Zara nodded approvingly, and in that instant, there was a knock at the door. Both women knew that it was time to switch their spoken language back to English as Iris said, "Come in, Damon."

Indeed, it was Damon and the propeller blade man, AKA, Emilio Zamora. As they entered, Damon was typically confident in his stride, whereas Emilio had a sheepish, somewhat withdrawn quality to his gait, as if he was leery or afraid of something.

"Gentlemen... let's get comfortable, shall we? On the Moroccan, please."

That said, Iris pointed at her favorite piece of furniture, a U-shaped sofa, handmade in Morocco with only the finest and most delicate fabrics imaginable. Wool, cotton, silk, and linen. Highlighted by rich, vibrant colors such as maroon, orange, corn yellow, and lime green. It was an eye-popping piece of furniture. Built for comfort and shaped to keep its guests closely linked to one another because of the curved U-shaped style of the piece.

Iris, Damon and Emilio all sat around the sofa. She was at the middle, where the U bridges in the middle before it spreads to each side. "Come on, both of you, sit next to me. One of you on each side."

Damon, of course, with his strutting pomp and arrogance, didn't hesitate as he dropped next to her at her right side. Emilio was leery and more restrained in his enthusiasm. Iris, the ultimate tease, urged him over.

"Come, Emilio. I won't bite. Here to my left."

Reluctantly, he joined the two of them. Zara was still seated at the desk, watching and smiling at them from a distance. She seemed to be in on something that the men weren't even remotely aware of. "You all look very cozy," purred Zara.

"Join us, my dear," said Iris.

Lithe and catlike, Zara literally cartwheeled herself over to the group, taking a cushion on the far right end of the sofa.

"Here we all are," said Iris.

The men both nodded affirmatively. Zara merely snickered with amusement

. "The reason I choose to sit here, even when it comes to matters of business, is because the comfort offered by these Moroccan works of art allows for a degree of relaxation, unavailable and impossible to feel when sitting behind a desk or a... regular chair."

"Yes, this is... lovely," said Damon.

"Beautiful, Miss Ravenne. Thank you," replied Emilio.

"Of course. And when one is more relaxed, one is much more inclined to convey the truth about any given matter with a greater attention to... details."

Zara raised her eyebrows, turning her sultry gaze over to Emilio.

"So, my dear..." said Iris as she stared directly at Damon. He smiled at her wickedly.

And with lightning speed, she turned, focusing closely and completely on Emilio. The gesture caught him off guard, and he jumped slightly out of his seat.

"Emilio, darling... Tell me all about New Orleans."

Emilio looked over at Damon, searching for some unspoken seal of approval. Damon wouldn't give him the time of day, as he was simply staring out the window behind Iris's lavish desk.

"New Orleans went... fine, Miss Ravenne," replied Emilio.

"So you would say you enjoyed yourself and took in all the sights and sounds of that decadently lush city?" asked Iris.

"I'm sorry, Miss Ravenne. I'm not sure I..."

"Don't worry, I'm just teasing you, Emilio. You need to loosen up. Remember... Comfort equals honesty. So... I'm going to ask you a very specific question, and all I ask, is that you be honest with me when you answer. Fair enough?"

"Yes, Miss Ravenne."

Zara and Damon looked at one another momentarily, anticipating something unexpected from Iris, but not sure exactly what.

"Fine. So… I sent you, Damon, and a small part of his team to New Orleans with the principal task of acquiring the final property acquisition contract from Rhodesia En Rouge. They are the last, but undoubtedly most important establishment, remaining on Walnut Street, and my plans simply cannot go forward without it."

"I understand," said Emilio.

"The new toy that was created for you by our experts, the toy that was specifically designed for you to eliminate Miss Miller, and any of her associates, if there was a problem of sorts… I'm assuming it worked fine?"

Emilio felt increasingly tense, but subtly aroused as Iris used the tip of her fingernail to stroke the side of his cheek. She had her arm around his shoulder as they both were seated back on the Moroccan grand sofa. He looked at her with a combined sense of longing and fear as he mustered the courage to respond.

"Miss Ravenne, the device was fine… But Miss Miller and her companions are still… alive."

"Alive?" Iris suddenly stopped with her flirtatious gesture. She sat up, and Emilio sat up alongside her. She placed her hand gently on his lap, saying, "Explain this to me, Emilio."

"There was unexpected interference by someone we didn't anticipate would be there. An intruder. But I can assure you that the next time there will be no mistakes. We will be… prepared. I promise you, Miss Ravenne."

Iris looked over at Zara and Damon, and they all smiled warmly with one another, grinning from ear to ear.

"You see, the sofa truly works… miracles. I believe you, Emilio. Your honesty and attention to detail shines, and I thank you for that. Come."

Iris gestured to Emilio with her arms open so that they could embrace one another. They hugged firmly and seemingly with great affection. She then pulled away and looked at him closely in the eye, with her hands holding his face.

"Emilio, why don't we seal this promise of yours... with a kiss?"

Emilio always lusted after Iris. All men did, and he was no exception to the rule. He couldn't believe his ears, and he was compelled to look over at Damon first to get his silent seal of approval.

Damon winked at him and nodded accordingly. Emilio turned his focus back to Iris. Mesmerized by her hypnotic gaze, he leaned forward, and they kissed on the lips. There was a fullness to her kiss, inciting sensations of both ardor and intensity within any recipient of her sensuous lips and doting caress.

They pulled away from one another and Iris rose from the sofa. She walked seductively back to her desk, turning to face Emilio as she stood.

"That was a special kiss, Emilio. You certainly made my heart flutter."

Emilio found that compliment to be more satisfying than anything he had ever heard.

"I only hope that my lips were able to make your heart... skip a beat, the way you did mine."

Zara's smile quickly dropped, forming a slightly malevolent scowl across her face. Damon stood up, walked over to the window, overlooking the lovely lights of Barcelona, turned and waved sarcastically at Emilio. "Bye, bye," said Damon.

With that said, Emilio began to feel a shortness of breath, followed by a sharp stabbing pain in his chest. He clutched his hands over his heart. The pain intensified, and as he tried to release his scream, he stood with his last ounce of energy and hit the ground like a stone. He was dead, victim of a sudden, unforgiving cardiac arrest.

"Talk about the kiss of death," remarked Damon.

Zara, slinked across her chair like a sleek cat, began to snigger, covering her mouth with her hand.

Looking stern and severe now that Emilio had been eliminated, Iris carefully removed the strip of false lips from her mouth with the edges of her fingernails. She tossed them down the thin opening of her paper shredder, just adjacent to her desk. They belonged in the trash now that they had served their purpose. Made by her team of gadget masters, this was a pair of lips, dosed with a slight layer of cyanide on the receiving end so that once kissed, the victim feels the pangs of instant heart failure, resulting in immediate death.

"Amazing. Not exactly lips like sugar, but it certainly does the trick," said Iris, as she sat in her desk chair looking over at Damon, who was relaxed by the window seat. "So... what exactly was he referring to about interference and intrusion?"

Zara raised her hand like a teenager in a high school classroom, responding to her teacher's question. "I'll bet I know."

Damon and Iris both looked over at her.

"Stirling," said Zara.

Iris looked over at Damon, who nodded affirmatively.

This captivated Iris so much that she chose to stand and walked around the other side of her desk, so as to address them both. This was the power unit, the trifecta of individuals who comprised the organization that was Ravenne Industries... Iris, Damon, and Zara.

"So... we finally have a location on our friend, Dr. Stirling. It's been years. Fucking years," said Iris. There was a look in her eyes, one of reflection and satisfaction. She appeared to be remembering something. She asked, "How did he appear to be where Miss Miller was concerned?"

"Oh, they were definitely quite comfortable," said Damon. "It appears that her partners and their nephew..."

"Tyler Wilkes?" interrupted Iris.

"Exactly. Well, he appears to be some sort of security expert for her new business venture, and he made a special guest appearance at the Rhodesia En Rouge as well. Nothing earth shattering. But now we know who the key players are. I think that now that we're moving into Phase 4 of extraction where the Miller transaction is concerned. We'll need to turn up the heat. I suggest taking my entire team with us when we leave for Louisiana."

"Indeed you will, Damon. Indeed you will."

Iris turned her eyes and attention over to Zara.

"My dear, you're going with Damon this time. I think we'll expedite this assignment and accomplish everything much more effectively if the city is graced by your divine presence."

Zara instantly perked up and sat in the chair, facing her idol and her employer directly. "It will be my honor and my pleasure, Iris."

"Yes, I believe you'll enjoy getting acquainted with Mr. Wilkes. Should be right up your proverbial..." Iris gave her the elevator glance, looking at Zara up and down "...alley."

"I look forward to it," replied Zara.

"Seems that the worm has most definitely turned in our favor. Now that we finally have a location on Stirling, we can proceed with the larger portion of our plans, addressing the position of our friend Professor Thulin, while finally acquiring the secrets that will unlock..."

"Operation Beech Grove," said Damon.

"The three words that will undoubtedly change the course of history," replied Iris.

"Will you be joining us this time around, Iris?" asked Zara.

Damon looked over at Iris, tilting his head slightly to the side, as if to say that he approved of Zara's suggestion.

"Oh, my dear... I wouldn't miss it for the world," said Iris.

And with those words, the three of them all looked at one another and simultaneously burst together into what sounded like a symphonic cacophony of laughter. There was passion and vigor to the way they laughed in harmony, and the sounds of their ebullient celebration of the mission at hand drifted out the window, echoing like a distant wind in the nighttime Barcelona skies.

10

In the Warehouse District of New Orleans, the city's well-worn historical identity rubbed shoulders with contemporary cool. There were elements of New Orleans ranging from its deep past to its envisioned new horizons, horizons envisaged by those who thought the city could be contemporary and hip while retaining her centuries-old sense of place.

Across the street from the Ogden was the Contemporary Arts Center, where the cutting edge of contemporary art was exhibited. In contrast to the solid brick 19th and early 20th century architecture of the nearby warehouses, the flashy Contemporary Arts Center practically screamed its modernity to the city.

Just behind the ACC, in a slightly smaller structure, but with equal attention to its sense of off-the-wall design, was The Emerald Carousel, a combination restaurant, bar, and after hours gentlemen's club.

It was a cool, crisp evening that Thursday night, right around midnight, as Tyler Wilkes, dressed to the nines with his signature white blazer, walked through the front door. The interior spoke volumes of the sense of uniqueness and singularity that the Emerald Carousel brought to the entire Warehouse District. It was a popular dining establishment for locals and the signature tourist trade, but after hours, beginning at 11pm, the place really set the night on fire. The aesthetic, the food, and certainly the women, all of them professional exotic dancers, highlighted the deep tropical influences, from Southeast Asia to South America. Customers who visited, whether it was for the food, the atmosphere, or simply to lay their eyes on the evening's entertainment, always walked away happy.

Tyler made a quick beeline for one of the center booths at the front of the house. The show was about to begin, and one of the premiere exotic dancers was preparing to take center stage. He gestured with his hands to the bartender to please bring him a drink, his usual, and as they exchanged looks, Tyler acknowledged the bartender by giving him the thumbs up signal. He took his seat and looked up as he noticed the lights gradually beginning to dim. It was a packed house that evening. All the tables and booths were taken. The music began to swell, and she took to the stage. She was the main attraction of the Emerald Carousel. The song being played as she began her routine was "Pop Goes The Zipper" by Prince in an extended version.

She was an astonishing sight, and it was no wonder she was the star of the joint. Her name was Monica Ekland. She was 30 years old, and she had a face that could ignite true fireworks on a cold, winter day. Half-Filipino and half-Swedish, she was a true work of art on the stage. She owned it completely and utterly. Her movements were erotic and scintillating. This was a woman whose stunning looks and physique could easily wake the dead. But there was something much more to Monica. Something deeper which actually made her infinitely more desirable. She was an art history major at Tulane. Her parents were both lawyers, and she was essentially using the gig at the Emerald Carousel to fulfill and realize what had been her lifelong dream and passion to open her own art gallery and help catapult the careers of the talented local artists whose work was in need of greater recognition and exposure. Yes, Monica Eklund was all that and a bag of chips. A great admirer of art history and an advocate of the arts, she also had tremendous love in her heart, and she was devoted to the one man in her life...

As her routine continued, she locked eyes with the man who was seated at the booth just below, near the center of the floor. Tyler caught her attention the moment he sat down. There was a gripping familiarity when their eyes met, and with all the leering gazes enraptured by her stunning presence on that stage, she couldn't take her eyes off Tyler.

A pert, upbeat waitress made her way to Tyler's booth to serve him his cocktail, a tropical looking concoction of some sort. Her name was Brenda, and she exuded positive energy.

"Hi, Tyler! How have you been?" asked Brenda.

"I'm doing well, Brenda! Great seeing you," replied Tyler.

"So, when are you going to take me out?"

Tyler was amused at her forwardness, but he set her straight without hesitation. "Come on, Brenda. You know me. You know I'm a one-woman kind of guy."

"So you've told me, but are you sure you've found the right woman?"

Tyler smiled softly as he looked at Brenda without strings. "I'm pretty sure."

Brenda was a good sport. A flirt by nature, but she was definitely sincere about her strong attraction to Tyler, and she respected his integrity when it came to his relationship. "She's a lucky girl."

"No, I'm the lucky one," said Tyler.

"Well, let me know if I can get you anything else."

"I'm all good. Thanks again, Brenda."

He handed her a twenty and gestured with his hand for her to keep it.

"Thank you, Tyler."

As she walked away, Tyler smiled and nodded his head, looking back up at the stage and casually sipping his drink. The song gradually reached its end, and the lights dimmed to black. Dark for a few moments, the lights slowly began to rise, the stage was empty, and the crowd, including Tyler, released a thundering round of applause. The music continued playing, and the audience eventually fell back into casual drinking and conversation.

"Fancy finding you here, handsome."

The voice sounded just behind Tyler, and the familiarity of it brought an immediate smile to his face. He turned and was greeted by the love of his life. Monica. She leaned forward and kissed him passionately on the mouth, the way lovers do when there is longing and passion between them. These two were very close, and they complemented one another perfectly. She sat right next to him.

"Nice show?" asked Tyler.

"Better now that you're here," said Monica.

They kissed again, a series of soft, gentle kisses on the lips. They weren't just madly in love, these two were constantly hot for one another.

"So, how was your day?" asked Monica.

"Life of a security man. A little rough, but nothing I couldn't handle," replied Tyler.

"How are your aunt and uncle doing?"

"They're fine. This deal though, this damn real estate deal. I don't get it. All the properties on Walnut have gone for it."

"All of them except yours."

With a slight measure of concern in his eyes, Tyler nodded affirmatively.

"What does Angie think of all of this?" asked Monica.

"She will not go for it. Her heart is set on turning Rhodesia En Rouge into the premier New Orleans resort getaway for tourists and locals alike. It's her dream, Monica. A dream she's going to see through no matter what the cost."

"I know the feeling," said Monica.

Tyler finished off his drink, realizing the implicit significance of Monica's remark. "Hey, that's right! What happened today with the realtor? That location you had your heart set on in the Garden District for the art gallery?"

Monica had a wise sense of humor. She pouted and began to shake her head, knowing this would get an immediate rise out of Tyler.

He looked at her with sadness and regret.

"Baby, I'm so sorry... They didn't take the offer?"

Monica looked him dead in the eye. A smile from ear-to-ear gradually formed across her face. "Yes, they did!"

"Oh my God!! Baby, I am so happy for you!!" They reached across the table and kissed again. Several times. "So the company accepted?"

"Sure did. I take ownership of the building at the first of the month. As soon as that happens, I contact all my artists, and we start having auctions, shows, events, the works! My parents are thrilled. Those loans they took out on their business paid off. I didn't want to let them down. I'm just so glad they're finally going to be able to see my dream realized."

Tyler couldn't contain himself. He was incredibly proud of her. This only reinforced why he was so deeply in love with her.

"Look at you, you're going to be living the dream. Not too many people in this world are able to look at themselves in the mirror on a daily basis and say that they are actually doing what they love in this life. But you... You had your passion, and now you are going to make it happen. I'm so happy for you, baby."

A tear of heartfelt joy and sincerity formed in Monica's eye. Her feelings of love for Tyler were completely mutual. "You know, Ty... living the dream won't matter to me if you're not with me... to share everything by my side."

Tyler was overwhelmed with emotion. He did everything he could to suppress his feelings until the wellspring of joy he felt for her came forth in a single tear. "I love you, Monica."

"I love you." They embraced and kissed.

"So what's on for tomorrow?" asked Tyler.

"I have to sign the papers tomorrow morning with the former owners and the realtor, then I have a Zumba class to teach around 2."

Tyler nodded in understanding as a slight smile formed across his lips. "You want company tonight?" asked Tyler.

Monica smiled seductively upon hearing his words. "Of course I do."

As they rose from the table to leave, he grabbed his jacket and noticed something on the back of it, by the left shoulder, stuck to the fabric almost like a piece of chewing gum. He examined it closely. It looked like a very small miniature Rubik's Cube, except that it was completely white. The size and coloring explained why he neither felt nor saw it previously. But not wanting to dismiss the notion of it entirely, he placed it in his pocket thinking he would examine it further later on. Monica was slightly ahead of him and stopped when she realized he was still standing by the table.

"Everything ok, Ty?"

"Fine. We're good. Let's go."

* * *

Just outside the club, there were stragglers and night owls still making their way through for an evening nightcap and to catch the final round of dancers doing their thing.

Monica and Tyler stood outside by the main door, but before they got into their individual cars to head back to her place for the evening, something important occurred to Tyler. "Hold on, baby. I almost forgot."

"What is it?" asked Monica.

"There's a business dinner tomorrow night for the Rhodesia, so I have to be there. Last minute emergency type of thing. You know how it is."

"I understand. Will you come by after my last show?"

They smiled and kissed.

"You know I will. I'll see you at your place in a few."

Monica got into her car, a red Alfa Romeo SUV. Always the gentleman, Tyler closed her door as she entered. He walked over to the opposite end of the lot and went over to his car, a beige Denali truck. He opened the door, threw in his jacket and closed the door. He started his engine and slowly followed Monica back to her home as they turned left out of the parking lot.

Further off in the distance, at a darkened corner of the lot, Damon Chambers sat in a grey Prius. He removed an earpiece from his left ear, with a very satisfied smile painted across his face. He started the car, switched on the vehicle lights and quietly drove away. He turned right, the opposite direction from which Tyler and Monica left, driving out into the night to an unknown destination.

11

When the New Orleans night skies were clear and the lights outside the structure were blazing, the Rhodesia En Rouge was truly a magnificent sight to behold. It was a Friday evening. Guests were arriving. Valets were parking cars. Traffic was heavy. It was business as usual at what was soon to become one of the hottest vacation spots in the country.

The most elegant of the five restaurants in the Rhodesia En Rouge was easily Lautrec on Walnut. Seated in a closed section of the restaurant in the private dining room were the six guests of the hour. This was not just an informal gathering amongst friends and professional associates. This was vital business. At the table, wearing the most elegant men's and women's evening wear, were Tyler Wilkes, Rockne Bail, Diane Bouvier, Bernie Llewelyn, Angie Miller, and Kent Stirling. They were in the main course of the evening's dinner. Half of them had chosen the roasted quail in plum sauce with asparagus spears drizzled in olive oil and Rice Pilaf. The other half elected to go with the Prime Rib served with garlic mashed potatoes. Each of them were nursing their favored cocktail of choice.

"I think we can all agree that the chef has most certainly outdone himself," said Bernie.

"Agreed," replied Diane. "The Prime Rib is succulent like never before. Perfectly cooked."

"Ditto for the quail. This is truly one of the best dishes I've ever tasted," said Angie.

Stirling merely nodded his head in agreement.

"So, Kent...," asked Rockne, "what are your thoughts on our fair town?"

"Rock, this is and always has been one of my favorite places in the states. I have quite a bit of history in New Orleans. Professionally speaking, of course."

Rockne and Diane clearly had their interest piqued as they leaned in, intrigued by whatever Stirling had to say. Tyler was the only one in the group who seemed slightly remote, not fully engaged by either the group or the conversation at hand. Something was clearly gnawing at him. It was all there in his deep set eyes as he focused his attention solely on the plate of magnificent Prime Rib in front of him.

"Professionally speaking, Kent?" asked Rockne.

"Yes, Rock..." Stirling said, as he stole a quick glance over at Bernie and Angie. They were the only ones who were aware of his covert operations generated and executed in that part of the world, but they remained silent, allowing Stirling to regale them with his story. "I'm not sure whether or not Angie had mentioned to you at some point that I'm actually a doctor."

Rockne and Diane looked at one another with astonishment and curiosity.

"Interesting. My brother's a doctor as well. One of the best in his field," said Diane.

"Really? Which is that?" asked Stirling.

"Neurology," she said. "Edwin Bouvier. His practice is in Chicago. What about you?"

"Cardiologist. I'm also a vascular surgeon. I had a residency period in New Orleans several years ago. I've always loved it here."

"I see. Where is your primary practice now?" asked Rockne.

"To be candid, I had been living in the Yucatan for several years. Dividing my time between Merida and Belize where I was head of the cardiology departments for each central hospital But... things happened."

As Stirling began to reminisce about the past, Bernie could see that he was still affected by it. The sting of what had happened in the Yucatan was a wound that hadn't completely healed.

"Kent was very advanced in his techniques. Very concerned about the welfare of his patients. Modern medicine has a tendency to dovetail and progress in mysterious ways. The local governments there found some of Dr. Stirling's methods too radical for their conservative mottos. But make no mistake, Rockne and Diane, Kent Stirling isn't just one of the finest human beings I know... He's also one of the very best cardiologists and vascular surgeons in the world. For him, the welfare and well-being of all of his patients has always been priority one. For Kent Stirling, life... is what matters most."

Upon hearing Bernie's incredibly moving dedication, Stirling raised his glass, toasting Bernie. Angie was almost moved to tears. Even Tyler was swept away enough in Bernie's unofficial sermonizing that it took him away from his private concerns, if only for a moment. He looked up and toasted Stirling as well. "To you, Dr. Stirling," he said.

Stirling was definitely moved, but his natural tendency was to always keep his true emotions close to the vest. "Thank you, Ty. Sincerely... And please, call me Kent."

Angie placed her hand on Stirling's shoulder. He looked at her and leaned towards her. They kissed warmly and affectionately. As she pulled away, she swiftly wiped a tear away from her face. "And on his off time, his hobby is delivering babies on trolley cars," she chimed in.

The entire table suddenly burst out into unhinged, unanimous laughter, not sure if what they were hearing was designed to merely lighten the mood, or if in fact, general obstetrics were another of Stirling's many hidden gifts and skill sets.

"Kent, is that really true?" asked Diane.

"Not to that extent, Diane. But there was an unexpected incident the other day when Angie and I were riding the St. Charles Trolley over to the Garden District, and there happened to be a pregnant woman on board."

"And you ended up delivering the baby?" asked Rockne

Stirling nodded affirmatively.

"Mother and child are alright?" asked Diane.

"Both of them are perfectly fine. Happy and healthy."

"Certainly can't ask for a better ending than that," said Rockne.

In that instant, Diane smiled and leaned forward, focusing her poised gaze and elegant charms onto both Angie and Stirling.

"So I really would like to know more about the two of you. How did you both end up finding one another?"

Angie and Stirling looked at one another in unspoken delight Slight smiles formed across their faces, but they both knew how to react quickly and think on their feet, because there was no denying that as loaded as Diane's question was, it had clearly been posited to them before, so they knew how to muddle through in a way that was charming and conversational without any indicators or clues as to the truth or any of their secrets from the past. Angie leaned forward and began to engage with Rockne and Diane, delivering her version of their story.

In that moment, Tyler noticed that his aunt and uncle, along with Stirling and Angie, were deeply engrossed in their private chatter. Bernie was just wrapping up his meal, enjoying the company and sipping his drink in between. Tyler was seated at the head of the table, and Bernie was sitting next to him. He leaned over to ask him a question, and he tried to be as inconspicuous as possible because he didn't want to be heard by the others, nor did he want to attract their attention. In a very hushed tone, almost a whisper, he said, "Bernie, can I ask you something?"

"Sure, Ty. What's going on?" Bernie was always razor-sharp in reading people, so he knew how to mirror someone and play along. As such, he answered in a fairly whispered tone as well.

Tyler reached into his pants pocket and pulled out the small, white Rubik's Cube type object, handing it over to Bernie. It was approximately the size and shape of a small ice cube.

Bernie only needed to examine it and place it to his ear for a scant couple of seconds to assess it and analyze precisely what he was looking at. "Where'd you get this, Ty?"

"I actually found it at my girlfriend's place of work. It was just... lying on a table. The look of it caught my eye, but it seemed almost like it was there for a reason. I figured I'd let you check it out as soon as I saw you."

Bernie looked closely at Tyler as he spoke. Tilted his head slightly as he looked into his eyes. The fact was that he knew he might be lying about having found the thing on a table. But he played along, and shared the information with him as to the true nature of the object.

"Well, to tell you the truth, this is actually a high density bug."

"A bug?" asked Tyler.

"That's right. It has a very low level of frequency, but with expansive range and an extreme degree of clarity. It catches all ambient sound and even the quietest levels of conversation. You can hear practically anything with these."

A veiled look of concern swept across Tyler's face. "Is it on right now?"

"No, I switched it off when you handed it to me."

"How the hell did you do that?"

A slight smile formed across Bernie's face. "I've created a few of these in my time, Ty. Let's just say that I know how to handle them, and I'm very familiar with this particular model."

He handed it back to Tyler who immediately placed it back in his pocket. The look on Tyler's face was easy to read. He had the weight of the world seemingly bearing down on him, but Bernie wasn't about to probe too hard because he knew that with the inaugural opening of the new restaurant/ballroom just around the corner, he and Stirling needed to stay close to Angie and in the vicinity of the Rhodesia En Rouge.

"Thanks, Bernie. Listen, I don't want to make a big deal here with the whole group, especially my aunt and uncle."

"But?" asked Bernie.

"I've got a couple of my security team who checked in late to their posts, and I just need to make my rounds across the entire place, make sure it's still all quiet on the western front... Know what I mean?"

"I know exactly what you mean. It's your job. Don't worry about it. I'll cover for you here. Do what you have to do."

Tyler was grateful, patted Bernie on his shoulder. "Thanks very much, Bernie, I appreciate it."

Bernie nodded affirmatively.

And without stirring up too much commotion, Tyler was out gracefully and stealthily through the back door exit, leading to the exterior of the hotel and the main parking grounds.

Angie, Rockne and Diane were still heavily enmeshed in their conversation, but Tyler's sudden disappearance from the group was enough to distract Stirling and capture his attention.

He looked over at Bernie, signaling him with his eyes, so as to assess the situation. Bernie merely closed his eyes and nodded his head, indicating in an unspoken manner between them that everything was fine, nothing to be concerned about. Stirling acknowledged Bernie and rejoined the group conversation. But for a split second, Bernie looked over at the exit door thinking that what had Tyler so quietly concerned, causing him to rush out of there, could indeed have been very personal.

* * *

Outside the hotel, Tyler ran full tilt towards his car. He got in and sped off, heading out towards the Warehouse District and to the specific location where Monica, his girlfriend, was presumably celebrating a going away party with her co-workers at the Emerald Carousel.

Mercifully, traffic was light that evening, allowing Tyler to maneuver in and out of lanes at fairly high speed. Police looking to give speeding tickets at this time of night were prevalent but not excessive. Tyler didn't care. Bernie got his wheels turning as soon as he realized the white cube was a listening device. He thought the worst and prayed for the best. In the dangerous world Tyler inhabited, that was the safest and only way to live. He approached the Ogden and went behind to where the Emerald Carousel was located. He parked. It was later in the evening, and it was closed to the public for purposes of celebrating this private staff party in honor of Monica. Tyler scanned all around the perimeter. Everything seemed fine. There were magenta and yellow neon lights flashing from the inside of the structure. He surreptitiously walked towards the club so as to get a closer look inside. This was Monica's night, and he didn't want to be noticed. As he walked to the edge of the walkway, allowing him to peer through the windows from where the light was emanating, he caught a complete glimpse of something that instantly relieved him. Monica and her co-workers, a group of about twelve other women, were dancing, drinking, socializing and generally having a good time. The music playing in the background was classic 70s disco. The Bee Gees, to be exact. Tyler exhaled a sigh of relief. He could leave Monica to her own devices to enjoy her party. But as he walked away, he paused for a moment mid-step. With a smile, he thought this would be a nice opportunity to surprise her. He turned back around to knock on the main door to access the party, and then it happened—

The Emerald Carousel exploded into a massive ball of orange and yellow flame.

Cork, metal, glass, and splinters of wood rained across the entire parking lot. The concussion of the blast was so enormous that the fireball reached 50 feet into the sky above. Tyler was lifted off his feet and catapulted backwards like a rag doll. He crash landed through the windshield of Monica's car. The blow shook him to his core as he bounced off the car and landed on the asphalt with a coarse, resounding thud. He suffered some slight cosmetic scrapes across his face and upper body. Nothing too severe. He was shaken but more stunned as he came to his senses and gradually got back on his feet. There was smoke rising from his jacket as he walked slowly and steadily towards the decimated structure that was once the Emerald Carousel. There were incoming sirens wailing in the background. Police and Fire Department were on their way. Tyler could only stare at the building as it burned. No one would have survived that blast, and he knew it. He began to shake convulsively as he stood there, followed by tears and a rattling form of crying that struck him to his core. Monica was gone. She was more than just the love of his life. She was his complete world, and now that world was shattered and taken away in the blink of an eye. He couldn't contain himself. The pain and grief of losing her was overwhelming. And in that moment, Tyler looked up at the skies above and screamed.

12

The city of Reykjavik was more than just the capital of Iceland it was also the epicenter of Iceland's cultural, economic and governmental activity. It had always been a popular destination among foreigners, and it remained one of the cleanest, greenest, and safest cities on the planet. Reykjavik was located on the southern shore of the Faxafloi Bay, and it was the world's northernmost capital of a sovereign state. The surrounding capital region had a population of roughly 250,000 which constituted more than half of the country's population. There were landmarks to be savored, studied and explored, among the most notorious and revered of which were the Perlan, the Reykjavik Cathedral, and the Harpa. Of the most artistic and regional significance was the Hallgrimskirkja, the largest church in Iceland and the second tallest structure in the country. Known for its uniquely curved spire and side wings, this was where the skyline view of Reykjavik in all its vivid, glorious splendor could truly be appreciated.

And nestled most curiously in the northeast corner of the principal village adjacent to the Hallgrimskirkja was a patently boring-looking one-story warehouse, surrounded by various small businesses scattered and combined with the occasional smaller derelict warehouse or abandoned facility. There was no signage either in front of or behind it. There were never any cars parked in front, and it had no connecting parking structure. For all intents and purposes, it very well could have been abandoned, just like others in this portion of the village. But it wasn't...

Inside the building, the dank corridors gave off the scent of alcohol. There was a modern, battered decadence to this place, tinged with the design of a Frankenstein-type lair. There were experiments going on here—studies in human aberration and mutation, taking exceptional beings who were construed as gifted individuals and doing whatever it took to maximize their unique gifts. The corridors led to serpentine hallways which had doors leading to rooms or chambers within the walls. One seemingly endless passageway climaxed at a spiral staircase which consisted of no less than 250 stairs. It was absolutely enormous and seemingly endless in its endless tracking spiral. But therein lay the most seismic revelation this place had to offer...

As soon as one hit the bottom of the stairwell, there was a short corridor of about twenty steps leading to a doorway. Once the door was opened, it revealed what appeared to be a hotel lobby filled with offices, consulting areas, experimental rooms and training venues. There was even a spacious dining area and conference room. This was designed to be an indoor, underground small city of sorts, but what happened down there was an insidious mixture of science and evil, merging in the most inconceivable ways possible. Known simply as the Lair, this was the principal domain, headquarters, meeting place, experimental facility, call it what you will, of Max Thulin, the principal architect of the secret society and organization known as the Sandbox.

On this particular day, there was a bizarre series of tests being performed on a gentleman named Wolf Relling, a half-German, half-Danish operative, who in recent years was having problems on missions due to issues with his very peculiar gift of being able to control the minds of others. He was not inhuman. He was a mortal man, and he took pride in being a formidable asset who successfully accomplished the assignments that were tasked to him. But a recent string of high-priority hits resulted in aborted failures, and this was a luxury Max Thulin could not allow. His method of handling disappointments of this nature was unorthodox to say the least. Never a man of principles, but a man devoted to the powers of science and scientific exploration, he was interested in bringing out the best of those he considered to be his "children" while exploiting their talents to advance his own personal lust for power. Money was never a concern as he was ostensibly born into millions, the product of a very aristocratic pair of European families on both his father's and mother's sides.

Thulin was in his mid-sixties, extremely formal and elegant in his precise but mannered way of speaking. He was fluent in eight languages and able to communicate through signing as well. His was a mind difficult to comprehend and equally challenging to circumvent and defeat. Bald since his mid-forties and able to stun one into submission through the penetrating gaze of his deep-set blue eyes, he was a force to be reckoned with and a man who understood that the balance of power was always in question.

On that somber afternoon, Thulin and his chief biophysicist/ genetic engineer, Graham Berenger, were performing a technique that utilized a combined fusion of science and mental stimulation to provoke a given reaction. By firing rampant streams of disconnected imagery deep into the inner vortex of the mind's eye, they intended to take the cerebellum of Wolf Relling and supercharge it to the point where he could actually manipulate other human beings' minds. Besides Wolf Relling, there were two other individuals on the planet, known by Thulin, with the ability to achieve similar extraordinary results. But they were not of primary concern right now, not while he was using audiovisual hypnosis, a peculiar avant-garde approach to mental awakening and reappraisal, on Wolf Relling.

Thulin and Berenger, in the evaluation room, watched through one-way glass at the activities being imposed upon the unsuspecting Wolf Relling, who was seated in the room known as the Game Changer. Presumably, the results were designed to alter and improve the subject, but this was the first time they were attempting this specific technique, with Wolf Relling as their guinea pig.

Relling was seated in a steel swiveling chair. His extremities were firmly tied, and he could not move his arms or legs one single inch. His eyes were taped open via a skin-like substance that had the potency and strength of masking tape. It blended into his natural complexion, so it was virtually impossible to see a trace of it. It simply looked as if his eyes were wide open as though he had been shot out of a cannon. There was a savage irony as to why Thulin was really utilizing this technique to generate this change in Relling, but the end result still remained to be seen. How he would proceed moving forward would be exclusively informed by how Relling reacted to the induced hypnosis.

"Wolf, are you ready?" asked Thulin in his velvety Scandinavian accent. His English was nearly perfect and accent-free, but you could still hear the strains of Danish background. "We're about to begin. I simply need you to relax and clear your mind. It's extremely important that you vacate any thoughts or concerns you may have had before we began prepping you for this."

Graham Berenger was completely subservient to Thulin's needs and desires. He hung on his every word and gesture because he worshipped him in a strange sort of way, almost as if he saw Thulin as some sort of all-powerful deity. He was Oxford educated and malevolent to the extreme, but with a hint of breeding and impeccable good manners.

"Professor, the levels are modified now to approximately tier 5," said Berenger. "Any higher, he could crack under pressure. We need to assert the viability of the procedure before we start calibrating for any future subjects."

"Yes, Graham. Proceed as indicated. We'll... improvise if necessary."

"As you wish, Professor."

Wolf was relaxed, completely under the deluded impression that he was being tested that afternoon to prepare for a mission of a highly delicate and grave nature. He never questioned orders, and he was only there to serve the greater good, which he believed to be the sole intent of everything involving the Sandbox.

The hot, white lights of the Game Changer room gradually began to dim, and the chair on which Relling was seated began to rise and pivot. The swiveling tripod on which the chair rested slowly began to swerve and move in all directions. The equipment was being tested before the experiment began. Relling was firmly in place with a clear mind and a receptive attitude. Fear was not in the equation for him. He trusted how the Sandbox treated him completely and utterly.

"Professor, I'm ready when you are," shouted Relling, uncertain as to what extent they could hear him.

"Equipment is secure. Images are ready. Audio is prepared," said Berenger.

"Proceed," replied Thulin. There was an ominous feeling permeating the dimly-lit evaluation room. A very strange sort of trance-inducing New Age music emanated from the walls, designed to invoke an atmosphere of rest and relaxation.

As the experiment began, it became clear from the outset that the velocity of the imagery and the swiveling movement of the chair was designed to amplify and increase in short round bursts, informed not by the speed of the images or the loudness of the sound, but rather by the reactions of the subject. This was designed to be a total mind bend through and through. But how it would evolve and conclude for its initial subject remained to be seen.

Echoing throughout the Game Changer were dissonant sounds of traffic, like screeching cars careening on a highway desperately trying to avoid getting into an accident. The images on the screen were a combination of aberrant sexual acts performed between men and women, fused with rampant acts of arbitrary violence involving murders with all forms of weaponry—edged instruments, firearms, flame throwers, grenades, bare hands breaking necks—anything and everything that could potentially dispose of a human being and end a life. The neon-lights began to pulsate a bit more rhythmically. The imagery became more and more rapid in its cutting but emphatically hybridized in its nature. This was a very heady cocktail of sex and violence being fed into the cerebral cortex of its subject. For the moment, Relling was taking it all in, but his brainwaves were stable. This was not what Thulin was looking for. He needed to see that there was additional stimulation affecting the brain scan so as to amplify the strength of the cerebellum whenever the subject placed focus on a potential target to induce a sense of mind control.

"I'm not seeing any immediate changes or modified effect on our friend, Mr. Relling. Increase the dosage and the speeds by 50 percent," said Thulin.

"But Professor, we're operating right now at what is presumably maximum resistance for any subject," replied Berenger.

"I understand that, Graham. But as you and I both know, Wolf Relling is no ordinary subject. 50 percent. Do it."

Berenger was there to serve, but there were occasional instances when even he felt torn as to the real intent behind Thulin's scientific experiments. He looked at Thulin beneath hooded eyes, but acquiesced to his request.

"Yes, Professor."

Inside the Game Changer, the lights suddenly began to dim to near blackness. The sound dropped to a level of total muteness. The imagery from all four walls suddenly disappeared revealing only the blank spaces of all four corners in the room. Relling was confused but not shaken by the sudden shift in environment.

"Professor! Mr. Berenger! Is something wrong?"

There was absolute silence until Thulin's soothing, authoritarian voice rose out of the unseen speakers in the room. "Just relax, Wolf... We just made a few minor adjustments to the procedure. We'll begin again momentarily... Are you ready?"

"Yes, Professor! Whenever you say!"

The room was so quiet Relling could hear his own breathing and heartbeats. Then out of nowhere, chaos ensued. The screeching sounds were nearly deafening. The barrage of sexual and violent imagery began riddling the walls at such rapid fire speed that the human eye could barely follow it, but above all else, the steel swiveling chair on which Relling was seated began to move at an inhumanly rapid pace. Relling tried desperately to keep up with the streaming torrent of images bathing the four walls, but it was impossible to focus on anything, and the screeching sounds of tires and crashing were off the decibel chart.

Inside the evaluation room, the brain scanner and the accompanying brain waves began to accelerate from the overdose of induced stimuli. Thulin began to smile like a child in a toy store who couldn't contain himself because he'd just found the toy of his dreams. But he kept his voice down even though his enthusiasm was nearly through the roof, repeating, "It's happening. It's happening."

Berenger watched Relling being thrown around the room violently, reacting in total extremis to the sights and sounds within the Game Changer, while focusing on the brain scan monitor alongside Max Thulin.

Now, Relling was in undeniable physical pain. His head was throbbing and his temples were pulsating as he turned with every contraction of the incessantly violent swiveling chair. He began to scream uncontrollably. Thinking at first that this was the desired effect that Thulin was looking for, Relling resisted showing any kind of opposition or defeat. But as the sounds and images intensified to a degree of cataclysmic proportions, he could no longer contain his fear and paranoia at what was happening. He screamed to no avail, and pleaded, "Professor!! Please!! Make it stop!! I cannot continue!!"

Seconds afterwards, he began to bleed. First out of his eardrums, followed by his eyes, and eventually more profusely from his mouth. Inevitably he passed out and finally succumbed to the ultimate reaction... fatal cardiac arrest.

Thulin and Berenger saw that the movement on the brain scanner completely halted.

"It's over," said Berenger.

Thulin thought for a moment. His brow furling and raised, he couldn't fathom the notion of stagnating when it came to the potential results of Operation Beech Grove. Not now. Not when he was this close.

"This will not stand, Graham."

"I'm sorry, Professor?"

"I said, this cannot be... It is more essential than ever that Dr. Stirling be acquired and brought into the center. Time is of the essence... Where do we stand?"

"Our operatives in the U.S. and in Mexico have been alerted of the current position of our targets, but they also know that the Beech Grove Files are in the wind. Seemingly unattainable."

"Good, let them baffle and ponder and concern themselves. When we truly are in desperate need of their activation, we'll establish contact."

Berenger was sullen, secure in the knowledge that Thulin would never stop pursuing this ultimate goal of creating his vision of a brave, new world.

"As you say, sir... It would be the most prudent course of action."

Thulin nodded affirmatively and with total assurance.

They both looked over at the deceased, bloodied body of Wolf Relling, a tragic victim of their experiments. The blood from his orifices had stained virtually all of his clothing as he lay there, still and lifeless.

"A pity about Mr. Relling. The Game Changer failed us today."

Berenger thought for a moment. And he smiled when something potentially useful dawned upon him. "True, Professor. But remember... we had the potential to expand the subject's brain waves if they already had a cerebral gift of sorts like Mr. Relling.

We were looking for growth to maximize impact and control. But... what has been proven with this procedure is brainwashing."

Thulin knew exactly what Berenger was implying. They leered at one another.

"Yes, Mr. Berenger. You're so right... if we can't improve what is already there, we can change what it has the potential to become."

"That is exactly right, Professor."

Thulin knew they would reach the conclusion of their journey with the results he was looking for. It was simply a matter of how and when. He was marginally distracted by the lingering sight of Relling's dead body. He was a calculating man with no remorse or pity. To him, Relling was merely another experiment waiting to be examined and pushed to the limit. But now that he was gone, Thulin viewed him as nothing more than a space-taking eyesore which needed to be removed. "Graham?"

Berenger was in the corner of the room looking through files from previously completed experiments. Deep in thought, he was snapped out of his studies upon hearing Thulin calling him.

"Yes, Professor?"

"Get our local cleaning crew to come here right away to dispose of our problem. We have work to do."

Berenger turned his view to the Game Changer room and Relling's fallen corpse.

"Yes, Professor. Right away."

13

It was a gloomy, typically overcast day on the afternoon that Monica Ekland was laid to rest at Cypress Grove Cemetery. It was known for its distinct Egyptian entrance pillars and wall vaults. The cemetery was actually situated on what was once the Hollywood Plantation. To be more precise, it was in the mid-city area of New Orleans. Founded in 1840, it was also one of the older cemeteries in the city.

The sermon on Monica's behalf had concluded and at the corner of the gravesite, near her final resting place, Tyler was standing by her parents. They were all somberly attired in black, and all three holding hands. It was clear that they were remembering the ray of light that Monica was, always eager to please and filled with the ambitions and hopes to make her way towards a better life and the realization of her dreams. Tyler separated and hugged both Monica's parents. Their cars were nearby, and when they done saying their goodbyes, Monica's parents got into their vehicle, Tyler got into his Denali, and they drove off in opposite directions.

* * *

At home later that evening, Tyler was grief-stricken in a way that didn't simply imbalance him emotionally. The loss of Monica struck him to the root of his core, the seed of his soul, in a way that was unfathomable for the degree of pain he was feeling. He anticipated this, but he also knew that in spite of the reservoirs of anguish cascading through him, life had to move forward. He needed to move on, and he had obligations to fulfill. Not simply to his aunt and uncle, but to Angie and the Rhodesia En Rouge. There was a major event looming on the horizon, with hundreds of people expected to be present. It was the inauguration of the brand new Conference / Ballroom at the Rhodesia En Rouge. The name Angie had decided to bestow upon the resort's latest creation was the Silver Palace.

Tyler had a job to do, and he needed to be on point that evening. People were counting on him—Angie, his aunt, his uncle, his entire team—and he wasn't about to let any of them down. In his heart of hearts, he felt instinctively and intuitively that that was precisely what Monica would have wanted. She would not have wished for Tyler to be sullen and grieving for her. She would have wanted him to be positive and bright whenever he remembered her and the deep singular love they shared during the time they were given.

Tyler's place was modest in size but very richly designed with furnishings from various parts of southeastern America. It was a two bedroom condo located in the Warehouse District. The area had seen significant redevelopment, transforming historic warehouses into stylish condos with high ceilings, exposed brick and modern finishes. This particular structure had a lovely rooftop pool, and Tyler lived directly beneath it. It was a three story building, including the rooftop pool area.

Inside of Tyler's place, he had converted the second bedroom into a home gymnasium, tricked out with all the latest fitness gear and cardiovascular amenities including a spinning cycle and treadmill. The wall was perfectly aligned with weight bars and dumbbells.

Tyler was seated in the main bedroom. Soft music was playing in the background. Enya. He and Monica had a shared mutual appreciation of her soothing and evocative music. He took a picture frame from the side table next to the bed they once shared. As he studied the photograph, a smile worked its way gradually across his face. The photo was very lovely and invoked a feeling of nostalgia. They were seated at the poolside bar at the Hyatt Resort in Cancun, Mexico. It was where they first met and consummated their relationship, instantly knowing they were made for one another. In the photograph, they were crossing arms as they shared and sipped each other's drinks. Their expressions were glowing; they clearly were in the throes of newly discovered bliss.

He inhaled, and as he smelled the evening air from the slightly ajar bedroom window, it subtly fused with the natural scent of the room itself. He reluctantly reached over and grabbed Monica's pillow. He placed the pillow beneath his nose, grabbing a whiff of the rose-scented memory of Monica's beautiful hair, and he just let go. His tears began to flow, and his body stirred and shook convulsively as he stared at the photo while clutching the pillow close to his heart.

The light inside the kitchen of Tyler's condo switched on. He walked in slowly and walked over to the refrigerator. He opened it and realized that the night before Monica was killed, they had actually been discussing that they needed to go shopping for Tyler because he was running low on groceries. He acknowledged it with a slight nod of his head and closed the refrigerator door.

Later that evening, Tyler walked out of the neighborhood corner market holding two full bags of groceries. Stocked with vegetables and other items, the greenery was brimming and peering out the edges of each bag. Then Tyler heard it.

A scream, echoing from the adjacent alleyway. It was a woman, and as she turned the corner of the alley leading to the midway section of sidewalk where Tyler stood, she tripped and fell, landing hard on the asphalt. Tyler set down the two bags of groceries and immediately ran to her aid.

She was groggy and disoriented as he kneeled carefully before her. He raised her slowly and turned her around gently. Her hair was matted, some stuck to her face. He moved the strands of hair to reveal one of the most striking pairs of eyes and luminous faces he had ever seen. It was Iris Ravenne's protege... Zara Zimmermann. Her face trembled from the shock that she had clearly endured. Seemingly on the run from what seemed to have been a violent encounter, she gradually calmed down. Considering how frantic and uncertain of her surroundings she appeared, she looked remarkably unscathed. There were bruises around her legs and arms, but her face was essentially undamaged, save for a few cosmetic scrapes just above both of her eyebrows. She was remarkably stealthy in the manner in which she fell because she broke the impact by covering her face with crossed elbows when she hit the asphalt.

She pulled herself away from Tyler, and they simply sat across from one another. He remained quiet, allowing her to get her bearings. She kept eyes trained on him, at first warily, but when she realized she could trust him, they softened. He cautiously reached out and touched her arm. She didn't flinch. Speaking softly, he asked, "Miss, are you alright?"

Zara tilted her head slightly, looking at him with piqued curiosity.

"It's important we get you checked out. Get you to a hospital. Make sure that you're OK."

Zara still did not utter a single word. Tyler seemed more curious than concerned, but he was eager to help out what he perceived to be a woman desperately in need of help and perhaps medical attention. He knew she was visibly shaken, and he approached her as delicately as possible, moving slowly and speaking softly. Still sitting, she leaned back against the brick wall. He sat in front of her, watching, one leg bent with his arm resting on his knee. She slowly crossed her arms across her chest, signaling a lingering sense of both insecurity and fear.

"Look, are you from around here?" asked Tyler.

Zara slowly shook her head no.

"No, alright..." He searched for just the right words to say. "Do you happen to know who did this to you?"

She was reluctant to reveal too much of what had actually gone down, but with a decisive sense of affirmation, she relented and nodded affirmatively, indicating that she was aware and familiar with her attackers.

"You do... Good. Look, let me just ask you... What's your name?"

She looked at him closely and carefully, knowing that once she opened this door, she had to be prepared to walk through it. She formed a magnetic smile across her stunning lips and answered, "Sara." She was very precise to not pronounce the Z of her name.

Tyler nodded, he smiled from ear to ear in his typically warm and ingratiating manner. As they locked eyes and connected in that moment, he reached out to her by extending his hand forward. Zara looked at it cautiously at first, then placed her hand in his.

* * *

Behind the principal building that was the Rhodesia En Rouge resort hotel, there was a concrete flight of just over 400 steps. This stone staircase led up to the private residence of Angie Miller. She made the very deliberate decision to make her mark in New Orleans because of her own family heritage, and if she had the ability to do so, she wanted to build her dream home behind what would be her definitive place of business. She ultimately fulfilled that dream. At the very top of those 400 concrete steps rested the one story home of Angie Miller, and it was a sight to behold.

Favoring the indigenous style of architecture that was native to New Orleans, Angie's home was a Shotgun House. Known for their long, narrow, and rectangular shape, this was the predominant architectural style in New Orleans. Her home was raised on brick piers, and it featured a narrow porch with a roof apron supported by columns and brackets. Hers was augmented by some very ornate Victorian detailing. But the most distinguishing feature of Angie's home was the floor plan because the rooms were arranged in a straight line from front to back, hence the name, which implied a straight "shot" through the house because of the way the doors were aligned.

At the very far end of the vast, cavernous hallway of the four bedroom home was the master bedroom, Angie's room, and that particular evening, the sounds emanating from the interior were those of unparalleled erotic heights.

Stirling and Angie were both completely nude, their bodies firm, fit and perfectly formed. Their proportions were stunning, each of them graced with a bronze, toned ass that would make most men and women green with envy. The heat of their erogenous zones was pulsating. They stood kissing passionately and fully on the mouth, and Stirling's cock gradually began to rise and stiffen. As the tip of his engorged shaft grazed ever-so lightly against the inner thigh of Angie's inviting region, she could feel herself surrender to his incomparable masculinity. Her wetness consumed her, and she longed to feel him deep within the moisture of her peaked state of excitement. She ran her fingertips across the muscular curves of his tight gluteal muscles, which only made Stirling more attuned to her desires. He slowly worked his way down, cupping her smooth breasts in his hands, while allowing his tongue to flicker ravenously across the width of her warm areolas. Like a harmoniously synched opera, they knew each other's hot zones and trigger points. In conjunction with his attending to her every inch, which he worshipped like a sacred temple, she stoked his flames further as she reached for his stiffened rod and began to stroke it. The fire in his balls was gradually brewing, and as he went down even lower, he slowly began to devour her labia, gently kissing her clitoris, feeling the warmth of her desire consume his overpowering state of arousal. Slowly, he lifted her off her legs, taking her in his arms and holding her delicately by her gorgeous ass. The ease with which he did it gave off the air that her 130-pound frame was as light as a feather. Angie ran her long-nailed fingertips across Stirling's broad, powerful shoulders as he laid her down across the bench at the foot of the king-sized bed.

He stood up, gently opened her legs and placed her feet on his shoulders, and just as he prepared to enter her completely, she caught a quick glimpse of the glistening head of his fully aroused penis. The sight of it alone sent her into shuddering waves of unhinged ecstasy. And as he entered her, they moaned together. Low, guttural moans of mutually felt ardor. Only this was not an elemental passion driven by unhinged lust. These were waves of deeply felt love. The type of love felt by two human beings who invariably always connect and become one person through the power and communication of sexual consummation.

Slowly and carefully, his shaft throbbed inside her and rhythmically they began to move in unison, hitting each other's hot spots and turning each other on like they had never been before. The love Stirling and Angie felt for each other was a type that was indescribable if only because the intellectual connection made by the two had already sown the seed for everything else that would follow throughout the decades and turbulent times they shared with each other. As his thrusting intensified, she popped her height of orgasmic delight, which in turn released his torrent of passion, cascading and filling the walls of her inner being. They embraced and kissed, followed by Stirling, making a pithy remark which always amused them both.

"And once again, we couldn't even make it to the bed."

They both burst into spontaneous laughter, recognizing that their bond was a truly unique one, seldom felt or shared by any two people on the planet.

* * *

Stirling and Angie stood side-by-side on the veranda of her bedroom. It was a lovely space, overlooking not only the Rhodesia En Rouge below, but with a sleek view of part of the French Quarter and the underlying New Orleans skyline. The colors that evening were bold, vibrant and intoxicatingly beautiful. The sky was clear, the stars were bright, and the moon was full. They each had a couple of drinks resting on the ledge of the balcony. Seven and Sevens. As they sipped, Stirling looked over at Angie. He gently caressed the side of her face, moving her lion's mane of hair away to glance at her perfectly structured profile. She felt his gaze on her and smiled. And as she turned to look at him directly, their eyes connected in a way that signaled their love was a fragile, delicate thing, and they both treasured every second they were in each other's company. She leaned forward, and they kissed delicately on the lips. As she pulled away from him slowly, she turned and faced the magnificent sights of her hotel and the city skyline just behind it.

"Beautiful view," said Angie.

Stirling's eyes remained fixed on Angie's singular profile.

"It certainly is," he replied.

They both smiled as she continued to face the outward view of the city she so adored.

"You know," said Sterling, "there's something you still haven't explained to me... and I asked you about this a while ago."

Angie looked over at Stirling with a slightly perplexed expression. "I'm not sure I know what you mean."

Stirling took another swig from his glass, looking out towards the multi-colored skyline. "You mentioned those visions. That you were seeing images of... yourself. The headaches. The occasional blackouts. When did that start?"

Angie shot him a quick look with concern in her face as she closed her eyes.

Sterling said, "And tell me exactly what Max Thulin and the company have to do with it." His tone was severe. Not because he was grilling her and forcing an answer he suspected had been kept away for personal reasons, but because he was worried that her well-being could be gravely compromised for reasons he was trying desperately to comprehend.

Angie shook her head. "Stirling..."

"Miller, come on... Don't keep this from me."

She looked at him with a depth of sadness in her eyes.

"I'm here for you," said Stirling.

"Stirling, I swear I wish that Bernie had never told you anything about this. Of all people. Not you. Not now... You don't belong here."

"Fuck that way of thinking!" Stirling snapped at Angie, and it was a tone and a side of him she had never experienced. "Listen to me... No one on this Earth could ever love you the way I did... And the way I still do."

Angie fought hard to keep back her tears. She knew she needed to come clean with him, and the last thing she wanted to do was to break down.

"Angie..."

Her eyes widened. He had never called her that before in all the years they had known one another. She was always "Miller" and he was always "Stirling." Unable to hold back, a single tear streamed down her face, which she wiped away instantly.

Stirling recognized that this was difficult for her, but as was always the case when it came to Angie Miller, he completely placed his heart in her hands. "I came back to the world and back on the grid for one reason and one reason alone... You."

Angie placed her hand on the side of Stirling's face. He took it in his hand and kissed it gently, holding it in his own hand as he bore his soul to the woman he never stopped loving. "Please... don't shut me out."

She nodded, kissed Stirling's hand and pulled away slightly, taking her drink and finishing it with one final swig. Stirling knew she was mustering the strength to come clean and he gently placed his hand on her back. She looked up to the sky as she began to speak.

"You know, it took me a long time to find my way back. Here to New Orleans. At the same time, when we were basically forced to separate because of the whole Vienna debacle, I knew that 'better left apart' would be preferable to 'better off dead.'"

Stirling listened intently, hanging fiercely on her every word and gesture.

Angie bit her lip, tried to take another swig of her drink, not realizing the glass was already empty. She reached over and took a sip from Stirling's glass. She was in deep confessional mode, and Stirling simply allowed her to be because he could tell she was finally coming clean.

"I made my decision somewhere between Jakarta and Hawaii that I needed to keep moving. But along the way, I noticed that I was able to just read people's thoughts and get into their minds in a way that... even you couldn't do back in the day."

Stirling stayed completely still and quiet. Whatever was running through his mind as Angie spoke, he kept it to himself.

"One day, in Oahu, I think I must have just gotten into the mind of the wrong person. I got made that day, and I started running from that incident forward. Never able to sit still anywhere for more than a few weeks before I was suddenly detected and marked again... Stirling, I have so much blood. So much fucking blood on my hands you have no idea..."

She paused to release her tears. Stirling arched his eyebrows, holding back his own emotions. He felt pain because her pain was his heartache, but he consoled her with his gentle touch and loving embrace, allowing her to continue.

"I had to kill. Programmed to execute the way we were trained at the Sandbox. But not in the name of King or Country. No, I was being forced to kill in the name of simply being left to my own devices... They simply refused to leave me alone... Fucking Thulin, he was the one. He was the one giving the orders. At the same time, I had crossed paths with so many different enemy agents along the way that something must have snapped in my head from the stress because that was when I started seeing these double visions... of myself... So one day, I did what any sane person would have done."

"You disappeared," said Stirling.

"Better. I just went ahead and faked my own death. Reckless driving along the serpentine cliffside highways off the Amalfi Coast."

"What did you do?" asked Stirling.

Angie looked out into the vast nighttime sky and clearly began to remember the exact day that she officially died. It was a clear day on the Amalfi Drive. Skies were clear, and so were the waters of the Tyrrhenian Sea below. Azure blue-green. She drove the circuitous path of the Strada Statale 163 Amalfitana. Breathtaking views, with a highway carved into the side of the cliffs, and hairpin turns and bends that earned it the nickname 'the road with 1001 turns.'

Heading into the picturesque town of Positano, her charcoal grey Porsche 911 sped along the snakelike road, curving around each and every turn with the finesse of a gazelle on wheels. Reaching a straight run with no curves, the car hit a top speed of 180 miles an hour, swerved off the main road ever so slightly and broke the metal retainer. The Porsche flew through the air and a black clad figure wearing a mask in a one piece leather jumpsuit opened the driver's side door, pivoting away from the car. The lone figure landed feet first straight as a knife cutting through the azure waters of the Tyrrhenian. The Porsche nosedived straight into the jagged rocks below, exploding on impact, setting forth a mushroom shaped ball of flames which wafted into the skies above, a plume of billowing smoke and flames.

Beneath the waters of the ocean, the masked figure swam elegantly and quickly through the dazzling realm of translucent liquid space. Approaching a compact mini-submarine designed for two occupants, the masked swimmer approached it from below and knocked on the lower hatch. A tube extended, descending from the hatch like an extended ladder through which the figure could climb and gradually ascend into the vessel's inner core. As the swimmer climbed, the tube chute gradually closed and ascending behind the mysterious figure. Once the Porsche driver was safely inside, the chute locked and sealed itself, allowing the miniature submarine-like vessel to turn in the opposite direction and drift away through the endless sea.

Nestled and dry in the sturdiness and security of the vessel, the mystery figure's hand extended itself to the engineer and operator of this mini-sub. It was a feminine woman's hand. Angie's. She had driven off the Amalfi Drive, allowing her Porsche to crash and burn, knowing she could easily escape detection. No body was ever recovered, and they had her on high alert for detection and extraction while she was taking refuge off the Amalfi Coast. That was when she decided it was time to disappear… forever. And the man who extended his hand to pull her up to the warmth and safety of the sub was the gadget master himself, Bernie Llewelyn. As Angie and Bernie looked at one another they smiled and hugged warmly. Angie exhaled, relieved that now she might be able to resume a normal life.

"Thank you," she whispered into Bernie's ear.

When Angie finished telling her amazing story, Stirling was both relived and amazed. "So it was Bernie who saved you. Helped give you a fresh start. He was the only one who knew everything from the very beginning."

"Because, like you, ever since the very beginning with the Sandbox, Bernie has always been the only one I could completely trust."

"Not the only one, Angie," said Stirling.

Angie loved hearing Stirling say that. She also knew that he was right. There were two people in the world she knew she could trust with her life.

Stirling looked out to the sky and reflected before he spoke. "Look..."

Angie gave him her undivided attention.

Sterling continued, "The Silver Palace is having its grand opening in a few days. All eyes will be on you. It's your night. Your dream is finally becoming a reality. There's no way we're not going to see that through. But... we stay frosty, and we keep a sharp eye on all corners because all I can tell you is this... I'm here to stay. I lost you once... And I'll be damned if I'm going to lose you again."

Angie looked at him with unconditional love as tears formed in her eyes once again. Stirling wiped one off her cheek. He brought her towards him, and they kissed fully and deeply as lovers who are also soulmates would do. They embraced, holding each other tighter and closer than ever before because at that exact moment in time, everything else simply fell away. That was when Angie Miller and Kent Stirling realized that come hell or high water, they would always be there for each other.

14

There were cars lined as far as the eye could see the evening of the grand opening of the Silver Palace ballroom at the Rhodesia En Rouge. The traffic along Walnut Street was jammed to absolute gridlock as the queue of stretch limos and luxury sports cars began arriving at the front entrance of the Rhodesia, depositing a combination of the New Orleans Elite coupled with high-rolling clientele from all across the globe.

The interior of the ballroom was an eye-popping sight to behold. It stood to reason that Angie named it the Silver Palace, with silver linings literally bathed all across the corners and table centerpieces. Even the chandeliers, standing light fixtures and chair corners were accented and conceived with a bold emphasis on silver. Angie's late mother, Helene, had been a jewelry designer, whose most memorable pieces were focused on the creation of silver in its most dazzling forms.

Additionally, the design team of the Silver Palace focused on the scale, composition, and proportions of the architecture. The use of color adorning the various sofas, cushions, and fabrics was loosely inspired by Lake Como and the Mediterranean. Overall, the atmosphere was elegant, sophisticated, and contemporary. And capping it off, directly above the central dance floor was a ceiling-sized skylight with a gorgeous view of the Heavens beyond.

Slowly but surely, the guests began to arrive and fill the room by taking their seats at their assigned tables, lining themselves up for drinks at the ornately dressed silver and glass bar, or taking their first, casual spins on the dance floor. The band was a local favorite called the Purple Hues, specializing in blues, reggae, and modern Jazz with a touch of vintage disco thrown in for variety.

Stirling was in typically elegant form that evening, dressed to the nines in his signature off-white tuxedo dinner jacket, form-fitting black slacks, a peak lapel, a single mother-of-pearl button closure, a white-on-white striped shirt, a black batwing bow tie, and a red carnation boutonniere to complete the ensemble. He walked, sleek and catlike, across the main floor of the room and was stopped dead in his tracks when he noticed the sight which lay before him. Guests were walking by and brushing past him, even occasionally grazing his shoulders admiring his looks, but nothing could break his distraction because he was entranced...

Angie had arrived. She was a vision in green. The sleeveless dress caressed her flawless curves and was designed to accentuate the fullness and shape of her irresistibly feminine form. Slit across the right leg and made of the finest silk fabric, her elegance and grace was in peak form as she moved in step with the band's music. Stirling walked towards her. They held hands and looked into each other's eyes.

"You're indescribable, Miller... In every way, shape, and form."

She savored every inch of his chiseled, handsome face, admiring how equally refined he was in his choice of special evening attire.

"That makes two of us, Stirling."

They kissed softly on the lips. The world seemed to be spinning all around them as they took a 360 degree turn together, holding each other's hands as they admired the scope and scale of Angie's dream and lifelong ambition finally coming to fruition.

"Remember this moment, Miller. We're all here because of you. Never forget that you and you alone made this possible. I'm so happy to be here to share this with you."

One of Kent Stirling's gifts, although he had several, was his gift of language, knowing what to say and exactly when to say it. He didn't mince words... ever. He said what he meant, and he meant what he said at all times, regardless of the occasion or circumstance. And at this particular moment, he rendered Angie Miller completely speechless. She could only respond to him right then and there with the heartfelt expression of the way he truly made her feel. She looked deeply into his eyes.

"I love you, Stirling."

Now Stirling was at a loss for words. For once, and possibly the first time, he was truly aware of what it meant to be in the presence of unconditional love.

"I love you... Angie."

They kissed once more and embraced. She pulled away and looked over at the crowd that was gradually growing and culminating at both the bar and the dance floor.

"I think I better start greeting some of the guests."

Stirling nodded approvingly. Angie turned and walked towards the center of the ballroom. He scanned the perimeter once more, always vigilant, forever alert, keenly attuned to the sights that belonged and the anomalies that didn't. In familiar fashion, he caught the eye of Bernie Llewelyn, who had just arrived. Bernie was wearing a dark blue suit accented with a beige ascot. With his full but perfectly groomed beard, he resembled a cool, silver fox. Stirling and Bernie shook hands as they met by one of the side door entrances leading into the ballroom.

"Silent and smooth just like always," said Stirling.

"After a little over forty years on the job, I would sincerely hope that's the kind of entrance I make at all times," replied Llewelyn.

They smiled with one another as Stirling patted him on the shoulder.

"Guys!" an exuberant male voice called out to Stirling and Bernie.

As they looked over to see who it was, they were approached by a very slick looking Tyler Wilkes, whose well-selected evening attire was more than adequate to the occasion.

"I just wanted to say hello before I get to work. Just need to make sure all of my team are on point for their details and individual assignments. This is Angie's night, and I just want to make sure everything runs as smooth as silk for her and for these wonderful guests who have come here to celebrate the occasion."

"She's lucky to have you leading the troupe, Tyler," said Bernie.

"Absolutely... The best man for the job is also the only man for the job, and we're looking at him," chimed in Stirling.

Tyler was slightly moved by their mutual vote of confidence because it stood to reason that he had tremendous respect and admiration of both of these men. He looked up to both of them. "That means a lot, gentlemen, coming from both of you. I mean it." Stirling and Bernie both smiled as Tyler addressed them. "Hey, and before you know it, we might have something else to talk about sooner than later."

"How so?" asked Bernie.

With a slight degree of hesitation, Tyler responded. "I met this girl..."

Stirling and Bernie were stunned as they looked back at him. "You're serious?" asked Stirling.

"It's not what you're thinking. I met her shortly after Monica..." Tyler struggled to say the words as Stirling rested his hand on his shoulder. "I mean, you know, she's a friend, and I'm just... you know... glad I met her. She's been very special, and she kind of... needs my help right now... You know?"

Stirling actually knew exactly what he meant. The longing to assist a helpless individual in need was a powerful emotion, one that Stirling understood intimately. "Ty... I know just what you're saying."

Tyler looked over their shoulders across the length of the ballroom and smiled. "Ok, gentlemen. I just need to check in with Angie and my aunt and uncle before I confirm my team's positions and details. I see the three of them over there at the bar." Stirling and Bernie noticed them conversing and sharing drinks together. Their mood seemed upbeat and enthusiastic. "Let's make it a safe night for everyone, guys."

"You bet, Ty," said Bernie.

Tyler walked towards the bar to join his aunt, uncle, and Angie.

"Kid doesn't waste any time, does he?" quipped Bernie.

"Things happen, Bernie. Sometimes people fall into our lives when we least expect it. You, of all people... should know that."

Bernie nodded in agreement. "You make a good point... But, I actually wanted to share some good news before you become completely occupied for the evening."

"Tell me," said Stirling.

"Your new place tucked away by the French Quarter is finally ready for you to start living there."

"Took a little longer than usual, Bern. I was almost ready to propose to Angie that we move in together."

They laughed together momentarily.

"I'm sure you'd love that, but I just had to make a few minor adjustments to the construction and unexpected additions with a few pieces of furniture to keep you safe and sound... To keep you both safe and sound."

"Ah, yes... our very special lady. Is she there as well?"

"She's there, and she's spending time also at the other place we talked about."

"I'm so glad. How is she adapting to these changes?"

"She's doing great. Better than expected."

"God, I'm so glad to hear it."

Bernie smiled in approval with Stirling's gracious consent. "Oh, before I forget... You packed this evening?"

"Only standard issue," said Stirling.

"Holstered?"

"On one side, the other's vacant," replied Stirling.

"Good. Take this. It's a prototype with a few... hot details that take it over the top."

The object was taken out of Bernie's jacket and surreptitiously handed to Stirling. It was an oddly-shaped pistol-type utility device, almost like a crossbow pistol, but minus the cradle in which to insert the arrow. Made of rubber and steel, it was perfectly aligned and fitted to conform with Stirling's grip. There were two buttons on the trigger finger latch. One trigger rested on top of the other. Stirling held the weapon firmly.

"Alright, real quick," said Bernie, "it's a dual trigger release."

"Shape charge?" asked Stirling.

"Not exactly. The top trigger prepares the release, and the bottom trigger fires the charge."

"What does it fire?"

"Just aim sharp and treat it as you would a bullet. We'll leave it at that. Knowing you, I'm sure you'll master the use of it fairly quick."

Stirling never overthought anything related to Bernie Llewelyn's weapons and gadgets. He trusted him implicitly with everything, including his own life. He holstered the weapon inside where he would have normally placed his gun. He had the Glock 9mm on one side and the secret weapon on the other. They were now both carefully stocked and holstered beneath his dinner jacket.

Bernie glanced around crowded ballroom. "I think I'll look for my seating assignment at one of these tables."

"I'll see you soon. Thanks, Bernie."

Stirling and Llewelyn shook hands, and Stirling strolled towards the cluster of the tables adjacent to the stage where the band was still playing. The dance floor was crowding with couples dancing. Other guests socialized at the bar, while dinner was beginning to be served. Stirling quickly shot a glance over at Angie. She was seated at a table by the bar with Rockne and Diane on either side of her. An attractive blonde female server in her early 30s with hair tied firmly up in a bun, dressed in traditional black and white evening wear and black flat shoes, approached Angie, handing her an envelope. Stirling studied Angie as she held the envelope, her expression becoming more serious. She looked up searching for someone and waved as soon as she caught Stirling's eye, signaling him to wait there so she could come to him. He acknowledged her signal and waved back.

Angie leaned into Diane and Rockne, excusing herself. As she casually walked away from the table, approaching Stirling, her smile suddenly dropped to a look of veiled preoccupation.

"Everything alright?" asked Stirling.

"I have no idea. One of the servers handed me this letter. In a blank unmarked envelope."

"Did you read it?"

"No."

They looked at one another sternly, not certain of what the letter may mean or who it may be from. With a pinched degree of reluctant certainty, Stirling nodded, indicating to Angie to open and read the letter. As she carefully removed it, she noticed that it was written in a large felt tip marker on coarse, beige paper. There were five individual pages with a single comment on each page. She flipped through them quickly, reading each one aloud.

"It's your special day and a time to celebrate... So let's take a trip down Memory Lane... Do you remember Operation Beech Grove?... And if you don't... Just ask Dr. Stirling."

That was it. Angie folded the pages and placed them back in the envelope. She looked at Stirling with extreme consternation.

"What is this, Stirling?"

"Where's the woman who gave this to you?"

Angie carefully scanned the vast space of the ballroom. Sharply focused, she checked out everyone in a server's uniform as if she was a human searchlight. At the far east door stationed by the lobby, she locked eyes with the mystery blonde and pointed her out to Stirling. So as not to raise a panic, she said in a hushed tone, "That's her. There she is."

The server quickly disappeared out the door once she realized she'd been made by Stirling. He ran after her as if he was shot out of a cannon. His instincts told him that danger was afoot, and it was most likely tied to the Sandbox or Ravenne Industries. The partygoers were so enmeshed in their frolicking and social activities that they paid absolutely no mind to the fact that Stirling vacated the ballroom like a bolt of lightning. Angie looked over at Bernie, who was instantly concerned. She then turned her attention very slowly as if she was being silently called to the main entrance of the ballroom once again and saw her... the doppelganger, smiling and staring straight at her. Angie turned away, flinching in controlled pain as she placed her hand against her right temple.

Outside, in the main section of the hotel where the gift shops, restaurants, and casino were situated, there was a full-throttle foot chase in progress between Stirling and the mystery blonde. The stretches of carpeting and flooring were spaced out, and they periodically had to dart out of the way of hotel guests, employees, and bystanders who were walking or merely standing in the way.

The mystery blonde was incredibly adept, moving with the skill and finesse of a trained professional, possibly even skilled in the art of Parkour. As there were numerous obstacles in the way needing to be traversed throughout the hotel, the path of pursuit was not exactly a clean one for either the mystery blonde or Stirling. They each adapted to the environment as they moved skillfully across the inner space with an emphasis on jumping, climbing and running, but always executing their physical movements with a combined sense of safety and precision. Periodically, the mystery blonde would shove a man or woman who happened to be obstructing her exit. Stirling was not so cavalier or reckless, mindful of the path before him, and doing everything in his power to keep the mystery blonde in his sight.

They were both exceptionally adroit athletes, and they were not even slightly winded or spent as they approached the door leading to the rooftop. Now, the mystery blonde was only about forty to fifty paces ahead of Stirling. She pushed through the rooftop door with relative ease and began her ascent to the top of the building. With long elegant strides, she traversed six steps at a time with her powerful legs, giving her a solid start before Stirling even arrived to the stairwell.

Once he pushed through, it became clear they were completely alone as he pushed hard and fast to catch up to her. She was approximately five flights ahead of him for the total 21-story building. As he turned the corner leading to the fourth story stairwell, a gunshot whizzed past him, barely missing him. He unholstered his Glock, cased the surroundings, and when he calculated there was an opening he fired four rounds upwards and curved towards the island of the stairwell where she was positioned. She quickly pulled back to take cover, shaken by his well-timed, sudden retaliation. Cradling her Beretta 92SB with both hands, she continued running. Stirling took cover and resumed his pursuit, holding his 9mm Glock firmly in one hand as he traversed the concrete stairwell.

She reached the top of the building at the roof on the 22nd floor, completely relieved at the sight she saw waiting before her. Stirling followed closely behind, pushing harder, and as he finally reached the end, he burst through the door only to find... she was gone.

His eyes looked up to the sky. He could hear the faint noise of the helicopter blades slicing through the night sky and realized she had been extracted. He watched, catching his breath, as the helicopter made its way across town away from the Walnut District. But as they quickly made their getaway, Stirling heard the steadily approaching sounds of what seemed to be more than one helicopter bearing down from the opposite end of town, getting closer to his location, the Rhodesia. Without missing a beat, he knew they were being targeted. He moved like lightning back down the stairs to warn Angie and Bernie of the incoming threat.

Back inside the Silver Palace ballroom, Stirling rushed through the same door from which he had exited, a little more winded but with adrenaline fueling his strength and determination. He saw Tyler standing alongside Angie. As he approached them, it was as if they were already conferring about what had happened.

"What happened to her?" asked Angie as Stirling arrived at their side.

"She got away on the rooftop. There was a chopper waiting to extract her." Stirling quickly pivoted his attention to Tyler. "Ty, I need you to get your team ready. We're about to be hit."

"I'm on it!" Tyler didn't flinch or question Stirling for a second. He bolted away.

The ominous sounds of the incoming helicopters became increasingly louder. Stirling quickly shot his glance over to Bernie. He simply raised two fingers and pointed at the door. That was their coded signal that they were in deep shit, and Bernie needed to leave immediately. Without hesitation, Bernie signaled with a wave and raised two fingers to his eyes, followed by putting up six fingers. This meant that the message was received loud and clear and Stirling should watch his back.

At the same time, Angie's gaze flipped over to Rockne and Diane. They were already huddled with one another at their table, subtly aware that they may be in danger as they rose from their seats and proceeded to one of the exit doors. The roar of the incoming helicopters grew increasingly louder. Angie locked eyes with Stirling with grim steeliness.

"Get all these people out of here," said Stirling.

"Stirling..." she said in a hushed tone.

"Angie, there's no time to waste. Get everyone the fuck out of here now." As he turned away to prepare for the unexpected, she stopped him by firmly grabbing his forearm.

"Stirling... what the fuck is Operation Beech Grove?"

He exhaled with what seemed like the weight of the world on his shoulders. In that moment, the helicopters sounded like they were directly above the stained glass skylight.

"Beech Grove... is the end."

Angie's eyes widened in terror, and in that moment, a team of assassins shattered through the skylight, rappelling on ropes from the choppers above. It was a 12-person unit, dressed in combat gear with black masks and goggles. Glass rained down, cascading over the ballroom like so much razor sharp confetti. Some guests screamed. Others took cover and fled. This was clearly a tactical insertion, and this team was taking no prisoners. The team was armed with Heckler & Koch Mp5 submachine guns, and the goal was defined by their actions—kill as many as possible. The firefight began.

People fell as bullets flew and blood sprayed across the walls. Thankfully, the vast majority of the guests had fled in time before it transformed into an unabashed massacre of innocents. Stirling had taken cover, moving stealthily between pillars and light fixtures. He removed his dinner jacket, freeing up his range of movement.

A woman of about fifty, dressed in a peach-colored sequin dress, trembled as she cowered helplessly in a corner by the main bar. Her hands were over her mouth to keep from screaming or being detected by the killers. One of the assassins spotted her and took aim. But before the shooter could pop off a single round, Stirling approached from behind, grabbed the masked man by the mouth and snapped his neck, throwing the assassin to the ground stone cold dead.

Commandeering the Mp5 submachine gun as the assailant fell, Stirling switched to tactical combat mode and aimed at three adjacent assassins approaching in line formation. They were unaware of Stirling's hidden presence, until he rose from behind the counter and strafed them with a perfectly delivered stream of automatic gunfire, sending all three of them to their proverbial maker. A fourth assassin jumped from behind the bar with a jagged knife in hand. Stirling merely swirled his entire body around and simultaneously pulled out his 9mm Glock, emptying the remainder of the magazine into the attacker. The assassin's body flew backward, smashing into the glass display case above the mirrored wall behind the bar, sending a rainbow array of alcoholic beverages streaming down onto the fallen killer's body.

The team of twelve was now reduced to a team of seven. Stirling had no additional clips for the 9mm pistol, so he unleashed the mystery weapon Bernie had given him earlier in the evening.

As he traversed the spaces and checked carefully behind each light fixture and marble pillar, he remembered what Bernie had said about treating this weapon like a pistol by aiming and firing the discharge as if it were a bullet. He knew exactly what to do with the dual trigger mechanism, but he had absolutely no idea what to expect.

The room was so expansive in its design that there was actually a second level, slightly slanted, tilted like a curved hill and behind the main floor below, forming a perfect circle. There were tables, chairs and even a separate but smaller bar on the second level. Stirling had eyes focused directly ahead of him, but there were two other killers flanking him from behind where he had an unforeseen blind spot. He heard rustling ahead of him, took aim at what he felt could be another unseen assailant, and then in a matter of seconds, it happened.

"Stirling!!" Tyler called out.

Shots were fired and Stirling looked behind him to see two more from the team of unknown assassins fall to their deaths from above, crashing lifelessly on to the ground of the first floor below. He looked up and left towards the other direction of the floor above him to find that Tyler had his pistol brandished and aimed, and within seconds, he had eliminated two of the other assassins, who unbeknownst to Stirling were primed to terminate him.

Tyler and Stirling exchanged looks with one another. For better or worse, Tyler had saved Stirling's life. They acknowledged one another like fellow soldiers. Tyler winked at Stirling, while Stirling returned the approving gesture with a signature thumbs up. As they assessed the damage and current environment, there was still random gunfire and screams of people dropping dead in other sections of the cavernous space. They could have been members of Tyler's team, or hotel employees, or other innocent bystanders. It was impossible to be sure. But Tyler and Stirling assumed a parallel round position by dividing the space accordingly, with their weapons brandished and ready for what was next. Tyler remained on the second floor while Stirling remained on point on the ground floor.

The ceiling mirrors remained unnoticed by the killers, but Stirling caught a quick glimpse of their northwest position, several yards ahead of him, by using the canted angles provided by those mirrors. He glanced around trying to catch a glimpse of Angie, but she was nowhere to be found. Stirling smirked slightly knowing he had the upper hand on the three assassins who were prowling the space ahead of him, blind to his incoming presence. Their team was now five strong after the two who were summarily dispatched by Tyler.

Stirling was confident that this uninitiated weapon would provide the requisite firepower he needed to eliminate his opponents. He approached the standing three, who had their backs to him, took aim, released the top trigger and had his finger firmly placed on the bottom trigger ready to fire.

He whistled very quietly, and they turned. He released the charge from the mystery weapon which turned out to be a spear of flame. This was literally a custom made hand-held flamethrower which spread once it came within ten inches of its designated target, causing the flames to burst and expand like a fireball. So this was a perfect three-tiered kill because the trio of assassins were standing within a foot from one another, allowing the flame spear to burst, spread, and roast all three of them to perfection. Each one screamed and writhed in agony as the flames cooked through their masks and clothing, transforming them into human skewers of charred flesh and bone.

Stirling approached the three of them, looking down at the ground as they lay there frying to a toasted crisp. He looked at the weapon once again, nodded and smiled as he thought about Bernie and looked back up only to find the first of the remaining two on the attack, ready to pounce on him.

A well-placed spinning kick was delivered by the masked assailant to Stirling's gun hand, sending the hand-held flame gun flying across the room, landing right next to the northeast exit door. The assassin was clearly unarmed and wanted to disarm Stirling to take him on hand-to-hand. As Stirling was also out of ammunition for his Glock, he readily obliged, taking his traditional Karate-based fighting stance. But he wanted identity and closure from these assassins before anything else.

"You want me? You've got me. But let's do this in the traditional manner like real warriors. Truly face to face."

In that moment, the unseen killer assumed a normal stance and removed the face mask, throwing it on the floor and revealing a man of about 35 of Filipino extraction, proficiently trained in the martial arts. They glared at one another with their own versions of the death stare, attempting to break the other's will and resolve.

"Who are you?" asked Stirling.

"What difference does it make?" replied the nameless assassin.

Knowing that was the verbal prelude to a duel, the two men approached one another and circled one another slowly, gradually coming to a halt and assuming fighting position. Stirling's stance was that of the art of Aikido. His opponent assumed the position of traditional Japanese Karate. And the fight ensued.

The wily nameless assassin was excellent. He connected hard with a few of well-placed kicks and punches to Stirling's midsection and face. Stirling shook the blows off and decided it was time to switch gears and kick it up a notch. He began to employ the signature Aikido tactic of turning the opponent's force and aggression against them. As such, he began flipping and sending him against the mirrored walls, causing the glass to shatter and spread. The assassin rose and charged at full speed. Stirling threw him over the couches, causing him to go flying and smashing against the marble pillars. Stirling decided it was time to bring this battle to a halt. As the assassin tried to strike Stirling's head with a spinning elbow strike, Stirling intercepted the blow by catching the arm, twisting it and pinning him to the ground. He placed his knee firmly on the nameless killer's chest, immobilizing him completely.

"Time to talk. You've got ten seconds to tell me who sent you and why you're here."

The assassin smiled evilly and shook his head.

"I don't think you've got too many options here. Better talk fast," said Stirling.

The killer scowled with rage, made a look of slight frustration and looked at Stirling coldly in the eye. "What you don't know and what you cannot even begin to imagine, Dr. Stirling, is precisely what you will never understand."

"Go on," replied Stirling.

The killer's eyes widened into an almost maniacal stare.

"Tomorrow is forever!! The future is now!! The Raven will show us the way!!"

Stirling knitted his eyebrows, trying to understand what the assassin's words meant. But in that instant, the killer closed his mouth, released something from beneath his tongue, and bit down hard. Stirling knew exactly what it was—a suicide capsule. As soon as Stirling crushed his cheeks to open his mouth, the torrent of foam came spilling outwards. The second-to-last team member was dead and left Stirling with nothing more than an extremely cryptic message.

Frustrated, he tossed the man's face from his hand and rose to his feet. In that moment, everything seemed to stop and cease to exist because Angie appeared behind him, looking a bit shaken but relieved and happy that Stirling was standing before her. They smiled at each other for only a mere split second as something behind Stirling caught Angie's immediate attention. She yelled out as she dove to her right to take cover.

"Stirling, to your nine!!"

Stirling understood the code and deftly dove to his own right, taking cover, as a powerful stream of automatic gunfire rained in their direction, fired by the last member of the team of assassins. Angie had landed by one of the stone pillars. Stirling's first instinct was to insure that she hadn't been shot. Her body was completely clean as she lay on her stomach, perfectly still with her arms wrapped around her face and neck.

Stirling then turned around swiftly and focused on the shooter. They looked at one another for a few seconds that felt like an eternity. The killer wanted to show his face to Stirling, and so he removed his mask revealing that it was Damon Chambers.

Stirling's look of concern swiftly transformed into an expression of unrepressed rage. Chambers smiled from ear to ear, like a crazed fanatic, an indicator to Stirling that their paths would cross again soon enough. As soon as that was acknowledged, Chambers made a beeline for the exit door behind him and left the building.

Stirling then pivoted to make sure that Angie was alright. He ran to her side and, with a hand on her shoulder, rolled her over to face him. Seeing her face, he was instantly stunned and heartbroken...

One of Damon Chambers' bullets had penetrated Angie's temple. She was shot through the head and killed instantly. The bullet went through and through, entering one side of her head and exiting the other. Stirling was shattered, immediately consumed with pain as much as rage. He held her close, cradling her in his arms. He began to cry silently and then his body convulsed with sobs. He had never felt this degree of emotional loss and personal agony before. He looked at her eyes one last time, kissing her gently on the lips before taking his hand and closing her beautiful, almond shaped eyes forever. As he lay her down, he knew he would find the bullet. He scanned with his razor sharp vision and froze the minute he connected with a crack in the pillar at the corner of the room. He rose and stepped to the pillar. Scanning the floor, he caught the feeble glint of a shiny object, no more than an inch in length, lying among the shattered glass and debris. He picked up what was indeed the bullet that had taken Angie's life. Damon Chambers' bullet.

But as he examined it closer, he saw there was a distinguishing mark engraved on the bullet. This was a calling card, and it was a symbol he would never forget—a raven in flight. A deep black raven with its wings spread out at full span. He put the bullet away and without even flinching, he picked up Angie's now deceased body in his arms and carried her towards the exit.

The smoke had cleared. The dust had settled. All that remained of the chaotic mélange which seemed to have transpired in the blink of an eye were the corpses left behind. As he approached the door, a familiar voice called out.

"Kent!!"

Stirling turned and was mildly relieved to see the familiar face of Tyler. He was in no mood for conversations or apologies, but he saw the anguished sense of sorrow and the register of pain in Tyler's face when he realized she was gone.

"Oh, no... Kent, I'm... I'm..."

"They're all gone. The perimeter's clear. Just find your aunt and uncle. Stay safe, and I'll be in touch soon."

Tyler just stood there in somber resignation, acknowledging Stirling with a slight nod.

With Angie's body held in both arms, Stirling pushed the exit door open with his hip and left. Alone, slightly battered and concerned as to the whereabouts of his aunt and uncle, Tyler surveyed the violent aftermath and shook his head in total disbelief. He set his pistol down on the bar counter and spoke quietly to himself.

"Oh, Angie. Dear God, I am so sorry."

He hung his head and closed his eyes, fighting to hold back the tears.

Outside in the main parking lot of the Rhodesia En Rouge, Stirling carried Angie's body and approached his car, a light brown Lamborghini Countach. No longer in production, this was a classic 1981 model, tricked out with Bernie's magic touches to include additional enhancements and some tech-themed amplifications. The radical wedge-shaped design and scissor doors were present as Stirling pressed a button on his watch that opened both doors. He gently placed Angie's body inside the passenger seat and closed the door. Moving around to the other side, he got into the driver's seat, yanked his door shut, and took off into the night.

As he drove, he pressed the radio console switch, which doubled as a car phone. The speaker was on as the phone rang twice and Bernie answered on the other end.

"Kent!"

"Bernie! Are you alright?"

"I'm fine, I'm at the local safe house." "Listen, I'm going to need you to prep the charter plane for three. We need to take a trip to the Florida Keys."

"You, me, and Angie. Got it. How is she?"

Stirling was quiet. His face fought hard not to burst into tears. His voice trembled notably from the pronounced lump in his throat as he answered. "The Keys were her final wishes, Bernie."

In that instant, Bernie knew the truth. "Oh, Christ, no... Kent, I'm so sorry."

"Please, just do it. Make the preparations. I'll be there soon."

Stirling hung up. He looked over at Angie and ran his fingers along her face. Then, refocusing on the road ahead, he switched into 5th gear and sped off into the unknown realm of the New Orleans night.

15

The Mississippi River Trail was also known as the Levee Path, where dedicated paved paths snaked along the Mississippi River, often on top of the levees. There was one particularly nice section, located near Audubon Park, known as "The Fly", and it offered lovely scenic views of the river. Extending for miles, it provided a long, straight route alongside nature. On an atypically breezy morning, there were several runners and joggers exercising along the path. Tyler was one of them. Remarkably fit and agile, staying in shape was part of his daily regime.

After his morning run, he returned to his condo, somewhat shaken and disturbed to find what was waiting for him.

"Stop calling, me!!! Please just leave me alone!!!," pleaded Zara as she clicked off the call on her cell phone.

Tyler closed the front door with a thud that startled Zara. Barefoot, she wore sweats and a form fitting t-shirt. After being there for nearly a month, she had clearly become comfortable in his home.

"I'm sorry, I didn't hear you," she said.

"Just finished my run by the park," said Tyler, adding, "What was that all about?" He dried himself off with a towel he kept by the foyer whenever he returned from morning workouts.

They don't stop calling... I don't understand... How did they find me?"

Tyler registered what she said and knew she was preoccupied with good reason.

"Just give me a minute," he replied.

He walked over to his bedroom and threw the towel into the laundry hamper in his closet. Strolling back to the kitchen, he took a seat by her side at the dining table. She had just finished eating and was nursing a cup of coffee.

"Now... You mind telling me who was on the phone?"

She gritted her teeth and clinched her jaw, worried that she was bringing him into an issue that could get both of them hurt, or possibly killed. She placed her hand over her eyes and slowly began to cry. Tyler was put off by her response. He only knew how to care for and support the people in his life who were important to him. He wasn't sure yet what to make of Zara, but his heart and his instincts told him that she was in trouble and desperately needed his help. He reached for her hand, and she clenched it urgently. They wrapped their hands around one another, forming a fist of sorts. She squeezed his hand tightly.

"Zara?"

She looked up slowly, wiping away the tears from her eyes. Tyler kept his voice calm. "Who was on the phone?"

Reluctantly, she opened up and brought him into the fray. "It was them... They found me... Somehow, they found me."

He looked at her with a mildly puzzled expression, and hazarded a guess—"The people you were running away from the day I met you?"

Zara nodded affirmatively.

Tyler couldn't comprehend how this could have happened. "But we changed your number. Got you a new phone."

"I know, Tyler. I'm as confused and as... nervous about this as you are."

He leaned back slightly in his chair, letting go of her hand. Crossing his arms, he looked at her closely. "Zara, I need you to come clean with me. All you've told me since we met is that they were former business associates of yours, and they couldn't be trusted because they were dangerous, and they could hurt you."

"Yes, that's right."

"Not enough... I need you to tell me everything."

Zara seemed to collapse into her chair and exhaled, wiping away the remnants of her tears and running her hands through her lush mane of hair. She leaned forward and kicked back the last of her coffee. Finally, she fixed Tyler with a sullen gaze. "Alright, Tyler. The truth is that this whole thing was partly connected to you."

"To me?"

"In a way. To your Aunt Diane and Uncle Rockne to be exact. My old associates are not just involved in any business, you see... They deal in high end real estate, and they were in the process of taking over a very large section of Walnut Street with every business and home that existed in that area. And they meant to close on every property there, by whatever means necessary... including the Rhodesia En Rouge."

"Why? What was so important about that area?" Tyler's wheels began turning, gradually piecing together the fragments she gave him into a cohesive whole.

"Tyler, Walnut Street Properties are some of the most valuable commodities the city has to offer. In turnaround, they would be worth a fortune, but my partners had plans that extended beyond that, and I didn't want anything to do with it. That was when I pulled away, but they wouldn't let me leave because by then... I knew too much."

Tyler knew she was coming clean about everything. He needed to assure her that she had his absolute confidence, that he could be trusted. He uncrossed his arms and leaned forward in the chair, looking closer into her eyes. "How did you get involved with them in the first place?"

She turned away slightly, a surge of shame passed through her. "Tyler, please..."

"Zara... don't leave me out. Trust me. I can help."

She hesitated for a moment before she spoke. "My ex-lover, my old boyfriend... He is one of the main partners in the business. He asked me if I wanted to join the organization. To help by investing. I come from money, and... it was a way to get away from my parents because we... never got along."

"I get it. I understand. So you gathered some money to help your old boyfriend in a business venture that seemed on the surface like a noble venture that could have turned into something bigger and better for the two of you."

She was relieved that he was not only so sympathetic and understanding, but that he was clearly on her side. It lightened her mood to a small degree. She managed to give him a slight smile. "That's right," she said.

He took her by the hand reassuringly. "Listen to me, Zara... I'm going to get to the bottom of this. I have yet to figure out what's behind the disappearance of my aunt and uncle... But now that you're telling me all of this... I have absolutely no doubt that what happened to you and what happened to them... it's all connected. I promise you... Together, we will work this out."

She was moved by the grace of his warmth and the sincerity behind his words. In a final, decisive gesture to seal the bond between them, he took her cell phone, broke it in half, dropped the sim card on the table and tossed the busted pieces of the phone across the room. She stared at him with her mouth slightly agape. They both began to form large smiles, and as they laughed together in unison, they reached across the table and embraced one another firmly.

* * *

Sunset Key was a private island off Key West with residences and a resort known for its stunning sunsets. It was also where Bernie Llewelyn maintained his yacht and his Florida-based residence. That evening was awash in Day-Glo colors that streamed across the evening sky. Purple, orange, yellow, and red cradled the sun just as it was beginning to set. Stirling and Bernie stood on the deck of the balcony overlooking the tranquil seas and otherworldly skyline, both still, and deep in thought.

"That's it, Bernie."

Bernie turned to him with a look of paternal concern creasing the lines of his face.

"Angie's gone," said Stirling. "Her ashes scattered at sea as she always wanted... All we have left now... are the memories."

Bernie held his emotions firmly in check, but was clearly finding it difficult to hold them back as he turned to face the ocean.

"Where do we go from here?" asked Stirling. "When all seems lost... how do we find our way back to who we once were? How do we move forward? I've been asking myself those questions... for a few weeks now... I'm still not sure I have the answers."

"I'll tell you something, kid... I ask myself the same questions time and again... But the truth is... I can only come up with one answer. But it's the right answer because in its own way, it seems to address the core of each of those questions. And you know what it is?"

Stirling shook his head as he kept his look fixed towards the ocean.

"A better tomorrow... What keeps us moving forward... is the search for a better tomorrow. Because one thing I know to be true is that in this fucking, insane world that we live in... It's just about the only damn thing that makes sense."

Stirling felt the impact of what Bernie said, but kept his eyes deeply fixated on the sea before him. "Maybe you're right, Bernie... Maybe you're right."

"The heart... is what keeps us human and ultimately makes us who we are, Kent... You, of all people, should know this best."

"Time mends all wounds," said Stirling.

"No, people do... And you have a few... special people in this world who truly care about you, Doctor."

"Thank you, Bernie."

Bernie turned away from the ocean view and looked back over at Stirling to address him directly. "I'm not the only one. Someone else. Someone from the past... and very special, reached out to me because they were looking for you. This is someone who... will definitely help you heal."

Stirling's curiosity was piqued. He finally turned around to face Bernie directly. They now stood facing each other. "Who are we talking about here?" he asked.

Bernie smiled. "Go home, Kent. I'm going back home tomorrow morning to my place in Vail. I've got a few projects I need to complete... And you... just go back to New Orleans and be at the City Park by the oak trees tomorrow afternoon at 3pm. This person... will find you."

Stirling walked over to Bernie and stood right in front of him. He knew Bernie would always have his best interests in mind, and as always, he trusted him with his life because Bernie Lleweleyn was much more than just a mentor and a professional colleague— he was the closest person on the planet who Stirling considered to be like a father.

Bernie placed his hand on Sterling's shoulder. "Just do it, son... You'll be glad you did."

Stirling nodded affirmatively, and he and Bernie embraced on the balcony overlooking the calm seas of the Florida Keys.

* * *

Located in the oldest section of the park near City Park Avenue was a massive greenscape defined by the centuries-old live oak trees surrounding the area. This section was known as the Dueling Oaks, though one of the massive trees that gave it that name had been lost in a hurricane in 1949. In one of the most secluded spots in the area, Stirling looked at his Omega Seamaster Planet Ocean watch. It was two minutes past three. He was standing at the center of the green. No one else was in sight that sunny afternoon, as he admired the gnarled, aged textures of the oak tree.

"Kent?" a woman's voice called out just behind him.

The voice from the past clearly shook him to his core. At first, he felt his heart sink like a stone because he firmly believed he would never hear that voice again. He turned very slowly to face the woman. And sure enough, it was her...

Iris Ravenne, head of Ravenne Industries, AKA the Raven, stood there dressed in a sleeveless, form-fitting one-piece yellow velvet pants suit. Her figure looked beyond spectacular. Her hair was tied and in a bun. Her complexion was as flawless as Stirling had always remembered her, because to him, and certainly to Bernie Llewelyn, she was also Irina Contreras, his fiancé who was presumed dead, when their yacht exploded off the Yucatan coast near the island of Belize.

He approached her delicately as she stared at him longingly and with all the love in the world shining through those seductive, dark brown eyes. Like a nervous child, he pounced and grabbed her, bringing her towards him and holding her tight because he could not believe she was alive and well. Iris smiled and exhaled, relieved that he reacted this way because it was exactly the reception she was hoping for. She had already proved beyond a shadow of a doubt that betrayal and duplicity was a way of life for her. She was the stunning embodiment of evil, and she took no prisoners, but this was a hard truth and reality which Kent Stirling had hardly even begun to discover. He pulled away from her slightly, placing both of his hands tenderly on her face, looking deep into her eyes.

Irina was so deeply into character that tears streamed down her face as she gazed lovingly at Stirling as though he was the only man in the world for her.

"Irina... Dear God, Irina... It's really you."

Immediately, like a hairpin trigger, she turned on the Mexican accent with which Stirling had been so familiar when they were together and engaged to be married. This was second nature to her. She knew exactly how to turn her former identity on and off at the drop of a hat. "Of course, it's me, my love. I'm so glad that I found you."

She moved fast with her brand of getting reacquainted because she wanted Stirling to not only remember, but to become completely comfortable with her again right away. And so, she leaned into him and they kissed full on the mouth with an ardor and passion that was indicative of former lovers. But this was a kiss completely different from Angie. With Angie, the kissing and lovemaking was informed by a mutually felt emotional bond and nurturing love for one another. With Irina, the physical connection was what most inflamed and drove their passion. These two were incessantly hot for one another. Initially driven by unhinged lust, theirs was a bond which, through time, blossomed into what presumably became heartfelt love for one another. And Iris knew this to her core. She knew exactly which buttons to push and which triggers to pull when it came to Dr. Kent Stirling.

He remembered what Bernie had mentioned to him back in Florida about how people, not time, heal all wounds. Now, more than ever, he grasped the true nature of those words because the other love of his life was standing there before him now, and this time, he had no intention of losing her again.

* * *

Stirling and Iris spent the remainder of the afternoon at Lilette Restaurant. It was abnormally cool and breezy that day, so they sat outside on the patio, reminiscing and generally getting caught up with one another. Stirling hadn't erased the image or memory of Angie Miller from his mind. That was impossible. She was his lifelong confidante and closest example of a soulmate he had encountered, but the feelings for Irina had truly never died. They were simply dormant, but as these things go, they were now emerging to the forefront in a manner that he never could have anticipated. An elegantly dressed and groomed server of about sixty brought them their main dishes, two orders of Filet Mignon with asparagus spears and Lemon Basil pasta.

"So, Kent... Here we are."

Stirling nodded his head in total disbelief as he took a bite of his steak. "Irina... I thought you were dead. It's been almost three years."

She seemed to be savoring the asparagus spears as she considered the weight of Stirling's words. "I had to see you again, Kent. I just couldn't stay away any longer. But now... I have to ask you something."

"Of course," he said.

"Why is it you never tried to find me? So much time... lost. Time that we could have been together. This, I don't understand... I'm asking you, Kent... Why?"

The question was decidedly marked, and Stirling knew he had to be careful, cautious with his response because the one thing he knew was that Irina only knew him as Dr. Kent Stirling. She never knew that he had led a life as a secret operative for the Sandbox. The only link Iris had to the Sandbox in Stirling's eyes was her close friendship to Bernie Llewelyn, who had initially been introduced to her as a close friend of the Stirling family. So he knew he needed to keep his identity intact where Irina was concerned.

"Irina, no one could have survived that blast. The yacht was incinerated into cinders. And I remember that day so clearly. I was on shore gathering items for the boat and some supplies I needed for the hospital. I asked if you wanted to join me. You said that you were tired and you were going to try to get some rest. So now I'm asking you... how in God's name did you get away?"

Now it was Iris's turn. She was in the hot seat, and she also knew that her answer needed to be deftly considered. Her way of manipulating Stirling had always been turning on what he incorrectly perceived to be her inability to lie and her unwavering sense of honesty. She wiped her mouth with the edges of her napkin, took a sip of red wine and looked at him with longing and sadness in her eyes. He was captivated as she addressed him.

"Yes, it's true. I tried to sleep that afternoon, but I couldn't. I was extremely restless. Something in me didn't allow me to relax. Like a terrible feeling I had that something was going to happen. Something that would forever change the course of our lives."

It was fascinating because Iris had this uncanny ability to transform her state of being into a virtual fugue state. As if she was transfixed by her own fabricated history. Believing it herself in the process, and hence, convincing others that it was the absolute truth. Stirling always bought whatever she told him, and this was no exception.

"Change the course of our lives? How do you mean?" asked Stirling.

Before she proceeded to concoct her elaborate work of personal fiction, she flashed back to that day, remembering in exact detail what in fact did happen when the yacht exploded.

Iris got up out of bed and looked at her watch. She had on nothing more than a light summer dress, allowing her to move quickly underwater. She stood at the far end of the rear of the yacht. There were no crew members or other guests in the immediate vicinity. As she perched herself on the ledge, she adjusted a pair of deep-sea diving goggles onto her face and jumped off, executing a perfect swan dive into the warm Yucatan seas. She moved quickly and gracefully underwater at extremely high speed, as she was able to hold her breath for an unusually extended period of time. As she pushed forward and at a great distance away from the yacht, the blast shook the waters. The fireball from the explosion lit up the sky with a burst of yellow-orange flame that colored the glimmering veil of water above her. The destruction didn't even faze her as she swam and swam until she finally reached a jagged rock formation in the near distance. She rose to the surface and inhaled the fresh air, somewhat winded but not entirely out of breath. She looked over at the burning wreckage of what was once her close friend's extravagant yacht. A wicked smile formed across her lips as the flames rose higher into the sky. In that moment, she heard the sounds of an approaching speedboat nearing her location. She turned, smiled and waved. The boat pivoted and pulled up alongside her. The driver of the boat extended his hand downwards to help her out of the water. It was Damon Chambers, and they smiled together as they reconnected. She quickly got onto the boat, threw off her goggles and sat alongside Damon as they sped off together to an unknown destination.

After the recollection was complete as to what really happened that afternoon, Iris gathered her thoughts and began to convey her story to Stirling with unabashed conviction.

"Alright, Kent... Here's how it went... I got out of bed and was about to walk onto the main deck when the blast happened. Thankfully because our bedroom was in the rear of the yacht, and the door was wide open, the concussion of the blast managed to send me out and away from the yacht. God only knows how long I was airborne. But when I hit the water, my head bashed against a rock, knocking me unconscious. I could have easily drowned because I could hear what was around me, but I was in too much pain and completely disoriented to actually come around. I must have lost a lot of blood from the impact because the water next to me was red as I raised my hand to feel my head. Then, almost like a Godsend, I heard an incoming engine. I looked up, but it was blurry. It was a fisherman's vessel. I couldn't speak. But the husband and wife who were the owners of the vessel were kind enough to take me to Cozumel where I recovered for weeks in the local hospital."

"Why weeks," asked Stirling.

"Kent, I couldn't remember who I was. My name. Where I came from. How I got there. Nothing."

"Total amnesia," said Stirling.

Iris nodded affirmatively. "In time, I recovered, but by then..." She was shaky, and her lower lip began to tremble as she fought to hold back her tears, remembering the details that supposedly pained her the most.

Stirling held her forearm gently trying to console her. "It's alright. Just... take it easy"

She wiped away her tears with the back of her hand and continued. "By then, I was told that you were nowhere to be found. You had disappeared completely. There was no trace of you at either hospital in Merida or Belize. Nobody could tell me anything about Dr. Kent Stirling."

Stirling knew that what she said was true because by then he had dealt with the Sandbox incident orchestrated by Gavin Weller and moved to Florida. By his way of seeing things, he had avenged Irina and eliminated what he thought were the final remaining vestiges of the Sandbox.

"What about your parents?" asked Stirling.

Iris struggled to maintain her composure. Her parents were a sensitive subject. Of course, their fate and demise was another lie, but she filled in those gaps in typically fine and deceitful form. Her mother and father were, in fact, her adoptive parents, and this was why she was known to them as Irina. She had been orphaned by her real parents, Jean-Paul and Nathalie Ravenne. One day in Merida, Yucatan, she needed to eliminate all loose ends to resume her position within the Sandbox, and as her parents, Mr. and Mrs. Contreras, shared a couple of mimosas on their second-story bedroom balcony, Iris pulled up in a stretch limo. The passenger window lowered. Irina's head emerged. Her parents noticed her and waved with ear to ear smiles on their faces. Irina smiled back, and then pushed a button on a remote detonator. Mr. and Mrs. Contreras and the entire house which she had shared with them throughout her formative years went up in the smoke and flames of an enormous C-4 driven blast. The limo drove away as the house slowly cooked and sank to the ground. A satisfied smile formed on Iris's face as she threw the detonator to the side, and the limo drove into the distance.

But the story she laid out to Stirling was another elaborately illustrated bullshit scenario.

"My parents were contacted by the local authorities in Cozumel. They chartered a small aircraft, but it hadn't been serviced properly in much too long. The pilot lost control of the engines shortly after they took off from Merida Airport, and they crashed somewhere in the jungles of Quintana Roo. The pilot and my parents were killed instantly. After that... I tried to do whatever I could to start over, to put the pieces of my life back together, and then I dedicated myself to trying to find you, and one day, it clicked. I remembered Bernie... And here we are."

Stirling had no reason to question or doubt her versions of what had happened. After all, she shared her life with him, and they had once been engaged to be married. He was all too happy to see her again, and he exhaled as she relayed the news which he felt must have been exceedingly painful for her to recollect in such vivid detail.

He held her hand and kissed it softly. "Irina... I'm sorry about all of this. Sincerely, with all of my heart, I am deeply and genuinely sorry. But I think that what matters is that by fate or accident or whatever the case happens to be, we're here. I know that we've lost time, even years... But I'm just... I'm just glad that you're here now."

Tears streamed down her face as she reached across the table and kissed him passionately.

16

That October afternoon in Vail, Colorado, the snow was casually beginning to sprinkle down from the overcast skies. Along the circuitous main highway leading to the private residence of Bernie Llewelyn, a lone champagne-colored Range Rover drove at moderate speed. Arriving at what would be considered his front gate, a few seconds passed before the gate eventually opened. As the Range Rover drove through and up the driveway leading to the main estate, the gate closed slowly behind it.

Bernie Llewelyn stepped out of the front door to greet his visitors. As the car parked and turned off the engine, the doors opened revealing his guests. Bernie was delighted as he greeted them, "Great to see you both again," he said.

It was Stirling and Tyler, come to pay their old friend a visit.

"Good to see you, Bernie," said Tyler.

Bernie gave the Range Rover a little once over, impressed by Stirling's choice of car rental. "I like your new wheels," he said.

"Yours are better," replied Stirling.

Tyler and Stirling got their bags out of the trunk. They both individually shook hands with Bernie as they greeted him at the front door.

"Alright boys, how would you like to check out some new toys?" asked Bernie as they made their way through the front door of the house. The door had a sturdy oak-like feel as Bernie closed it behind them.

* * *

The backyard of Bernie Llewelyn's home was a massive outdoor space that extended as far as they eye could see. He owned acres of land at his private abode in Vail, and the merging of nature and primary colors was a singular sight to behold. There were targets involving wooden boards, hanging dummies stuffed with feathers plus cork to add weight and density, and bottles.

The three men chose their preferred weapons from a selection of beautifully-cared-for firearms on display along a thick wooden plank that served as both table and cleaning station. This was Bernie's way of bonding with his friends, and also a way of keeping their individual shooting skills sharp. Soon, the firing of weapons echoed and volleyed throughout the mountainous valley.

Tyler's weapon of choice was the latest 9mm pistol from Walther, the PPD Pro-E. This gun was a variant of the PPD line, offering a blend of features from the standard PDP and the high-end Pro SD models. It included a flat-face polymer trigger, an aluminum mag well and an increased magazine capacity of 20 rounds for the full-size model. This was the 4.5-inch full- size version, modified by Bernie to include gold titanium nitride plating and ported slides. For targets, Tyler chose the bottles which were placed a little over a hundred yards away. He took aim and fired, discharging a full load. He was clearly highly skilled as the vast majority of his shots were right in the kill zone. It was an impressive grouping, but Tyler was comfortable handling firearms due to his extensive prior military experience.

Bernie was situated at the opposite end of his personal outdoor range with his preferred weapon of choice. The winds were mild that day, the air was moderately cool, and the mountains were lightly snow-capped. He cocked, loaded, and began closely surveying the targets he was about to take down with his favorite weapon—the Remington 870 ATC-14, a compact 12-gauge shotgun featuring a pistol grip and a short barrel, designed for home defense. It was based on the Remington 870 platform but lacked a traditional stock, combining the proven reliability of the 870 pump-action with a shortened barrel and a pistol grip, which was precisely what made the weapon highly maneuverable. Bernie took aim at the hanging dummies stuffed with feathers and cork, utilizing the newly-added laser sights he had recently implemented. As he fired off 5 rounds at the perfectly lined figures at a distance of 300 yards, the hanging doll-like bodies burst into a sea of floating feathers coupled with a hail of heavy cork. Bernie's grouping was flawless, decimating each of the dummies. He had served with honor in the Marines, and he was a multi-awarded marksman on top of his design and fabrication skills.

Standing silently and coolly in between Tyler and Bernie was Stirling. He had chosen the most unconventional weapon, not a run-of-the-mill firearm. To be precise, this wasn't a firearm at all, but it was one of Stirling's preferred extras, as it had always served him well on some of his earlier assignments during his active days working for the Sandbox. Anything that was available on the market where weaponry and electronic gadgetry was concerned was always guaranteed to get a powerful facelift from Bernie, due to his mastery as both a craftsman and an inventor. He could fully strip, analyze, and assess the features of virtually any object, calculate its worth and fallibility, and within minutes ascertain how it could be improved to maximize its absolute potential. His lifelong commitment was to be the best at what he did in any undertaking, and Stirling was always the key benefactor of Bernie's specific brand of excellence.

On this bristling afternoon, for his personal target practice session, Stirling had chosen the Ravin r500 sniper. This was not a firearm. It was a crossbow of unmatched accuracy. The Versa Drive system with the internal screw drive allowed for easy and silent cocking and de-cocking, stopping at any point, and the illuminated scope gave it improved accuracy for night shooting. Extremely compact, with a narrow axle-to-axle width when cocked that enhanced the weapon's maneuverability, it could fire arrows at speeds up to 500 feet per second, making it amongst the fastest crossbow available.

Bernie, by virtue of his skill and ingenuity, was able to strip the weapon, and through adjustments and modifications he made in the releasing chamber via the trigger mechanism, managed to increase the firing speed to 750 feet per second. But he didn't stop there. The key additional ingredient to this signature masterwork, which he executed to perfection, was the revolving arrow holder, capable of holding six rounds without reloading a single arrow because the cylinder turned as each arrow was fired due to the automatic chambering device he installed within the central base of the crossbow. In Stirling's hands, this instrument of death was lethal to the core. As he loaded the sixth and final arrow into the slide gap, he removed the illuminating scope as he preferred to remain unencumbered by its additional weight.

Having finished their initial rounds of practice, Tyler and Bernie walked over to where Stirling was preparing to unleash his grouping and stood safely behind him at a distance, merely to observe him. It was obvious that Tyler was awed by the sight of this one-of-a-kind gadget.

Stirling looked across in the distance. At approximately 900 feet, he could make out the row of dangling dummies waiting to be obliterated. But these dummies were different from the ones Bernie had destroyed because they were made entirely of wood with carvings in the facial region to denote individual features. As he shouldered the Ravin, Sterling looked through the crosshairs of his irises, taking aim at the first dummy. There were yellow X marks on different spots of the body of each and every dummy, indicating that these were the specific bullseyes to be targeted for the definitive killshot. A few had them along the side, while others had it at the forehead and even the upper legs and ankles.

Tyler looked over at Bernie, who was more focused on looking at how carefully and methodically Stirling prepared before unleashing his group. Stirling looked down the path, exhaled and let them loose. His eyes were like lasers, his aim virtually flawless. Within seconds he had discharged all six arrows. Tyler grabbed a pair of binoculars from the wooden plank that doubled as their outdoor table. He looked through them to see that the arrows were far from being centered as they had penetrated varying parts of the wooden target bodies, boldly sticking out of sections which didn't appear to be accurate or properly connected. Tyler flinched, perplexed by what he perceived to be the poorly executed grouping of Stirling's shots.

"Stirling, I think you probably should have used the sight scope for this session."

Stirling smiled.

"Why is that?" asked Bernie.

Tyler lowered the binoculars to address Bernie. "Because he missed the kill zones on his targets like, big time..."

A few seconds of stillness and silence passed before Stirling chimed in.

"Did I?"

At that instant, a concussive wave of explosions rattled off in the distance. The sextet of dummies which had been shot by Stirling all blew up, releasing a furious storm of wood and cork across the distant field. Tyler snorted in surprise, put down the binoculars, his mouth completely agape, and looked over at Stirling.

"No, I guess you didn't."

Bernie smiled and walked away from the firing zone back towards the main house.

Sterling said to Tyler, "Whether your target is human or inanimate, your killshot will never be located in the same place twice. Especially when you find yourself in the heat of battle. Remember that."

Tyler considered the weight of the remark and nodded. Stirling laid his weapon down on the oak plank, and as he walked past Tyler, he patted him firmly on the shoulder.

* * *

Later that afternoon, the sun finally began to break through. The skies were no longer overcast. The three men were now inside the house seated around a large mahogany table with a screen projector at the center of it. There were three drinks on the table as well. Arnold Palmers all around. Bernie had his laptop computer in front of him. He stood and walked over to the room's entrance to close the door and turn off the lights. There was, however, ambient Mondrian light fixtures scattered throughout the four corners of the immense room, giving it a sense of illuminated balance and shape, highlighting the men's faces and allowing them to see one another in the darkness.

"So, gentlemen... Let's talk shop," said Bernie.

Tyler and Stirling turned their attention over to Bernie, knowing that whatever he had to share was of vital importance.

"The people responsible for the massacre at Rhodesia En Rouge and the killing of our dear friend, Angie Miller, was Ravenne Industries. Of that, we are certain... However, Max Thulin and the Sandbox also had absolutely nothing to do with it."

Stirling nodded reluctantly but affirmatively, almost as if he wasn't the least bit surprised to hear this.

"You're absolutely positive that no one was giving them orders from a higher place of authority?" asked Tyler.

Stirling, silent, listened carefully to what Bernie said. "No one... And you should also know, Tyler, that they were also directly responsible for Monica's death and the incident at the Emerald Carousel."

A look of rage and pain crossed Tyler's eyes as he remembered his beloved Monica. "Bernie," he said, "I need to be proactive on this... not reactive... what's our next move?"

Bernie shot a quick glance over at Stirling.

"Yes, Tyler," said Stirling. "We agree. But you also need to understand that when dealing with the enemy, information and intelligence are the keys to gaining the advantage... So first, we need to play it cool."

"Exactly... And first thing's first, Tyler. Have you had a chance to make contact with your aunt and uncle since the incident at the Rhodesia?" asked Bernie.

Tyler shook his head. "Nothing yet. Now, I do know where I'm going to look next because it's basically my final option. But as of this moment... still no confirmation as to their status or current whereabouts."

"Alright…" said Bernie. "In that case, let me run it down for you where Ravenne Industries is concerned." Bernie flicked the projector on, and began a very brief but important slideshow. "This is Damon Chambers," he said. On the screen, a candid photo showed Chambers wearing a smart suit and dark glasses, emerging from a car which had the door being opened for him by an unseen assistant. "He is the point man for Ravenne Industries. Nothing ever goes down without his involvement or direct supervision. He is methodical, ruthless and not without a sense of flamboyant style. Although he does not run the show, you could arguably make a case that he is their number 2."

"Yeah… at this point you could say that Stirling and I are familiar with Mr. Chambers."

"A little too familiar, I'm afraid," said Stirling.

In that moment, Stirling thought back to the evening he saw the maniacal smile on Chambers' face as he held on to the lifeless corpse of Angie Miller. He winced slightly as he remembered, and Bernie noticed it. In that moment, Bernie flipped the image on the projector with his remote.

The shot on the screen changed to something deeply harrowing and disturbing. It was the sight of a rollercoaster at an amusement park, completely derailed and demolished with at least fifty battered corpses lying on the asphalt at the bottom of the park grounds. It was a disastrous sight, and it caused all of them to squint as they tried to make sense of the carnage.

"What's this supposed to be? More Ravenne Industries handiwork?" asked Stirling.

"That's exactly what it is," replied Bernie. "Last year, they had an operative walk away because apparently he had an ailing wife and child, and he wanted to attend to their needs exclusively. This is what you get when you attempt to leave their organization... forty-eight dead, including the former operative along with his wife and child. This amusement park is located in Copenhagen, Denmark."

The three of them remained quiet and somber as they all assessed the loss of life with unmistakable disgust and contempt. Bernie switched the image on the screen yet again, this time revealing a shot of a woman whose face was completely hidden. He alternated between five different shots of presumably the same woman. In all of them, her face was obscured.

"Why aren't we able to see the woman in any of these shots?" Stirling queried. "She either has her hand covering her face, or she's always turning as she exits a car. There isn't a single clear view of her." Despite that, there was something tantalizingly familiar about the woman.

"That's right, my friends, you cannot see her because she is always aware of the possibility of being photographed or spotted whenever she happens to be in public. But all you need to know is that you are looking at the shot caller as well as the one-and-only CEO of Ravenne Industries..."

A chill shot through Stirling. If his intuition was correct, the woman in the photos was the former love of his life who had recently reentered it... Irina Contreras. Stirling looked over at Bernie with a borderline death stare. His fury was contained but undeniable.

Bernie continued, "Meet Iris Ravenne, gentlemen. As you know, she is also known in certain circles as the Raven. She is the current threat we are facing, and we need to contain this threat much sooner than later... Obviously."

Tyler thought to himself carefully. It was as if he was piecing together a puzzle.

"I have to ask a question... Who is this Max Thulin you both keep mentioning and how is he connected to Ravenne Industries?"

"I'm glad you asked, Tyler... Unfortunately, the answer is a bit more... complicated than you may imagine" responded Bernie.

"Why?" asked Tyler.

Stirling immediately interjected. "Because the Raven is dead to Max Thulin."

Tyler was puzzled. "I'm not sure I understand."

Stirling looked over at Bernie, who approvingly nodded, indicating that Stirling should run it down for Tyler. Give him the complete backstory, as it were.

"Iris Ravenne was once an operative for the Sandbox. I had no direct contact with her, but I knew of her because her reputation had preceded her. She was actually handpicked by Thulin and groomed for supposedly bigger things... From that standpoint, I suppose you could say our initiation processes to the world of the Sandbox were vaguely similar... We were raised in different parts of the world. Fairly close in age to one another, but because of the unique nature of our upbringing, training and assignments, our worlds never connected. They may have intertwined, but we never actually... worked together."

Tyler gave Stirling his full attention, while Bernie simply listened to the facts he had already been aware of for years.

"Anyway, Ravenne reached a breaking point where her services to Thulin and the Sandbox were concerned because she wanted the keys to the kingdom. She was making a stand for the ultimate power grab because although Thulin has always been trying to change the world in the name of science and human advancement, she is simply about power and control. Domination is the elixir that feeds her desires and soothes her soul for no other purpose other than to say that she will never allow herself to be inferior or subservient to anyone who stands in her way."

"I see. A person like that... is completely incapable of love. They don't care about society or the world at large because they only understand power, hate... and destruction," said Tyler.

Bernie nodded in agreement.

"That's true, Ty..." said Stirling. "But the Raven has made it her life's work to mask her true sentiments through duplicity, resilience, commitment to her cause, and above all else, a series of affairs with men from around the world, who in their own way brought her closer and closer to her ultimate goal..."

"Absolute control of the Sandbox," replied Tyler.

"Exactly...' Stirling said. "But by pulling away to create her own personal version of the Sandbox."

"Ravenne Industries," said Tyler.

Stirling nodded affirmatively.

"Now you see the big picture," said Bernie.

Tyler considered all this and said, "I do just have one last question."

"Which is?" asked Stirling.

"This recent real estate grab, on Walnut Street in New Orleans. How does that benefit Ravenne Industries? Why does something like that... bring her closer to her ultimate goal?"

"Another great question," replied Stirling. "But it actually has a fundamentally simple answer."

Bernie turned off the projector and switched on the main room lights. He sat back down and focused completely on Stirling, curious to see how he would break it all down.

Stirling continued, "Everyone knows that all of the properties on Walnut Street are prime buys, regardless if it's a home or business, and it would definitely capture top dollar and lucrative returns for the investor who acquires it. It became global news when that street got completely reassumed and purchased by Ravenne Industries, and it was her way of leaving her calling card to the world... even Max Thulin. One thing the Raven demands is attention, but she goes about it through very pointed acts of power and intimidation. The Walnut Street sweep was a prime example of her rabid display of unchecked power. Nothing more. But when Rhodesia En Rouge refused to become part of the deal... well..."

Stirling was hurt. Very notably hurt because this was a direct link and memory of Angie. One he was trying desperately to put behind him so that he could move forward, but it was next to impossible given the way he unconditionally adored her. But he suppressed his feeling and held his true emotions close to the vest, just like he always had.

"Kent, I'm sorry... I didn't mean to push," said Tyler.

Bernie looked away, buried in the sorrow of his own personal thoughts and recollections of Angie Miller.

"Anyway... it's all academic... because she's gone," said Stirling.

Tyler bowed his head down in restrained sadness.

After a moment's silence, Stirling said with conviction, "She's gone. The Rhodesia's done... But we're not."

Tyler and Bernie both looked up to consider Stirling. Fueled by what was clearly his renewed sense of vigor to continue the fight. "Mark my words, Ty... This is far from over, but it's important that you both know and seriously consider something else."

"What is it?" asked Tyler.

"Max Thulin... This is far from over for him. But his methods at bringing his plans to fruition differ from the Raven's greatly. He doesn't favor arbitrary violence against the innocent or rampant displays of random collateral damage... But when he marks or targets someone who he either is trying to eliminate or is in desperate need of finding... make no mistake... he will stop at nothing, and he will move mountains to make it happen. The difference between he and the Raven, though, is that he's methodical, deliberate, and will pace himself and even seem to disappear for an extended period just to lull you into a false sense of security. And as soon as you believe Thulin is safe and out of your life... that's when your worst nightmare begins."

The assessment was clear and present with a firm grip on danger to boot. Stirling knew Thulin only too well. He was marked in the past, and it seemed that once again, the past was coming back to haunt him. Bernie and Tyler were reserved in their consideration of Stirling's powerful declaration. They weighed all of it with the gravity it so solemnly deserved.

"I hear you, Kent..." said Tyler. "This is hardly over for me either. Monica is gone, and..." Tyler turned to face Bernie directly. "Bernie, can you run a make on absolutely anyone that's currently on the grid right there?" Tyler's eyes pointed down at Bernie's laptop.

"Absolutely anyone. What have you got?"

"Sara Kirkland."

"Sara with an S?" verified Bernie.

"That's right. Capital S followed by a-r-a. Then Kirkland, just the way it sounds."

Bernie keyed in all the information. The specs came through.

"There are nine floating in the database. I'll need specifics to narrow down the search."

Tyler thought to himself as Stirling looked over at Bernie.

"Right..." continued Tyler. "Approximately thirty years of age. Caucasian. Long, dirty blonde hair. Very striking looks. Green almond-shaped eyes. Probably half-Spanish or half-Mexican by way of the accent."

Bernie quickly typed in the additional details and waited for the response.

"Ok, looks like I have something... And by the sight of it, she seems to check out just fine."

"What did it bring up?"

"Sara Louise Kirkland. Age 32. German-Scottish father and Spanish mother. Real Estate Agent and Financial Analyst. Graduate of the University of Vienna with a master's degree in Business Administration. Top ten percent of her class. Absolutely no criminal record whatsoever. Last known residence appears to have been Barcelona, Spain. And not only is she completely clean, she is an absolute looker, let me tell you."

Stirling reacted to Bernie's remark with a slight but sincere smile.

"But now, here's the real litmus test, kid... Your confirmation. Take a look, and tell me if it's her." Bernie turned the laptop around to show Tyler. Stirling was very cautious to notice the any changes in Tyler's expression as he looked at the photo.

Tyler closed his eyes, exhaled, then turned to address Bernie. "It's her," said Tyler.

"Who is she?" asked Stirling.

"Just a friend," replied Tyler.

"You're sure about that?" asked Bernie.

"I'm positive. But as things stand right now... I'm extremely cautious about being seen with anyone... even if it is just a friend... Then add to the whole equation the fact that we still have no sign of my aunt or uncle as we speak... I'm sure you both understand."

Stirling nodded.

"Of course," replied Bernie.

Tyler stood up from his chair. Placed his hand on his brow. He seemed both tired and concerned.

"Kid, are you alright?" asked Bernie.

"Kent, Bernie, I just want both of you to know something... I'm not going to let anything happen to the people I care about. That includes the two of you."

Stirling and Bernie simply looked at one another, inexplicably moved by the nobility of Tyler's devotion to their friendship.

Tyler took a deep breath, exhaled, and said, "Gents, I hope you don't mind, but this has all been a lot to take in and absorb. It's been a long day, and if it's all the same to both of you, I think I'd like to just relax for a bit, take a shower and get ready for dinner."

"Get some rest, Ty," said Stirling.

"See you in a little while, kid."

Tyler turned and left the conference room, closing the heavy mahogany door behind him.

The weight of the world seemed to exit that room as soon as Tyler departed. Bernie and Stirling were silent for a moment until Bernie broke the lingering silence.

"The naive optimism of youth... you used to have it," said Bernie. "I know... I remember," Stirling responded.

With those words said, Bernie closed his laptop.

17

It was a quaint and quiet afternoon on the courtyard of Cafe Amelie in the French Quarter. Tyler and Zara Zimmermann, or Sara, as she was known to Tyler, were seated at a corner table, looking relaxed and comfortable as they each enjoyed a savory regional breakfast and nursed their mimosas. Tyler settled for the Eggs Sardou, which consisted of poached eggs with creamed spinach, artichoke bottoms, and hollandaise sauce. Sara was feasting ravenously on the crabmeat cheesecake. It was a local favorite and one of the more popular dishes at Cafe Amelie consisting of fresh crabmeat, a pecan crust, mushroom sauté and Creole meuniere.

This was actually a savory dish, though it was as tasty as a dessert."This is so delicious. You must try it," said Sara as she extended a forkful of crabmeat cheesecake towards Tyler's lips. He glanced down at it, opened his mouth and took the full bite, relishing its flavors as he swallowed. Impressed, he said, "Very good."

Sara smiled, but she saw that even the tasty treat didn't remove the look of concern he'd been trying to disguise all morning. With a slight twist of her head, she asked, "What's the matter?"

"Hmmm? Nothing, I'm fine."

"I can tell that something's on your mind. You might feel better if we just talked about it."

"Sara, I promise you... There's nothing wrong."

She settled for his answer and they sat in silence for a moment before she attempted to flip the mood by changing course. "Hey, there's something I wanted to tell you. Hopefully this will put a smile on that handsome face of yours."

Tyler did smile shyly upon hearing Sara compliment him. "What is it?" he asked.

"You remember when I told you that those old real estate associates of mine had reconnected with me and gave me that proposal about beachfront properties on the Amalfi Coast?"

Tyler nodded.

"Well, they acquired a string of them. The contracts are closed, and now they're looking for a few more partners to invest with the idea of taking what are basically vacant buildings and turning them into... whatever we want. Homes to rent. A nice hotel. A classy restaurant. Anything!! I said I would have to talk to my good friend Tyler, but I think that this might be a great opportunity for both of us."

"You're serious?"

"Of course... I mean we talked about this, no? You mentioned that you recently made some of your stock investments liquid and did fairly well, right?"

"That's true," replied Tyler, intrigued by both the prospect of a joint venture with Sara, and the emphasis she'd put on the word "friend" that suggested she was beginning to see him as much more than that.

"So think about it..." she said. "My money is in a Swiss bank account. Just sitting there. Cash from prior real estate deals that paid off extremely well for me. And you have the money from your stock investments, so it's accessible. It's there. You're good to go.

This is something that could represent a lot of money for both of us. A real future. I mean, come on, Tyler... this is the fucking Amalfi Coast we're talking about. You know the tourism that place gets every year. And believe me when I tell you, those people have money to spend, and that is no joke. We're talking serious money, and that means serious opportunity... for both of us," said Sara, with tremendous enthusiasm and conviction.

Tyler pondered the details of her proposal. It sounded amazing, and he was in a position financially where he could realistically entertain a prospect of this magnitude and potential. But he realized, too, that this was a crossroads—reading her body language and the tone of her voice, he sensed that what she was offering was a partnership that extended well beyond real estate. He looked deep into Sara's eyes, brimming with heartfelt sincerity and just a glimmer of glittering sexiness. He was getting that old feeling, one that washed over his entire being when he first fell head over heels for Monica Ekland. Now he sensed that same connection with Sara. The writing was on the wall. He was falling for her. The implicit nature of her expression was not lost on him. He was sold.

"You're right. You are absolutely right, Sara!"

They both raised their mimosas to make a toast. "

Let's do this... Partners," said Sara.

"Partners. One hundred percent."

They clinked their glasses. Each of them took a sip, then Sara leaned forward and sealed the deal, kissing him gently on the lips. The sensation of the touch of her lips pressing lightly against his was enough to get him completely aroused, and he didn't fight the feeling. On the contrary, for the first time since Monica's passing, he saw a glowing future for himself... with Sara.

***

Later that afternoon, Tyler drove along the main street through the Garden District. Rockne and Diane, his missing aunt and uncle, owned a gorgeous historic mansion in the Garden District, and this was the only place he hadn't checked to see if they were because when they weren't at their main residence in Audubon, they usually spent time at their beach home in the Hamptons. He drove slowly and parked on the street directly in front of the house. He turned off his engine and looked at the home, concerned that something felt off despite its immaculate exterior presence. Reluctantly, he got out of his car and walked through the main gate to the front door. He knocked. There was no response. He knocked again and still nothing.

He glanced through a window and saw that the furniture had been removed and the floors looked clean, yet there was no sign on the lawn to indicate the sale or acquisition of the home. It appeared to be abandoned. There was a slight mistiness layering the windows, which he wiped off with the back of his hand. With the moisture cleared from the glass, he could see the interior more clearly, but still couldn't quite make it out. He wouldn't feel satisfied until he went inside and walked both floors in their entirety. As he examined the front door, there was a lockbox dangling from the handle, the type of lockbox left by a realtor when a house is either in the process of being sold or has been recently acquired. Tyler was skilled at picking these devices. With a little stealthy effort, he had soon extracted the key from the lockbox and unlocked and entered through the front door.

"Aunt D!!" he called out. "Uncle Rock!!" His voice echoed off the high ceiling.

There was no response.

Tyler walked throughout the quietly, almost reverently, sensing that something was very wrong. There wasn't a soul living in this house. It had been emptied down to the last piece of silverware. Every single room on both floors was completely vacant and spotless, as though no one had ever lived there. There were no beds in the bedrooms, no towels in the bathrooms, no cookware in the kitchen, no signs of life whatsoever.

Tyler came downstairs slowly and cautiously, feeling profound sad. He couldn't understand why his aunt and uncle would suddenly evacuate their home so suddenly, without a trace, without giving any indication of their plans. Reaching the bottom of the stairwell, he tried calling out one last time.

"Is there anybody here??"

The silence was nearly deafening. A pin dropping would've sounded earth-shattering. It had the feel of a mausoleum, and as Tyler looked all around the home for what he instinctively knew would be the last time, tears welled up in his eyes. His Aunt Diane and Uncle Rockne were the truest form of parents he ever known, the final vestiges of family remaining in his life. With them gone, he had no one left he who was a blood relative.

He turned and gave the upstairs area one final glance, exited out the front door, and closed it behind him. Standing there, alone and in a state of unspoken despair, he weighed the gravity of their inexplicable Houdini act. Walking down the short stairwell leading to the front gate, he paused and turned to face the full exterior of the house one last time, then looked at the sky as if it might offer either answers or an explanation.

"I don't understand... Why did you both do this? I'll always love you... Thank you for everything... I hope we find each other... God bless..."

Tyler knew that no one could hear him, but he simply had to express himself by letting the words out. With that accomplished, he walked to his car, got inside, and sped back to the city.

* * *

That evening, night fell with a distinct coolness, typical for the fall season. The humidity wasn't as pervasive nor as consistent as during the odd warmer Autumn days. The front door to Tyler's apartment opened, and he entered, looking discouraged and disheartened from the afternoon's findings, or lack thereof. His eyes instinctively signaled him to look up, and he was both moved and stunned by what he saw before him.

In his kitchen, adjacent to his living room, the table was elegantly made for two, with a pair of lit candles, two plates, and two red wine glasses filled to the top, accompanied by the bottle itself. A serving tray was in the middle of the table with the quintessential seafood dish... Creole shrimp and crab gumbo served over a bed of rice. Tyler looked up slowly to see the truest vision of the evening standing beneath the light of the dimly illuminated foyer. It was Sara, standing casually and looking at him. Their eyes connected. He stepped up to her, almost at a loss for words as he looked affectionately into her eyes.

"What is all this?" he asked.

"Looks like dinner for two."

"I see that, but... what's the occasion?"

Sara took Tyler's hand in hers and gazed at him with a warmth and depth of feeling which had eluded her until that very moment.

"I just wanted to make something nice for you on your special day."

Tyler looked at her curiously, not entirely certain what she meant. "My special day?"

Sara smiled.

"Yes... I remembered that today is your birthday."

It had been such a physically taxing and emotionally exhausting last couple of weeks that Tyler had completely lost track of the days. He exhaled and embraced her as he smiled from ear to ear, grateful that she'd taken the time to acknowledge him with such personal, heartfelt detail.

"Thank you, Sara... Thank you so much."

* * *

A short time later. The candles were incandescent in their illumination, highlighting the natural beauty of both their faces. The serving tray was nearly empty. They had enjoyed a full, complete meal together, dedicated entirely to Tyler. She was a vision, and Sara's singular femininity was not lost on him as he looked at her with hungry eyes, admiring the fullness of her shape through the paisley-patterned summer dress she wore so flawlessly. He drank his final sip of red wine, savoring the flavor as he swallowed.

"The way you prepared that Gumbo..." he sighed.

"Yes?"

"The Creole version normally has tomatoes and okra, exactly the way you made it."

"I was hoping that's how you liked it."

"It's my absolute favorite."

Tenderly, Sara caressed Tyler's face with the side of her hand. He closed his eyes, gradually feeling the heat of his arousal beginning to rise. He took her hand and kissed it gently. She leaned forward, and they kissed fully on the lips. As they both pulled away slowly, he took her face into his hand and studied her expression closely.

"I'm so glad... that you came into my life. You were exactly... exactly what I needed," he said.

"It was meant to be," replied Zara.

* * *

Outside of Tyler's apartment, there was a legion of party revelers carrying on their night's escapades at a couple of the local watering holes. The evening breeze was inviting and unusually pleasant for a fall evening in central New Orleans. It blew through the open windows of Tyler's home, where he and Sara had made their way to the bedroom.

They stood nude by the bedroom window, silhouetted by the pool of neon light bathing them from the outside, caressed by the faint breeze. Gazing at one another, he was tender with her, longing to give her the unabashed pleasure she so effortlessly gave him with even the slightest touch. She wrapped herself around him tightly as he lifted her up off the floor. His hands firmly clutched her magnificently bronzed rear, and he was clever enough to open her slightly, allowing his stiffened member to enter her slowly.

Sara moaned with unhinged delight as she felt the tip of his cock lovingly slide in and grip the walls of her warm, moist space. They moved effortlessly, perfectly in sync with one another, rhythmically attuned to the other's hot spots. The notion of fucking while standing was nothing new to either of them, but they were sensationally euphoric at how their coming together peaked their state of ecstasy like never before. Tyler fucked like a champion, allowing each thrust of his powerful buttocks to bring them both closer to the point of mutual orgasm.

"Take us to the chair," Sara whispered to him.

He proceeded to the corner of the bedroom, where a brown leather chair accented his space with just the right touch of masculinity, with a hand-carved wood frame followed by a perfectly spaced bronze nail trim. As he approached the chair, he held her strongly with one hand while, with the other, he quickly grabbed the leather accent pillow and threw it to the floor.

He sat comfortably, and as she straddled him like an Olympic athlete, she arched her back so as to use her pelvic muscles to really stimulate the base of his cock and balls with maximum urgency. That was the key; he now moaned so intensely he could barely contain himself. To keep themselves a bit less rowdy with their sounds, he grabbed her mane of hair and kissed her fully on the mouth. In turn, Sara grabbed the edges of the chair with both hands, pushing herself onto the length of his steel bone, bathing it with her cascade of simmering wetness. Tyler's balls were brewing, his epididymis was pulsating and together they came, mutually and explosively.

As they kissed passionately in the afterglow of their fiercely engaged climax with one another, Sara gently and slowly guided Tyler's head to her perfectly shaped breasts. He cupped them together in his hands, kissing them tenderly, allowing his tongue to flicker across the length of her erect nipples as he sucked on them ravenously. She arched herself backwards allowing her hair to graze the very tip of the carpeted floor. A slight smile formed across her lips.

"How do you feel?" she asked.

Tyler grabbed her firmly as he lifted her back up to look deeply into her eyes. He then lifted her off the chair and carried her across the room, where they fell onto the bed, bursting into a sudden wave of genuine laughter. They lay there on the king-sized mattress side by side. He was just as enthralled by this woman as he had been with Monica...

"Like I haven't felt in a very long time," he replied.

Sara smiled wickedly. "I'm so glad to hear it."

Tyler slowly turned away from her and began to clutch his stomach. He winced in pain and within seconds, the pain began to accumulate and center itself right at the core of his being.

"Because sometimes... your true feelings can emerge in the most unexpected ways."

Slowly, he began to tremble convulsively. He was squirming now in extreme agony. As his eyes begin to water, he struggled to speak coherently. "What did you do to me?" he croaked desperately.

Zara stared at him coldly as she leaned back into the pillows and delicately used her fingertips to remove a very thin layer of skin from her nipples, invisible to the eye and undetectable to the taste. "Arsenic," she explained coolly. "We have some very clever scientists where I work who have perfected the recipe in powder form. A few microscopic grains is all one needs to ingest to bid farewell, and if it's actually consumed off the skin, the one wearing it is fine..."

Tyler's pain was now so excruciating that he turned off the bed and fell to the floor with a massive thud. His eyes began to roll to the back of his head. Steadily, he felt his heart rate slow as he crawled with his waning degree of strength to his desk, where his phone was. He stopped to scream, but it was no use. He was dying, slowly and surely.

Sara raised the transparent, poisoned nipple skin layers with her long-nailed fingertips and showed them to Tyler.

"As long as they're protected... Almost works like a condom, don't you think?" she asked him sarcastically.

And now, Tyler's lungs began shutting down. His breathing was labored. The pain in his stomach was much sharper, more pronounced. With his final ounce of strength, he reached up and took hold of the phone, but as he brought his arm down, it slipped from his grip and hit the floor on its edge, bouncing away from him. Tyler exhaled his final breath at that very moment. He was dead, victim of Agent Triple Z, Zara Zianne Zimmermann.

Almost as if handling a child's dirty diaper, she held the two toxic skin layers dangling by her fingertips as she walked to the bathroom, still nude, and flushed them both down the toilet. She then methodically and very expertly peeled off the skin layers from her hands, so as to prevent getting affected by any rogue arsenic grains which might touch her actual skin. Zara was more than just a ruthless professional… she was an exacting perfectionist who allowed absolutely no margin for error.

Next, she walked back into the bedroom and callously surveyed the fallen body of Tyler Wilkes one last time. She went to the bedroom window, still radiating the pastel-hued neon lights which reflected off her perfectly tanned complexion. An eternal narcissist, she stood there momentarily admiring her nude figure. Then she picked up her phone and made a call.

"Yes… It's done… As expected, this was enjoyable but sadly… predictable. Mmm hmm… Exactly… Actually, I'm going to need a disposal unit here… Untraceable… And besides the disposal unit, I would also send over a cleaning crew… Leave nothing to chance… I should be there in an hour or so."

Zara ended the call and placed the phone in her crossover purse which was hanging off the white Chiavari desk chair. She then walked back into the bathroom and turned on the shower.

18

October was, generally speaking, a relatively dry month in New Orleans, but during an October thunderstorm, the skies were always dark with roiling black clouds, highlighted by heavy rain, flashes of lightning, and powerful winds. This was one of those days.

Stirling stepped out of the bathroom of his newly acquired place in the heart of the French Quarter. With some sleek modifications and stylized additions implemented courtesy of Bernie Llewelyn, you could say that it was just what the doctor ordered. He had finished his shower and was nursing his daily mug of coffee. He had only a towel wrapped around his waist as he sat at his desk, placing the cup of coffee at the corner.

Stirling opened his laptop and proceeded to do some investigative research on his opposition. He began by tapping into the central nervous system that was covertly referred to as Sandbox Central. He followed by entering his password and waited as the computer loaded and the files opened. The page in question read "Eyes Only." He broadened his search with a few general key strokes.

The next page that opened was the file of Damon Chambers. He read through it carefully with principal attention focused on Chambers' number of kills, many of which were egregiously supplemented by reams of collateral damage. The slaughter of innocents meant nothing to Chambers; he was committed to the cause of Ravenne Industries with a zealousness bordering on religious fervor. His background involved precision-based terrorist attacks against rogue mercenary outfits. They were splinter cells which might have posed a threat to Ravenne's broader intentions where global domination was concerned. This spread out on occasion to mid-level hits, tactically executed with precise accuracy by Chambers himself. He was deftly skilled and impeccably well-trained, with knowledge of cyber-based counter-programming as well as top level training and expertise with light weaponry and virtually every discipline of martial arts imaginable.

Stirling had seen enough. He knew that Chambers was a force to be reckoned with and dealing with him would be no small feat. He would have to think quickly and effectively if they ever came face to face. As he continued to explore the "Eyes Only" files available within the Sandbox inner sanctum, he moved on to his next pending subject, Angie Miller. But something unexpectedly disturbing appeared on the screen when he entered her name on the search bar.

Her picture gradually appeared on the screen, unraveling from a series of pixilated dots. A warm, disarming smile formed across his lips as he saw her once again, but it was just as quickly followed by a look of consternation because what next appeared across her face, in bold red letters, was "File Extinguished."

This disturbed Stirling to the point of no return. In Sandbox terms, "Extinguished" mean all her files had been completely scrubbed, along with Angier herself. He couldn't fathom how the long-standing history of a deep cover operative like Angie Miller could be so readily dismissed and cavalierly disavowed. This type of total erasure was tantamount to saying that she never existed.

He knew she deserved better, and it led him to wonder what was so adamantly coveted by several powers that it could have led to Angie's untimely death.

He took some time to collect his thoughts before he keyed his next query into the computer, typing the words, "Operation Beech Grove." As soon as he pressed "Enter," the screen went completely black. Then slowly but surely, it rebooted in a glaring display of pure white. A beeping sound with the dissonant tone of a smoke detector began sounding off, followed by the words, "File de-activated," appearing across the screen in bold, green letters. Immediately, Stirling shut off the computer, uncertain as to why this was the reaction provoked by simply researching "Operation Beech Grove."

In that instant, his cell phone rang. Recognizing the number, he answered it instantly. "Bernie."

There was a long silence on the other end of the call before Bernie said, in a grim tone, "Kent... it's the kid, Tyler."

Stirling's heart sank as he imagined the worst. "What happened?"

"News report just came through. It was definitely a targeted hit, and he was the mark. His place was torched, and they left their calling card in addition to one of his severed hands, which was... found as they sifted through the ashes."

Stirling had a feeling. It was inescapable because now it was clear that they were taking a stand and eliminating all got in their way. " Ravenne Industries?"

Bernie said nothing, but exhaled deeply on the other end of the line.

"Bernie, was it the Raven?"

"Yes... they left their calling card. It was a pin of some sort, like a broach," Bernie responded, the weight of heavy sorrow in

Stirling thought to himself for a moment, ruminating about the past and the present.

"Bernie, we need to bring the fight to them. We can't continue lying around in wait in anticipation of their next move. If we do that, we'll lose everything we've worked so hard to preserve, over decades."

"I know. I'm already making preparations for how to go about doing this."

Stirling nodded, and his eyes widened at the same time with an atypical look of fear. "Oh God, no..." he said in a hushed tone.

"What is it?" asked Bernie.

"Irina," replied Stirling.

"I thought she was staying with you!"

Stirling closed his eyes, regretting his earlier decision to allow Irina to stay on her own. "She had some personal affairs to deal with before going back home. Said it was more convenient to stay at her hotel."

"What hotel?"

"The Four Seasons."

"Kent, get her. Bring her to your place and both of you take the charter plane and get over here to my Vail place ASAP! There's no time to waste."

Stirling was instantly struck by something else. "Wait, we might have to leave in the morning. Looks like we're going to get hit by a serious thunderstorm. Weather won't permit traveling this evening. But I'll get to her, and we'll be there tomorrow first thing."

"Be safe. See you soon."

Stirling disconnected and immediately dialed Iris's number. It went straight to voicemail. "Pick up the fucking phone," he muttered to himself.

Holding the phone tightly, he clicked off and prepared to dial again, but it was unnecessary. The phone rang. It was Iris.

Sterling immediately asked, "Are you, alright?"

"Honey, I'm fine. What is it? What's wrong?"

"No time to explain. I just need you to get over here right away. Once we're together under the same roof, I'll... I'll tell you everything."

"Is that all?" asked Iris.

"What do you mean?"

"Explain... Is that all you're going to do?"

Stirling closed his eyes. It was happening again. There was no denying it. Those old feelings were simmering and reaching a boiling point. He always held firm that she was the most sensual woman he had ever known in his life, and she knew exactly how to get his fuse lit. No other woman ever exerted that much power over him. Not even Angie. But the tone of his response signaled this was not a time for flirtatious banter. "Just... come to my place. It's important. And pack your clothes and personal items. We're going away for a few days. For our own safety."

There was no response on the other end. Iris was listening intently, but she did not acknowledge Stirling's request.

"Irina?"

"I'll be right over," she replied. The line clicked off.

Stirling hung up. He placed the phone on his desk and walked over to his bedroom window. As he looked outside, he could hear the distant rumbling thunder of the slowly approaching storm.

* * *

A few hours later that evening, in the not-so still of the night, torrents of rain shimmered across the windows of Stirling's second story compound, casting streaking shadows on the floor when the lightning bursts came with sharp cracks of thunder.

Stirling and Iris were creating their own fireworks in the silk sheets of his bed, unleashing themselves, fueled by their mutually aching desires. Her voracious sexual appetite always got Stirling uncontrollably excited, to the point of carnal bliss. The fire between them was further stoked by the fact that they always pushed their yearnings to the edge, doing absolutely anything and everything to and with each other.

Their dance of the flesh had begun with acknowledgment of each other's nude bodies by licking the beads of sweat off one another. They were both in peak physical shape with bodies to die for. Stirling took the initiative by going down on her. He so loved and obsessed over the thought of devouring her perfectly shaved landing strip. It was a literal taste of Heaven to him. She pulled him up and turned him, pressing him up against the cool, concrete peach colored wall with every intention of returning the favor.

The placement of this opening portion of their consummation was ideal because as she gradually lowered herself to a kneeling position, Stirling was looking at the full length mirror in front of him and through the shafts of light cascading through the windows, he was able to catch glimpses of her stunning snatch which opened, slowly exposing her aroused labia. This got him off and engorged his erection even further. He was moaning like never before, as she took him fully into her mouth. Her cock-sucking was slow and systematic. She attended to the needs of his riveted excitement in a manner that was peerless. She worked her way down his rod, reaching the edge of his slowly stiffening balls.

He lifted her slowly and whispered in her ear. She smiled excitedly, and the rain outside began to pound even harder, accompanied by the lightning and chill-inducing bursts of thunder. The storm was at its most primal and intense, and so were Stirling and Iris.

He picked her up effortlessly and turned her so that her face was in his genital region, and her welcoming heat was in his face as well. This was a standing 69 they performed on one another, and they were enraptured, loving every minute of it. After making each other come furiously, he then swept her in his arms, carried her over to the bed, and he turned her around so that her ass was staring at him longingly.

Even after firing his furiously enormous load, Stirling's cock was still stiff as a board. She wanted him badly, and the feeling was feverishly shared. He entered her slowly, maintaining his full erection. For what seemed like hours, they made unhinged love for what felt like an eternity, until they came triumphantly with one another again, reaching heights of unexplored euphoria through their mutually felt climax.

* * *

Later that evening, still completely nude, they slept. The rain continued falling, but the thunder had subsided, and there were only occasional streaks of lightning tearing through the grayish nighttime skies. Stirling was always a light sleeper, but Iris had so taken him over the edge that his state of slumber was heavy and impenetrable. But Iris's eyes suddenly opened, as if she had been awakened by some silent alarm which only she heard.

She lay on her back, while Stirling was lying on his side, turned in the opposite direction. Iris pushed up on her elbow and leaned over him, whispering into his ear, "Kent? Are you awake?"

Stirling didn't move a muscle, didn't even stir slightly because his slumber was as impenetrable as Fort Knox. Sensing intuitively that he could not be woken up, she kissed him lightly on the cheek before whispering in his ear, "Always remember."

With that, she rose from the bed.

* * *

Morning broke with skies overcast and the sunlight pushing through. The storm had passed with only drizzling pockets of rain washing through sweeping through New Orleans. Suddenly, Stirling snapped out of his deep slumber. He was lying on his stomach, and as he began to awaken, he rolled over onto his back, saying, "Well that was..." But as his extended arm fell across the bed, he let the rest of the sentence go unspoken. Iris was was gone. Then, a mounting sense of terror struck him as he heard an aberrant sound which shook his foundation to the core.

A strange hissing came emanated from the foot of the bed. Stirling was nude, with a light, white sheet covering him. Very careful and economical with his movements, trying not to move or shake the bed too vigorously, he slowly pulled away the sheet to reveal a hissing, slithering Eastern Coral Snake. These snakes were rarely seen due to their preference for burrowing in the ground, but they were nonetheless common in the city of New Orleans They were known for the bright coloration of their red, yellow, and black bands as well as for the fatal nature of their venomous bites.

Slowly, the snake undulated up his leg, its cold, scaly skin giving Sterling goosebumps. It slithered across his torso and rested its head along the chiseled gap of his muscular chest. It became a challenge of death stares between Stirling and the coral snake as neither removed their sights from the other for even a split second. They were completely fixated on one another, and slowly but surely, the snake's level of hissing grew louder and began to intensify, signaling that it was preparing to strike.

Stirling knew that he was completely and utterly vulnerable at this point, and it certainly didn't help matters that he also happened to be lying in bed completely naked. There was one solution, and if Stirling could make it work, he might actually make it out of this predicament. It would require precise coordination and timing unlike anything he had ever attempted before, even on the most hazardous of missions. Thanks to Bernie's stellar inventions and amped-up versions of household furnishings, the bed on which Stirling slept had a safety switch at the side, within reach of his hand, embedded against the mattress. By pressing it lightly, it released a compartment which could fit a weapon of any sort as long as it was no longer than ten inches in length and seven inches in width.

There was such a weapon stocked in that compartment, and Stirling knew it could save him if he could simply reach it in time. The snake moved up his chest about half an inch, poised and priming itself, flicking its forked tongue. Stirling stared back at it coldly without moving a muscle. Beads of sweat glistened and trickled down his forehead, dripping slowly into his eyes. He wanted to bat his eyelids, but remained absolutely still so as not to provoke the snake into attacking.

His index finger grazed the base of the button on the side of the bed. Stirling and the snake remained locked onto each other's eyes. The snake shook its tail and slowly began to open its mouth, revealing two short fangs filled with neurotoxin.

It was now or never, and Stirling knew it.

He pressed the button, but it was doubly reinforced. A lever emerged from the mattress which needed to be lightly lowered to release the final gift this gadget-laden bed had to offer. The snake began to arch itself backwards, getting ready to pounce.

Stirling struck first.

He flicked the lever down. It jolted the bed up and forward, allowing him to grab the weapon as the disoriented snake flew off Stirling and landed on the floor completely twisted. Stirling spun off the bed and went in the other direction, putting as much space as possible between him and the snake. Then, with the weapon primed and in his hand, he pointed it directly at the serpent which had now repositioned itself back into attack mode across the room.

The weapon in question was the flame gun in the shape of a crossbow pistol which Stirling had initiated back at the Rhodesia En Rouge the evening of the Silver Palace Ballroom party when Angie was killed. Now, he had the Coral Snake in his sights, and he knew this was a one shot deal. He took aim and fired the flame gun just as the snake pounced. Just like before, the spear of flame spread the moment it connected with the snake's body, spreading itself across the slithery scales and burning it instantly to a crisp.

Acting quickly, Stirling ran to his bureau and picked up a vintage seltzer bottle atop it. He sprayed the entirety of its contents over the roasting snake, the pressurized carbon dioxide acting like a makeshift fire extinguisher and smothering the fire completely. Once the flames were out, there was no question... the snake was stone cold dead.

Stirling shook himself back to his senses as he grabbed his silk house pants and stepped into them quickly. He looked all around for Iris and found absolutely no trace of her in the house. He knew she couldn't have been abducted, since he had converted the house that evening into a veritable fortress. But although no one could get in, it was easy to get out.

"Irina!!"

He checked every possible room and crevice to see if she might have been hiding from something or someone.

"Irina!!"

His cries went unanswered. She was definitely not there. He scanned the house for a trace of penetration within the perimeter. No one had breached it. Absolutely everything was intact. He began to think the worst, and then he thought about allegiances and previous alliances that had proven to be ruses. Betrayals waiting to be revealed from even the closest personal friends and allies. His heart sank as he began to look for the leavings of something resembling a clue. And then, as his eyes found the wastebasket next to his computer desk, he saw what revealed the ultimate but undeniable truth about the woman who he once referred to as the love of his life, his former fiancé, Irina Contreras.

He thought back and remembered... The prior evening when Irina arrived she noticed that his candles weren't lit. She looked in her purse and retrieved a small case of matches. As she opened it, she gave a look of relief.

"Last one," said Irina.

She struck the match against the case and threw the matchbox into his wastebasket. But he was more puzzled by the fact that she even had the matches in her purse to begin with. He continued to remember the previous evening's brief conversation with her...

"I thought you didn't smoke?" asked Stirling.

Irina smiled and thought for a moment, looking at him through typically seductive eyes.

"Cloves. They relax me. I only started recently."

Now snapped back to his present reality, Stirling reached down into the wastebasket, dreading what he might find as he pulled out the empty case. He opened it slowly, and his eyes widened with both shock and rage when he saw an all too familiar image...

It was the symbol of the Raven in flight. The call sign of the Raven. And it was the exact same look and position of the raven which had been engraved on the bullet that killed Angie the evening of the Silver Palace Ballroom celebration at the Rhodesia. Now, everything was clear, and the players were in the open. Stirling couldn't find the logic in any of this. He dropped the empty match case and sat down resting his arm on his desk and placing his hand on his furrowed brow.

There was one element which was as inescapable as it was undeniable. Somewhere along the road of her life, Irina hadn't simply turned... she had snapped. Her allegiances went to the wolves, throwing all sense of judgment and morality out the proverbial window in the process. Her justification for her choices and actions were no longer calibrated by anything even remotely resembling a moral compass. She was behind much more than just corrupt real estate transactions. She was making a pronounced and desperate grab for power. A level of power she wanted to usurp from one of the most powerful individuals and corporations Stirling had ever known and encountered... Max Thulin and The Sandbox. And in doing so, she had formed her own black ops-type corporation, skilled at more than just the necessities of capital gains and questionable business ventures. Ravenne Industries was a front for espionage, extortion, and murder. All in the name of Iris Ravenne, the woman Kent Stirling had come to know and fall in love with so deeply that he was on the verge of marrying her just before she was presumably killed in that yacht explosion off the coast of the Yucatan all those years ago. Iris Ravenne was the woman he came to know and adore as Irina Contreras.

But her psychology was warped now. In its own way, it was a fractured variation on the manner in which Max Thulin was trying to achieve something vaguely resembling a new world order... but whereas he favored a tactical and surgical approach marked by precision and the seeking out of the exact target, she was about making pronounced statements through the implementation of terror and fear. Hence, the chaos and carnage, which had all been dealt by the hands of Ravenne Industries, such as the massacre at the Rhodesia En Rouge.

But Stirling knew she was never going to stop there. It was no longer about following a scheme devised by Thulin. She clearly had no qualms about confrontation or consequence. If these recent displays of wanton violence exacted by Ravenne would bring Thulin out into the open, that was precisely what she was hoping for. Alas, the other collateral damage inflicted by her wretched conglomerate was about cutting everything belonging to Stirling at the root. He knew now more than ever that her so-called undying love for him was an extension of a wholly perverted masquerade. He had fallen to the extreme because he trusted her fully enough to expose his heart, and his feelings for Irina were completely untarnished. It was a love borne out of what he perceived was a mutual, spiritual connection. He knew now beyond a shadow of a doubt that he was wrong. He was made a fool of and betrayed, completely. He fought back tears, knowing that there was no room for pity, remorse, fear, and above all else... tears.

Then something in him snapped. Like a ripcord tearing through his heart. He realized then and there that to insure her obliteration of all that was linked to the Sandbox, she would go after everything and everyone Stirling held dear. No ties and no loose ends would remain or be left standing. Including...

"Bernie!!"

He bolted out of his chair and ran back to his bedroom. He needed to gather his essential belongings immediately. There was no time to waste. There was only one place where he needed to be and get to as soon as possible...

Vail, Colorado.

19

The first week of November in Vail, Colorado was particularly cold. Much more so than usual. There was a grip of snowfall imminently brewing, radiating gusts of wind that could strip your skin like razor blades if you weren't warmly and properly dressed. At the same time, the sun could quickly and unexpectedly break through, making way for a clear, blue, pleasant afternoon. Such were the extremes of weather in November in Colorado... unpredictable.

On this day, however, it was ominous and foreboding because something else was hanging in the air—a looming sense of impending doom. It was illustrated by a small train of three black Range Rovers all forming a line as they drove up the highway, approaching Bernie Llewelyn's hidden residence. They stopped about a quarter mile before the entry gate and driveway leading up to the residence, parking in a curved formation along the highway.

Four individuals got out of each vehicle—twelve men and women in total, all dressed in grey with long leather dusters covering their winter apparel. For better firing accuracy, they also wore matching leather gloves. Opening the trunks of the Range Rovers, they reached for gear and weapons. Moving with quick, practiced precision, they stocked and loaded their machine guns.

The team of twelve advanced at warrant speed in a straight line formation over and across the hill beyond the realm of Bernie's surveillance cameras and alarm system. Clearly, the location had been monitored and studied in regard to its countermeasure defenses; when it came to Bernie Llewelyn, it wasn't wise to leave anything to chance. The grey dozen slowly stopped and took point on a sloping hill which gave them cover and allowed them to take aim at the central residence itself. They were far enough out of range to avoid being heard, detected, or seen by anyone in the house. And as they raised the face shields of their helmets, it was no surprise who was in charge and leading this team...

Damon Chambers, Zara Zimmermann, and Iris Ravenne herself were on point, leading the team in groups of four. They stood separate but aligned, approximately a dozen feet from one another as they positioned themselves on the hillside, with a perfect view overlooking the main residence of Bernie Llewelyn.

Iris scanned the house with her binoculars, pulling and sharpening the focus to get a clearer view. As she lowered the lenses, she turned to Damon and Zara and with a slight gesture of her hand signaled to both to come to her. She addressed them quietly as they all stood side by side.

"The windows are either misted from the weather, or Mr. Llewelyn has added some sort of film-like substance to create the illusion of stained glass. Either way, I can't get a clear view."

Damon swiftly reached into the pocket of his pant leg across his thigh— the entire team wore these utility-styled jumpsuits with multiple pockets throughout the pants. Most of the team members had edged weapons and additional magazines stocked within them. Damon handed Iris a single-lens viewfinder with enhanced capabilities.

"Try the Raptor. A new gift created by our friends at the laboratory. Laser quality vision guaranteed."

Zara smiled in approval as Iris looked through the lens. It was a hyper-stylized device made to penetrate the thickest surfaces for pure, unfiltered vision. As she adjusted the coordinates of the crosshairs, Iris scanned the perimeter of the entire home. She stopped when she noticed that Bernie was actually in his kitchen, cooking a meal and preparing his dinner, while nursing what appeared to be a glass of white wine. She smirked slightly as she noticed the colorful quality of the ingredients he was using to prepare this meal.

"Dear Bernie..." said Iris, "still partial to the Chablis, as always."

"What was that?" asked Damon.

"It's nothing. He's there," she replied.

Damon and Zara looked at one another, the exuberance and excitement of what Iris had said lighting up their eyes like jaguars.

"How do you want to do this?" asked Zara.

"It's so strange..." said Iris. "Even when we knew each other when I was still living in the Yucatan, he used to tell me how much he loved having all his meals with fresh radishes. Looks like certain tastes never go away."

Damon and Zara looked at one another curiously, fully aware that the remark made by Iris involved something only she understood, clearly related to their personal connection and history with each other. A slight smile formed across Iris's lips, almost as though a pleasant memory had been activated. But she just as quickly snapped out of it, returning to the mission at hand, saying, "I want both of you to listen very carefully. This will indicate to you exactly how we are going to deal with Mr. Llewelyn."

Damon and Zara nodded and gave their undivided attention to Iris.

"When Stirling and I were still together, I was living in the Yucatan under the guise of Irina Contreras, and we spent a lot of time with Llewelyn. He used to regale us with stories of his past life when he was an active member of the CIA. Sharing some of his dreams, he also told us that architecture was his main passion, and he longed one day to build himself a personal residence that would be the equivalent of Fort Knox. Something impervious to natural disasters and any form of impending destruction related to offensive tactical maneuvers, such as a high level hit with heavy arms and explosives."

"And you believe this house is the realization of that dream?" asked Damon.

Iris looked at him with a stare that could cut through glass. "I know it is... Because he also used to tell us that Vail, Colorado was his favorite place in the world."

"So if the home is blast-resistant, probably with corrugated steel and reinforced concrete, how do we attack?" asked Zara.

"Simple... we don't blast him out. We tear the place to shreds and smoke him out. He's in the kitchen, but he has a radar sense like a jackal. So shoot out all the glass of every window and leave nothing to chance."

Zara nodded her agreement as she looked all around the perimeter. "He has absolutely no neighbors," she said.

"Yes, and that was a very deliberate choice on his part, I assure you," replied Iris. "Damon, contact the air unit. Tell them we're ready and to switch to whisper mode once they're five miles away from the target. Once they arrive, I want them above and slightly behind us. We will take out the ground level from down here. Have them focus on the second story only, and fire all three of the mini-missiles. Nothing more."

"Doing it now," responded Damon. He took out his Walkie and spoke into it. "Hawk One, come in."

In the distance, a Black Hawk helicopter gradually neared the air space parallel to the Llewelyn residence. As they steadily approached, the chopper switched to silent flying, also known as whisper mode, in which the propeller and engine became completely muted. Iris's instincts told her they were close. She looked up into the air and signaled them with her hands to go clockwise and flank them from behind, so that the ground team would be positioned in front with the air unit prepared and ready to attack behind the ground team's central position.

Now the air and ground units were both in place and positioned to strike. Iris looked behind her and above to wave to the helicopter pilot. When they locked eyes with one another, she pointed to the residence in front of them and pantomimed with her hand the slicing of her throat, indicating that the house was the target and to take no prisoners. The helicopter pilot, dressed in military garb and severe dark glasses, gave Iris a thumbs up. Iris turned back to address Damon and Zara one last time. "Position yourselves with your teams. Get ready."

Damon and Zara stealthily moved across the hillside and prepped their individual units as to how they would engage the target.

Iris took a last look through the Raptor viewfinder. Bernie was still in the kitchen, seated by the granite countertop, watching television and eating his meal.

She slid the Raptor inside her thigh pocket, raised her left hand and counted down to three. As soon as her finger hit three, she lowered her arm like a boom, and the entire team engaged.

A barrage of 9mm gunfire spread across the snowy terrain, tearing the windows to shreds. Immediately Bernie hit the ground and took cover. Without hesitating, he began to move across his floor in military format, crawling forward on his legs and the backs of his forearms.

Outside, the team mercilessly sprayed destruction across the entire perimeter of the house. Bullets from the three rows of Mp5 machine guns ripped out the windows and interior furnishings, sending splinters of wood, slivers of plastic, and shards of glass cascading through the air like so much rainbow-colored debris.

Inside the house, Bernie had taken smart, grounded cover, which was enough to prevent being hit, but his clothing was completely covered in glass, concrete, and wood. He looked just ahead of him and stared closely at a seven-foot tall supply cabinet. He arched his eyebrows as he looked at it with unbroken intensity, determinedly making his way forward while maintaining his prone position.

Outside, the Black Hawk targeted the inside of the second floor with all three miniature missiles. Firing the three projectile skimmers all at once, they concurrently shattered all the glass fixtures on the second floor, creating a massive interior fireball, causing the balls of flame to burst forth to the outside while blowing everything inside the second floor to absolute smithereens. But as the entire home was built like an impenetrable fort, the house remained standing and didn't teeter off its foundation a single inch.

"Target acquired and dispatched. Heading back to base," said the Black Hawk pilot as they resumed their flight pattern in whisper mode and flew east, away from the residence and back to their central base of operations.

On the ground, Iris and her team were fired their final rounds of ammunition, spreading 9mm hail across the lower level, decimating every square inch of interior space in the process. When Iris lowered her machine gun and stopped firing, everyone else followed suit and holstered their weapons. The stillness of the air was practically deafening, save for the chirping of a few rogue American robins, which made their way skyward as they peacefully fled.

Iris looked at her neighboring teams, clenched her fist and opened her hand forward, indicating to draw their weapons, maintain their cover, and approach the house carefully to insure that the target had been acquired and killed. It was extraordinary to consider that so much preparation and effort was taken simply to eliminate a single middle-aged man like Bernie Llewelyn. But Iris knew better than anyone that at the end of the day, Bernie Llewelyn was no ordinary man.

The twelve member team flanked the entire house, with Iris, Damon, and Zara on point. As they entered the dwelling slowly and with great caution, half of the team went upstairs while the other six swept the lower level. With her hand gestures, Iris signaled three of the team members to carefully scan the living room and rec room areas. She, Damon, and Zara would sweep the foyer, dining room, and kitchen.

As they all split up accordingly, Damon peeled off slowly heading into both the living room and rec room areas. Zara headed into the foyer, her weapon carefully pointed and drawn. Iris walked cautiously into the kitchen, and as she turned the corner behind the enormous counter space where Bernie had been eating, a look of unparalleled relief marked her entire expression as she looked down.

"Damon, Zara, please come here!" she called out to both of them.

Damon and Zara joined Iris in the kitchen and were aghast when they saw the sight before them. Iris was still staring downwards, seemingly delighted with her handiwork. As they all looked back down at the sight before them, it was indeed what appeared to be the fallen corpse of Bernie Llewelyn. His face had been completely blown off by the barrage of bullets. He was completely unrecognizable, but to Iris's eyes, it was over. He was gone. Damon and Zara seemed stunned, but were a bit more reserved in their initial reactions.

"Relax... both of you. Mission accomplished," said Iris.

Zara was shocked to hear the assertive tone of her assessment. "Llewelyn is dead?" asked Zara.

Iris nodded affirmatively with absolute confidence and a wicked smile.

Damon was a bit more reluctant to accept this assertion as being absolute. "How do you know for sure?"

"Because those are the clothes he was wearing when I marked him inside the kitchen."

The three of them looked back down at the decimated remains of the body. Bernie had been wearing a beige pullover, dark blue jeans and tan loafers. Exactly like the dead body. Besides the face being obliterated, there were bullet holes riddled throughout the entire figure.

Damon again asked, "Iris, how can you be absolutely certain this is Llewelyn?"

She replied, "Look at his socks."

Damon and Zara both looked down again. While Zara couldn't contain her mocking laughter, which she kept at a hushed tone, Damon's eyes widened in disbelief as he turned his stare straight back to Iris.

"All his life, and as long as I knew him, Llewelyn always wore two different colored socks... One black and the other white."

Indeed, the socks didn't match. Zara nodded her total approval, grinning from ear to ear. Damon locked eyes with Iris, and together, they smiled.

"Congratulations," said Damon.

"Yes, to all of us..." said Iris. "Angela Miller, Stirling, and now Bernie Llewelyn. Gone. Now, finally... we can proceed with our plans."

Damon and Zara were pleased their deadly actions had reaped the desired reward.

"Both of you, gather the rest of the tea," said Iris. "Our work here is finished."

* * *

The following evening, Stirling's 1981 brown Lamborghini Countach sped along the lone highway, racing towards Bernie's residence. It stopped once it reached the entry gate. Lowering his window, Stirling reached out and entered a key code on the console pad. A few seconds passed, and slowly, the gate began to open. The Lamborghini nearly flew up the driveway, with Stirling in shocked dismay upon seeing the damage. He parked along the curved brick path in front of the main house and shut off the engine.

Leaping out of his car, he stood in stunned shock for a few moments before dropping to his knees. He began to shake, anticipating the absolute worst. The house was in total ruins. The snowfall from the previous evening had actually quelled the flames on the upper level because the containment of the missile blasts didn't spread too severely. But both floors were shredded and the glass from both was littered across the entire driveway. It was still snowing lightly when Stirling burst through the fragmented remains of the front door.

"Bernie!!" he yelled.

There was no response. He surveyed the entire home for signs of life on both floors. His last stop was the kitchen, and he entered the deep, wide space very cautiously because this was where there was the most internal damage and destruction. Thankfully, the lights still worked as Bernie always kept emergency electrical panels on reserve and activated. He switched all of them on, giving the kitchen the brightness of illumination it needed for Stirling to be able to execute a thorough search of the entire space. Furniture and the remains of all the home's dressings were scattered all over the kitchen floor. Then he froze completely as he bore witness to the devastating sight before him. It was the dead body. He was terrified to confirm that it was Bernie.

What initially captured his attention was that the face was completely missing and the socks were each a different color. This traumatized him because, like Iris, he was completely aware of Bernie's propensity for wearing one black and one white sock. But then, he sharpened his focus when something about the body that was completely out of the ordinary captured his attention.

The right arm had the sweater sleeve pulled downwards and was flimsy, almost as if the right hand had been severed or perhaps shot off from the massacre. Stirling looked all around the kitchen and beneath the gap of the refrigerator bottom and the kitchen floor, he saw it lying there, but he had to confirm it. He reached underneath the refrigerator and pulled out the object. His suspicions were confirmed. It was a severed hand. But his anxiety was momentarily relieved when he saw something else—the knuckles of the hand had coarse, dark hair on them. Immediately, he smiled.

He left the severed hand on the floor and began to grab the walls of the kitchen, looking for an opening of some sort, or perhaps a panel. He opened the utensil cabinets, the glass cabinets, and even the standing supply cabinet. He swept each of them with his hands looking for a switch, a lever or a panel because he had a lingering idea which needed to be verified. There was nothing, and then he tried the final option in the kitchen... the countertop. He walked all around it with his hands caressing the granite, praying he would find the device he was looking for, and then he saw it—a button located right at the edge of the south side of the countertop. He pressed it. A mechanism sounded behind him, and it was literally like music to his ears.

He turned around, and he was even more relieved when he saw that the kitchen floor was opening, very much like the twin doors of an elevator. Slowly but very carefully. The dark hole revealed itself, and Stirling looked down with only one instinct... to call out his friend's name once again.

"Bernie!!"

Still, there was no reply.

"Llewelyn, are you there??"

The scattered sounds of shuffling began to slowly emerge from the dim space below. Stirling couldn't make anything out because the blackness of the void had no slivers of light anywhere. But the shuffling became clearer, and it slowly began to sound like footsteps. The feet were climbing up the ladder of the steps that led to the basement below. The footsteps eventually stopped, and as Stirling looked down, the shafts of light flowing downwards into the basement from the kitchen revealed a single hand reaching upwards from the ladder, extending itself towards Stirling. The hand had no hair at all on the knuckles. When he looked down, Stirling smiled so excitedly that he could barely contain himself. He reached down and pulled the man up to safety. It was Bernie Llewelyn.

20

On the road to Tikal, Guatemala, there was a palatial estate decidedly modern in its architecture and singular in its location, deeply hidden amidst the lush plant life and vegetation native to this part of the world. But the key to this not-so-isolated mansion was that all was not what it appeared to be at first sight.

Modern lidar technology, using laser-guided imaging, allowed researchers to see through the dense jungle canopy and map out previously hidden structures at Tikal. While these structures were significant, they were part of the larger urban layout of Tikal, not the isolated, opulent dwellings they were at first believed to be. Instead, they were part of once-thriving residential areas, ceremonial centers, and other functional parts of a booming ancient city. But this was precisely why an individual with enough intuition and resourcefulness could architect this environment to create whatever structure their heart desired. Such was the circumstance for Mr. Eric Yanel.

Brimming with confidence and worldly authority despite only being 35 years old, Yanel was Harvard-educated with Masters degrees in Civil Engineering, Interior Design, and Landscape Architecture, and he was clearly bound for greatness. Brooding handsomeness, forest green eyes, and a penchant for the ladies were his hallmarks. But he was also vindictive and currently bent

 Sins of the Raven

on the worst kind of revenge because he was intimately linked to Dr. Kent Stirling.

When the former head of US operations for the Sandbox, Gavin Weller, assigned a series of international assassins to eliminate Stirling a few years prior, a couple of the casualties who were killed in the heat of battle in Belize and the Yucatan were Yanel's parents, Ernesto and Consuelo, two of the Sandbox's top former operatives.

Eric Yanel had become deeply familiar with the cultural rituals of the ancient Mayans. He was a shrewd international entrepreneur, a skilled martial artist, an expert fencer, a former champion skier, and a medicine man. But revenge and the extermination of Kent Stirling was his primary motivator and brought him to the attention of his the man who became his closest personal ally, and for whom he was currently waiting.

The skies were overcast and the humidity overbearing, not unlike the climate of the Yucatan during the summer months of June, July, and August, as Yanel peered into the distance. From up the rough jungle road, a jeep approached. A satisfied smile formed across Yanel's lips. He was standing in front of a converted ancient Mayan palace which he personally designed from top to bottom and now used as a base of operations, complete with swimming pools, conference rooms, and outdoor shooting ranges.

The jeep came to a halt and from the passenger side emerged Max Thulin. Yanel walked towards him, and they embraced one another as they greeted, solid affirmation of their undaunted alliance. The jeep's driver was Thulin's personal chauffeur who went all around the world with him. His name was Magnus, and he was approximately 40 years old with a build like a brick wall.

"Professor Thulin, so glad you could make it," said Yanel. "I gather you had a safe flight?"

"It was fine, Eric, thank you. Unfortunately, my time is limited, but I felt I owed you this meeting to let you know that we are on schedule, save for a few incidental... changes we need to realize before moving forward."

"You know I'm at your disposal, Professor. Always at your service and willing to accommodate... whatever you may need to see to it that everything is accomplished as planned. You've been... like a father to me... especially since..."

And there was the rub. That was Yanel's Achilles Heel— his burning desire for revenge against the man he believed was directly responsible for his parents' deaths... Kent Stirling. Thulin knew that with Yanel's global resources and particular gifts, he had an ally who would remain as fearless as he was committed to their shared purpose. Through Thulin, Yanel had the gateway he needed to find the man for whom he'd searched around the world. What would ultimately become of their unholy alliance, however, was another matter entirely.

"Eric, there's no need to dredge up the past. The past is the reason we are who we've become in the present, and the motivating factor to build a better future for ourselves... and hopefully for the world in which we live."

Yanel listened to Thulin's and hung on his every word and gesture like a devoted disciple.

Thulin continued, "But I felt I owed it to you to come here to demonstrate my commitment to our unified cause. And, to let you know that we have a firm date for you to examine our base of operations and central training facilities for all global Sandbox operatives. I not only value your discipline as an agent, but I require your expertise to assess our current stronghold and make the needed improvements as you deem necessary."

Head bowed, Eric considered Thulin's words. But something else was on his mind, another important matter that he was contemplating, but keeping to himself.

"Eric, this meeting is vital before we proceed with the next step forward regarding Operation Beech Grove. Our target is the same... Dr. Stirling. But once we find him, just remember that your yearning for vengeance is not our first priority. We have plans for Dr. Stirling, and I know you understand that by cooperating to the fullest, you will be at the center of these plans, making your quest for retribution all the more... satisfying."

A malevolent grin formed across Yanel's face. The fact was that Thulin knew just what to say at any given moment. He wasn't just a brilliant scientist, a renowned international businessman, and a ruthless leader of a cunning criminal syndicate... He was also a callow, heartless emotional manipulator who knew exactly what buttons to push with anyone at any given moment to elicit the desired response.

"Of course, Professor Thulin. That is, as you say, priority one. When will you need me at the new training compound?"

"In exactly four days," replied Thulin.

Eric thought to himself and nodded slowly.

"I'll see you then, Professor."

Eric extended his hand. The professor shook it, and they embraced once again. Thulin turned and got back inside the jeep. Magnus entered the driver's side, started the engine. They swung it around in the opposite direction and drove back from where they came. Eric watched them cautiously. The sternness of his expression was tempered slightly when he saw a local Guatemalan woman named Odelia approaching. She was sensual, voluptuous, and clearly one of Eric Yanel's devoted followers. The moment she reached him, they kissed as lovers would, full and without reservations.

"Eric, the ceremony is about to begin," said Odelia. "We can prepare the ritual as soon as you're ready."

"Thank you, love. I'll be right there."

Odelia strutted away with an air of toxic seduction in every movement of her glorious hips. Eric smiled wickedly as she returned to their secret compound nestled in the heart of the lush emerald forest greenery. Then his eyes turned in the opposite direction of the expansive field on which he stood. He walked slowly, his head tilted upward as his look of lust for Odelia quickly switched to an expression of awe and reverence.

It was Temple IV, the highest pyramid in Tikal, Guatemala. A major Mesoamerican pyramid and one of the tallest pre-Columbian structures in the Western Hemisphere, it offered spectacular views of the surrounding jungle. Built around 741 AD and located at the western edge of Tikal's main site core, it was also known as the Temple of the Two-Headed Serpent. Via a wooden staircase attached to the pyramid, one could climb to the top of it.

As Eric walked towards its first step, he stood before it simply to admire its physical design and imposing features. He revered it obsessively as one would a statue of an idol. Then, in a moment of silent acknowledgment, he pressed his hands together in prayer mode and bowed before the astonishing stone fortress that was Temple IV.

21

Throughout the month of November, the snowfall in Vail, Colorado was so nuanced as to be borderline mystical in its singular ability to quell fires of any size or intensity. November always had its share of generous blizzards and even rainstorms, but the snow alone had the cooling effects of direct water application that was truly rare. Consequently, the fire which had decimated the second floor of Bernie's sacred compound was now fully contained. The winds were moderate, and there was a light sprinkling mist permeating the air. The house had been reduced to rubble and ash because of Iris Ravenne's recent assault of the residence, yet its foundation was so impregnable that it stood like a cinder block fortress.

What was even more extraordinary, however, was the underground basement that Bernie had created over the course of several months. It was a fully-functioning living environment where one could survive for an extended period of time without qualms or obstacles. There was an endless supply of food and drink. Living quarters consisted of four separate bedrooms. Everything was rigged and connected for full-service electrical, gas, and water related necessities. Bernie's makeshift laboratory and research center was a veritable conference room which could accommodate a dozen people with relative ease and comfort. In short, it was another Llewelyn-based invention which didn't disappoint and never ceased to amaze or inspire.

Stirling and Bernie were in the conference room facing one another from opposite ends of the table, each of them immersed in individual activity. Bernie was at his desktop, feverishly researching something of vital importance. Stirling was cleaning and examining the recently improved features of one of his favorite of Bernie's weapons tailor-made for him... the Ravin LR crossbow. He suddenly paused to look at Bernie, who was enmeshed in his data and research.

"I never could have seen this coming," said Stirling.

Bernie didn't react or turn away from what he was doing, despite clearly hearing what Stirling had said.

Stirling continued, "There was no reason for me to suspect her of all... of all people."

Bernie knew Stirling had issues to address, and they needed to set everything straight before finalizing their plan. "Yes, it's true... She blindsided both of us. But think about it, Kent, based on your history with her, you never had any reason to doubt her."

Not entirely convinced of Bernie's assertion, Stirling shook his head. "I'm not so sure, Bernie... Are you certain?"

"Absolutely... Stop torturing yourself over this. Irina did..."

"Please—don't. Don't refer to her by that name."

"Just indulge me. Set aside your doubts and your pain for a moment because we need to set this straight, or you'll never be able to clear your mind and your conscience, which at this stage, is all you can do, Kent. This is not about erasing the past... it's about setting everything right in the present. So do yourself a favor and please just... listen to me."

His comments were spoken like the both the knowing authority figure and the doting paternal figure Bernie had always been to Stirling. Now, he laid it all out as Stirling reluctantly nodded.

"When Iris came to me as Irina, desperate and in need of human connection, all she was concerned with was reconstructing the past. You were the center of her universe, and she had both of us believing that for years because from the moment you both met, she was given that cover. You were both her mark and her assignment. And by playing her role of Irina so dutifully and convincingly, she catered not only to my concern... but to my humanity. The same went for you, Kent. Above all else, she knew that you were grieving when she reconnected with you. The loss of Angie was insurmountable, and she preyed on that by reminding you of the love you both shared. Once that was established, the die was cast. You were all in. Not because you were a sucker, but rather, because... you're you."

Stirling weighed the gravity of Bernie's words, and in his heart, he knew there was merit and logic to everything he was saying.

"But why me?" asked Stirling?

"Iris was one of Thulin's prodigal children because at an early age, she demonstrated gifts which he believed he could exploit and harness into something greater to realize the Godlike visions he aspired to, which he was convinced would not only change the world, but actually make it a safe and better place."

Stirling shook his head in thorough disbelief and disapproval. "We know better, Bernie."

"Indeed we do, my friend. Indeed we do."

Stirling was silent then for several minutes, ruminating silently, until he reached for his cell phone.

"I see that look in your eyes..." said Bernie. "What's the plan?"

Stirling typed at lightning speed as he sent off the text message. "For starters, I'm sending them a message... letting them know I'm still alive, and that we need to meet... I'm taking Ravenne

Industries down. No matter what the cost. Thulin will always be there, but at this stage, we need to let him come to us... Playing his game is much more like commandeering a chess match. This is personal, Bernie."

Bernie completely agreed and nodded. "So... how do you want to play this?"

* * *

That evening in Barcelona, the castle residence which doubled as the headquarter base for Ravenne Industries was quiet and under close guard by the small unit of soldiers symmetrically placed along the structure's perimeter.

Inside the domain, Iris, Zara, and Damon went over the final details for the New Orleans real estate acquisition along Walnut Street. The mood was light and airy, with trance music playing in the background. They had just finished dinner and were scattered about the room, with Iris seated behind her desk. Damon stood by the enormous window overlooking the city lights below. Zara was sprawled, panther-like, across the curved shape of the Moroccan sofa. A text message vibrated on the desk, received on Iris's phone. Damon looked over at her.

"When are we actually going to begin the remodeling of the Rhodesia En Rouge?" he said. "Where New Orleans is concerned, there's nothing else to address before the closing of the deal except that."

Iris glanced at her phone. Her reserved expression of muted satisfaction was suddenly disturbed by what she saw. Her dramatic change of expression was noted by both Zara and Damon.

"Iris, is something wrong?" asked Zara.

Iris rose from her desk and stalked over to the Moroccan sofa to sit next to Zara. Damon moved away from the window and perched himself on the corner of Zara's desk.

"Well... it appears that we won't be consolidating the arrangements for Rhodesia En Rouge after all. At least... not right away," replied Iris.

Zara and Damon looked at her severely because they knew something was wrong. Iris read her text message again. Suddenly and without restraint, she burst into laughter. But it was not a laughter of sincerity or jubilation. It was an unhinged laughter driven by what appeared to be a borderline maniacal sense of rage and emotional extremity. Damon attempted to calm her down by addressing her in a very hushed, serious tone.

"Iris... tell us... what's happened?"

Slowly, Iris regained her cool demeanor and the laughter subsided. With solemnity, she said, "Stirling... is alive."

Zara and Damon's eyes widened like saucers.

"Where is he?" asked Zara.

"Seems he's still in New Orleans. He's given us a date and a place to meet him."

"Obviously a trap," said Damon.

"He doesn't realize we're back in Barcelona?," added Zara.

"Of course, and that is exactly why we will all proceed accordingly, so that way... he won't even know what's on the way. Both of you prepare to leave and take the entire unit with you."

"You're not coming?" asked Damon.

Iris smiled wickedly from ear to ear.

"Don't worry about me... I'll be ready for him," replied Iris.

* * *

Back at the underground facility in Vail, Colorado, Stirling and Bernie were finishing their review of the plans to deal with Ravenne Industries.

"I'm going to want certain adjustments made to how we would normally approach these scenarios," said Stirling.

"In what way?"

"I want to come at them in a completely low-tech manner. Analog is key because they know the way you normally operate. Especially Iris. And I've made precautions by choosing a meeting place that would make this method of attack I have in mind more...effective."

"Weapons?" asked Bernie.

"The usual array should do just fine, but this time I'm taking

"I noticed you were giving it a little once over a few minutes ago."

"I just wanted to make sure you hadn't made any unexpected changes to it."

"The mechanism and the bow are still completely the same as the last time you used it, with unmatched precision at much longer lengths than usual. You've also got enhanced balance and reduced recoil making it more stable for long-distance shooting..."

"But?" asked Stirling.

Bernie shrugged sheepishly. "I did make a slight improvement to the arrows."

"I'm listening..."

"They're now tipped with black powder. It's a material composed of charcoal, sulfur, and potassium nitrate. Basically if you prime your targets and align them accordingly, the effect on impact will have the register of a rocket launcher. That'll make the disposal of your targets a little more precise as well as more certain. You can take them out in clusters as opposed to singles."

Stirling nodded slowly, both amazed and impressed as well as feeling moderate disbelief. "What would I do without you, Bernie?"

"You'd be fucked."

Bernie's point blank remark registered a smile from Stirling. Rising from his chair, Bernie walked across the length ofthe conference room. He wanted to get a good look at Stirling as he laid down his theory on how to best realize their scheme for eliminating Ravenne Industries. Eye contact between these two had always been a pivotal component, not only for purposes of communicating, but also for truly relating to and understanding one another. Bernie stood next to him, admiring his own handiwork on the Ravin crossbow.

"It's a real beauty, isn't it?" Stirling nodded as Bernie reassuringly placed his hand on his shoulder. "Listen... I agree that analog is the way to proceed, but there's still one piece of newly-devised tech I want you to have at your disposal. Implement it only if it's absolutely necessary, because in a pinch situation... you just might need it."

"Is it what you were telling me about back in New Orleans?"

Bernie thought to himself and smiled.

"Yes and no." "You're the boss," said Stirling.

Bernie smiled. "No, I'm just the facilitator."

They looked at one another knowingly, with the unspoken understanding that one could never function without the other. They were a solid team, but they were also the closest of friends with a deep emotional bond that verged on being something akin to a father and son.

"I'm going to get my gear, get ready to head back to Louisiana," said Stirling as he stepped towards the conference room door.

 Sins of the Raven

Bernie nodded. "And I'll be back in Florida if you need me for anything."

Stirling turned the door knob preparing to leave, but turned to face Bernie one more time. "You know, this whole thing with Angie... Irina being the Raven... All of it... You know what it does? It decisively erodes what little faith I have left in humanity."

Recognizing the inherent nihilism of Stirling's words, Bernie bowed his head in solemn resignation, unable to meet Stirling's gaze.

Stirling closed the door as he left.

22

In Columbia, South Carolina, the Harrison State Forest was the site of the training facility for Geneticorp, an organization owned, operated, and overseen by Max Thulin. This is where elite groups of assassins stationed themselves to complete a rigorous training course designed to prepare them for missions involving high stakes and incalculable risks.

It was an atypical November afternoon. The climate was generally subtropical, characterized by short, warm, and quite humid winters, but this particular day was overcast and breezy with relatively little humidity.

Thulin was quite proud of how he had reverse-engineered the topography of the Harrison State Forest to meet his precise environmental requirements into something better suited to the needs of his trainees. He had stripped the principal vegetation which mainly consisted of pine and hardwood stands. By doing so, he was able to create a research and training facility, built entirely of concrete and corrugated steel, scenically enhanced by extensive xeric longleaf pine forests with species like saw palmetto. There were twelve-foot dividing walls resembling concrete cubicles which housed the twelve super-soldiers who were there to serve Thulin's needs. They were six men and six women, all of them professed in various skills including archery, sharpshooting, hand-to-hand-combat, demolition, recon and intelligence, counter-surveillance, and all manner of other espionage-related tradecraft.

Thulin was there with Magnus, his driver and constant bodyguard. They were surveying the latest fleet of operatives, and by the look on Thulin's face, he was undoubtedly impressed as they represented the Mount Everest of probable candidates, honed and fine-tuned to serve at the very peak of physical and intellectual performance. A revving engine sounded off suddenly, and Thulin turned his attention to the giant front entry gate with its GC emblem at the center as it opened to admit Eric Yanel, along with his stunning companion, Odelia, from Tikal, Guatemala. They were both casually dressed in bright, primary colors.

As they approached Thulin, he greeted them with open arms and embraced them. This was an unusual gesture for Thulin, as physical affection was not naturally embedded in his DNA, but he was all about placating and mirroring Yanel's behavior, which was all about tactile gestures and physical affection amongst family and business allies. After the two men greeted, Thulin turned his focus to the lovely Odelia.

"A pleasure seeing you again, my dear," said Thulin as he took Odelia's hand, gently raised it to his mouth and kissed it.

She reciprocated with by pursing her mouth in a self-satisfied smirk and slightly raising one eyebrow. Eric, looking on, merely smiled as he removed his dark sunglasses and placed them above his head.

"Eric, I'm so glad you could make it," said Thulin. "Please walk with me."

Odelia and Magnus ambled about six steps behind them as Thulin and Eric led the way. As they walked, Eric seemed unimpressed but indulgent of what was clearly Thulin's pride and joy. They strolled down the walkway, looking into each concrete cubicle to see the operatives in various forms of physical training involving weapons and fighting through various forms of martial arts, including Ninjutsu. The training outfits were one piece jumpsuits. Women were dressed in red, and the men wore blue.

"Professor, why did you ask me here? I thought we were prepared to lay down the gauntlet, as it were, with our mutual friend, Dr. Stirling. These delays are leading me to believe that there's a problem you're wary of sharing with me."

They paused in their tracks.

"Eric... There's no problem at all. I know you have your own agenda where the good doctor is concerned, but so do I. And it is only because I feel that we share a common goal where the outcome of that agenda is concerned that I have allowed you to partake in what I can assure you will be a momentous occasion for our organizations and even for the world as we know it."

"I've invested generously as a sign of good faith and allegiance to this cause, Professor. Is this place the final outcome of what you and I both know was a very sizable donation to our mutual agenda? An agenda which you promised me long ago would bring me closer to the man who was solely responsible for the death of my parents?"

Thulin knew Yanel was driven by his vendetta and need for family retribution. Indeed, he had dedicated his personal fortune to creating a private army of his own, steeped in the ways of the past, to become a force to be reckoned with among the world of international criminal syndicates. And it was all in the service of love... because Eric Yanel adored his parents, Ernesto and Consuelo, and when he learned that their lives had been taken, his sole mission became the pursuit and extermination of Stirling and all he held near and dear. His patience was now running on empty. He was in no mood for the platitudes and empty promises that were indicative of Max Thulin's powers of persuasion.

"Patience is a virtue, Eric... Didn't your parents teach you that?"

Yanel's eyes filled with barely controlled rage as he quietly responded to Thulin's sarcastic quip.

"Never speak about my parents, Professor." Thulin smiled and tilted his head slightly. Yanel punctuated the threat with a single word. "Never." Point made, he switched topics. "Now, my time is valuable. Why am I here?"

"Very well, Mr. Yanel... I have something to show you."

A bell, akin to one in a church cathedral, sounded off on various loudspeakers. Assorted staff members headed for the main building, while the twelve operatives all stood in a militaristic single line formation in front of Thulin, Eric, Magnus, and Odelia. Next to them was a large wooden plank table with an assortment of weapons on it.

Thulin explained to Yanel, "The instruments you see before you represent the latest in light and heavy weaponry designed by the finest arms manufacturers around the world. In the hands of the twelve men and women you see before you, they are guaranteed to deliver maximum efficiency in eliminating any target, human or otherwise."

"Professor, I've seen what your agents can do. I watched them train as we were walking, and to be perfectly honest with you... I'm not impressed." Yanel then proceeded to unload and eject the clips of each pistol and machine gun lying on the large oak table, insuring that no weapon was loaded. He placed the magazines into both his pant and jacket pockets for security.

"May I ask what you're doing?" asked Thulin. The curious thing about the way he addressed Yanel was that he wasn't even remotely nervous, with Magnus by his side quiet and cool as a cucumber.

The only other weapon on the table was an imposing-looking flamethrower, a Throwflame Xl18, which offered ten times more firepower than its predecessor. It was able to achieve a maximum range of 110 feet using a diesel / gasoline mixture, making it highly effective. Eric took it in his hands and slowly approached the twelve operatives standing next to each other in perfect alignment. He paused directly in front of them, while Thulin, Magnus, and Odelia all stood safely away to his right.

"Professor... I'm about to show you what it means... to achieve maximum efficiency."

The dozen men and women were fearless, looking at him coldly and without the slightest modicum of fear or panic in their eyes. He smiled at them and let loose, igniting the flamethrower and sweeping it across the entire line of twelve, burning them all to death with rapid skill and ruthless intensity. Each body fell to the ground crackling and disintegrating into ashes as their screams bellowed into the grey skies above. Magnus took a step forward, and Yanel quickly trained the flamethrower in his direction.

"Step back, my friend, or I promise, you will join them."

Magnus held his ground, glaring at Yanel.

"Step the fuck back!" Yanel repeated.

Thulin gently placed a hand on Magnus's bicep and pulled him back to where he had been standing. Odelia was calm and said absolutely nothing. Yanel then proceeded to break the flamethrower, smashing the release barrel repeatedly over the table until it shattered. He then swept his arms over the table, swiping the broken pieces to the ground. The twelve bodies gave off an ungodly stench, charring and crackling to a crisp as Yanel turned to face Thulin and Magnus, while Odelia slowly paced over to his side.

"As you and your minion are both unarmed, Professor, that means we're all safe now... I checked you both out as we arrived. So you wanted my feedback, and now I'm going to give it to you."

Thulin inhaled and crossed his arms, listening intently.

"This is an amateur's playground," said Yanel. "Nothing your so-called elite have to offer begins to compare with the incomparable strength of my soldiers. They are trained in the ways of the ancient Mayan warriors, able to eclipse modern man's most advanced weaponry and to steal away in the night by blending in with whatever environment surrounds them. Camouflage and escape artistry is a way of life for us, and when we find Stirling, we will finish what you and your organization started all those years ago."

Thulin stood glowering, his jaw tensing.

"So if that is all, Professor, we are going back to Tikal. I have important matters to attend to. I expect to hear from you sooner rather than later about the mysteriously absent Dr. Stirling. You claim to be monitoring his every movement. So show me, Professor Thulin, because where this matter and our mutual agenda is concerned, the time has come... to give it closure. I'll await your call."

Yanel took Odelia by the hand, and they strolled out of the training facility as casually as if they were leaving a garden party. The gate opened slowly as they approached the motion detectors, and they climbed into the car that was parked just outside. As it drove away, Thulin had an icy, forced smile on his face as he turned back to look at the charred bodies of his dozen operatives one last time.

"Magnus, see to it that the bodies... are disposed of properly."

Magnus gave a slight nod, acknowledging Thulin's request. "Yes, Professor."

Thulin prided himself on keeping his emotions in check. He didn't get angry. He knew, in due time, Eric Yanel would come calling again, and that was fine by him. That was the price to be paid for being in collusion with what he thought of as lesser beings. This was just another day for Max Thulin at Geniticorp as he removed his glasses, blew onto the lenses, rubbed them clean with a light cloth and placed them back carefully onto his face.

23

It was an unusually bright day at the Audubon Zoo in New Orleans as Kent Stirling strode across the bridge from the Reptile Encounter exhibit to the Jaguar Jungle. As he approached, he caught a glimpse of an old friend, and it was as though they had never parted since the day they first met in the Khangai Mountains of Central Mongolia. It was his beloved Himalayan snow leopard, Lilia.

Stirling had adopted her, taking her with him from place to place, always seeing to it that her surroundings and environment were either readily available or partially created for her, courtesy of Bernie Llewelyn. This was a decisive time for Stirling, and come hell or high water, he wanted Lilia near him. He needed her unconditional love and support through what he knew was going to be an arduous and grueling ordeal.

Stirling sat at a bench in front of the makeshift cave dwelling that was a perfect simulation of where Lilia lived in the Khangai region, complete with lush greenery and ample food and drink. She was home, and when her eyes connected with Stirling's, her heart was filled with the type of doting affection she knew he had for her because her intelligence was daunting, and in her heart of hearts, she never forgot that Stirling had saved her. All that divided them was the fence separating the exhibit itself from the visitors who would periodically stop to study the lair and take photographs.

Stirling was still as he pondered what had happened, who he had lost along the way, and above all else, what remained to be done. And in that moment, he heard the voice that soothed his soul more than any other...

"Fancy seeing you here," said the woman who brought more joy to Stirling than anyone he had ever known.

He turned and seated at the other end of the bench was Angie Miller. Life stood still, and for a moment, nothing else mattered and no one else existed. Stirling wasn't delusional. He knew she was gone. But this was a time of contemplation and recollection, and right now, he was conjuring the true love of his life, his one and only... Angie.

Stirling said softly, "We used to love the winter afternoons here back in the day. You remember how the jaguars would take refuge in the cave, keep each other warm and nestle one another on those special nights?"

Angie smiled warmly as she thought back. "This was one of our main refuges, wasn't it?"

He looked at her dotingly and said, "Always."

They sat there silently, on opposite ends of the bench, watching Lilia in her lair, who appeared to be smiling as she quietly. Gradually, Angie's expression changed from joyful to concerned.

"Stirling... Why are you doing this?"

"What do you mean?" he asked.

"No one, but no one, is capable of doing the things you do. Why not focus on building a future instead of erasing the past?"

Stirling looked at her closely as he pivoted in the bench to face her directly.

"I'm not erasing the past, Angie. I'm preserving it. Protecting it. The future as envisioned by Max Thulin could simply never be. The world... would be a deeply dangerous place to live. An inhuman place. And I won't allow that. No matter what I have to do, I need to make sure... that his plans, and the plans of anyone else even remotely associated with him, never come to fruition."

She rose and took a few steps forward, seating herself in the middle of the bench, a little bit closer to Stirling. He arched his eyebrows slightly, his eyes welling up as he looked at her, but he remained seated exactly where he was.

"Stirling, please..." she pleaded, "you need to do the entire world a favor." He looked at her quizzically. "You need to move forward. You need to to preserve the integrity of what you've always been fighting for. You need to keep doing what you were born to do from the moment you realized why you're really here... You need to keep saving lives. And preserving the ideal of what it truly means... to be human," said Angie.

After a pause, she added, "Please, Stirling... don't die for me."

In that instant, Stirling rose from the corner of the bench where he was seated. He cautiously approached her, and gazing into her lovely face, he slowly sat down and took her by both hands. They looked at one another lovingly, and internally embraced the undying love they always had from the moment they first met. He leaned forward, and they kissed tenderly.

"Excuse me, sir?" a young female voice spoke from behind. Her name was Tia, and she was a pleasant employee from the Audubon Zoo.

Stirling turned to face her, and as his and Tia's eyes connected, he realized that Angie was no longer there. The moment had passed, but the memory would surely remain with him forever.

"Yes, is something wrong?" asked Stirling.

"Not at all, sir. It's just that the zoo is going to be closing shortly."

Stirling nodded. "Of course... Look..." He glanced over at the name tag pinned to her forest green top. "...Tia, I was hoping I could just have a moment with Lilia, the snow leopard inside the lair over here."

Tia seemed puzzled by the request, but she was incredibly polite. "Sir, the animal exhibits are only meant for observation. You are welcome, though, to take photos if you like."

"I'm sorry, I should have mentioned to you that I'm Bernie's friend, Dr. Kent Stirling."

When Tia realized who he was, the look on her face quickly changed from bemused befuddlement to warm acceptance. "Dr. Stirling, my apologies. I had no idea. Of course, please feel free to take some time with her. She's been so amazing. Mr. Llewelyn did mention that you all were looking to find a permanent home for Lilia... Is that why you're here?"

Stirling arched his eyebrows and smiled slightly, almost as if he was indicating in silence that he probably would be taking her back soon.

"I understand," said Tia. "Well... we'll certainly miss her. Please feel free. Just go around the fence and walk through that gate. The code is 0218. I'll be back in about a twenty minutes."

"Thank you, Tia."

As she walked back towards the other exhibits to continue making her nightly rounds before closing, Stirling went to the entry gate to Lilia's lair. He entered the code and walked in, closing the gate behind him. He approached her moving slowly and cautiously and knelt before her. At first, they simply locked eyes and stared at one another. He then slowly raised his hand and began petting her affectionately across her head and back. She leaned towards his hand and proceeded to lick it as a gesture of warmth and caring. Then he came close and embraced her. The love Stirling and Lilia shared was mutual and unconditional. And right now, this was a moment he treasured and needed. She was his calm before the storm.

24

Very close to Tulane University was an abandoned football stadium. The field was desolate, immense, and during the evenings, appeared unusually sinister in its oddly enveloping pill shape. The two goal lines were still intact, between 50 and 100 yards, and the tiered structure of the stadium still maintained the original design which allowed spectators to either stand or sit to view the spectacle of the game. It was both ominous and impressive in equal measure, especially now that it was completely untouched and empty, at least, in this section of the stadium. The lights were notably dim, the greenery of the field floor was still well-groomed and maintained. And at the far ends of each goal line, there were two curiously placed glass boxes, almost the sizes of tool sheds. They were transparent, but they were dark on the inside. There were no plans regarding the fate of this particular stadium in the immediate future. There were no surrounding homes or businesses in this section of town, save for a store called Outdoor Universe, which was an enormous tri-level department store the size of a small shopping mall. that sold everything relating to camping gear, sporting goods and all the like related products involved with outdoor activities.

Outside, at the front entrance of the stadium, a six-person team of Ravenne Industries operatives was in combat gear and ready formation. They were there to take out a very specific target. All of them brandished light weapons including machine guns and sidearms with multiple clips and additional ammunition. Their outfits were dark, as were their shoes. As they approached the front door, they noticed a doorbell with a sign placed directly above it which said, "Ring for front door access."

The unit's leader, a woman of about 40,very hard in her look and demeanor, noticed the bell and thought it to be slightly curious. She lowered her chin to speak into the transceiver attached to the left side of her chest.

"Yellow 1, Yellow 1, come in, copy?"

Damon Chambers, leading his own six member team at the opposite side of the stadium interior, received and responded to the call through his own transceiver, saying, "Blue 1, this is Yellow 1. I receive you."

"We have an odd scenario here. This stadium is supposed to be abandoned, but I think we have a security detail on site because we need to ring a doorbell to access."

Slightly amused, Damon smirked sarcastically and responded, "Then ring the bell, and if they ask what you're doing there, just... show them your invitation."

The Blue Team leader knew exactly what Damon meant, and smiled wickedly. "Will do. We'll see you shortly," she replied.

"Copy that," said Damon.

They cut their transmission to one another, and without missing a beat, the Blue Team leader pressed the doorbell.

What followed was literally mind-blowing. The instant she pressed the doorbell, there was an explosion. The blast radius was expansive but precise blast radius, taking out the team leader and her fellow operatives. All six flew backwards, impacting the ground hard, completely decimated by the violence and concussive force of the blast. As they landed, some of their bodies were intact, but others had missing limbs. All were killed instantly by the unexpected welcome at the entry door.

As Damon and his unit proceeded below, exploring the bowels of the stadium, the sound of the blast posed a mere distraction and nothing more. From their vantage point, they couldn't really hear it clearly, and the rumbling of the blast sounded almost like a massive AC unit kicking on and into high gear. Nothing more. Damon had no idea one of his teams was eliminated in its entirety. He raised his hand and formed a closed fist, indicating that the unit should stop in their tracks. They had come to a metal door, leading to the outer portion of the stadium. The other entry doors had been made of wood and a surface composite like plastic. He grabbed the door handle gingerly and turned. The door opened, and everything was fine.

He lowered his hand, releasing his fist for the team's hold formation. They proceeded to move forward. As all six members walked through the door and proceeded another twenty feet forward, the door suddenly closed behind them automatically, as if their crossing its threshold had triggered some sort of remote timer mechanism switched on by bodily motion. One of them frantically walked back to try and open it. It was locked. Damon turned and looked forward. His eyes widened when a series of metal poles descended from the ceiling, smashing onto the ground below, then tilting forward, chasing them almost like rows of dominos caving in on them. The door suddenly opened, and Damon shouted the order.

"Get the fuck back!! Back to where we started!!"

In line formation, they reversed their marching orders and ran at full tilt to the opposite end, back to the outswing exit door from which they initially entered the bowels of the stadium. Damon was at the back of the line, and as the operative in front grabbed for the crash bar to push the door open, it happened.

Another massive explosion.

The flames and force barreling through the interior ripped the entire unit to shreds, except for Damon. He was saved by being at the back of the line. But there was now rubbish and stone debris cascading from above, pinning him down. He looked up, barely able to see anything through the smoke and dust, shaking off his fear and panic so he could focus on finding a way out. The weight of the debris holding him down was extremely heavy. As he surveyed the floor in front of him, all he could see were the bloodied and torn remains of his five fallen comrades. Nearly all of two of the black ops units for Ravenne Industries were now stone cold dead.

Damon strained with all of his physical strength to pull himself out of the rubble gripping his body, but the weight was too overbearing. He couldn't budge. Then he looked all around and caught sight of the one instrument that might save him from imminent disaster. His Mp5 machine gun had fallen out of his arms when he reeled backwards and landed on the ground following the initial impact from the explosion. If he could simply reach the gun, he could literally shoot out the surface of rocks and concrete which had him pinned down and make his flight to freedom. He stretched as hard and as far as he could with his arms despite being a few inches from being able to grab the weapon's shoulder strap. He screamed desperately as he struggled once more to reach it. It was merely a matter of inches.

Up above, on the actual football field, the dimly lit surroundings eventually revealed the sextet of approaching silhouettes, nearing the heart of the stadium. This was the third and final unit consisting of half a dozen more Ravenne operatives. They gallantly crossed the field and approached the power box that gave the stadium and field full-throttle electricity, resulting in the hot, white lights which would emanate throughout the stadiums during night games. As the team leader, a lean, sturdy-looking fellow of about 30, reached the power box, he leaned his head slightly to communicate a message on his transceiver.

"Yellow 1, this is Green 1. We are on the stadium floor. No sight of the target here, but the lights are on conservation reserve, so we need to pull the switch on the main power box unit to get a better view of our surroundings."

Damon heard the call, but his transceiver had ripped off his clothing when he was catapulted from the blast, and it was also lying on the ground near the Mp5. He desperately screamed out to his team member out of sheer rage and desperation, despite realizing that they could not hear him. "Don't do anything!! Leave the fucking power box!! Get away from there!!" shouted Damon.

The Green team leader tried to make contact with Damon yet again. "Yellow 1, do you copy. I can't make out your response."

He looked back at his other team members, who were all standing still with their weapons at the ready.

"Fuck... they're underneath the stadium, and he probably can't transmit."

The Green team leader scanned the dimly-lit perimeter carefully surveying every inch of the area. "Target is here..." he said. "I can feel it. We'll just have to shed some light on the situation."

And with that said, he flipped the switch on the power box.

The shining white lights immediately went on, giving ultra-bright illumination to the field and all of the seating areas encircling the entire enclosed outdoor space.

As they spread out carefully in twin formation, they were spaced out in pairs right by the south end zone. Suddenly a whizzing sound pierced through the air. The Green Team leader spun back around and was astonished by what he saw—a steel-tipped arrow penetrated the power box. The leader was perplexed. His enemy was there. Maybe if he called him out... he looked up at the sky and shouted, "Is that the best you've got?!" The team members chuckled, clearly not feeling threatened by anyone who'd bring a crossbow to a gunfight.

Then they heard the beeping, emerging from the power box. Within moments, the ground on which all six team members were stood rose up ever so slightly, giving way to the exposure of a trio of perfectly placed and positioned Claymore mines, which then detonated in three-way harmony.

The trifecta of explosions sent all six soldiers catapulting through the air like lifeless, floating dummies, their bodies ripped to shred by tiny steel fragments. They all crashed back onto the field with heavy, lifeless thuds, like bags of wet cement.

Down below, in the underground of the stadium bowels, Damon heard the rocking sensation of the blasts. Anticipating the very worst, afraid it would make even more rubble rain down upon him, he redoubled his efforts to get free. He was almost but not quite able to reach the strap connected to his Mp5. But above him was a low-hanging piece of metal pipe, protruding from the ruptured ceiling. The ceiling portion seemed stable enough that it wouldn't crush him if he tugged on the pipe, the length of which, if he could work it free, might be enough to hook onto the shoulder strap. He now focused his attention on the pipe, making that his urgent micro-mission. Sweating profusely and gritting his teeth, he edged his way closer to it, millimeter by millimeter.

On the body-strewn football field, a dense layer of smoke wafted through the air, and through it suddenly emerged Kent Stirling, surveying the aftermath of his brilliantly executed handiwork. He had concurred with Bernie Llewelyn that taking out Ravenne Industries and everyone within it was going to require both the tactical and surgical precision of a heart transplant, a procedure with which he was extremely familiar. Holding his preferred weapon of the Ravin R500 crossbow ,he surveyed the bodies carefully, stepping around each one with his weapon primed, just in case any of them happened to still be breathing.

Directly behind Stirling and unbeknownst to him, a phenomenon occurred that almost seemed like something out of an old issue of EC Horror Comics. Inside the end zone at the south end just next to one of those mysterious glass sheds, a portion of the earth literally began to rise, revealing a compact female figure wearing a scuba mask for protection. Quiet and stealthy in her movements, she appeared like a zombie rising from the dead because the earth carved coffin was cut out in this woman's exact measurements, so she fit inside the light burial space perfectly. All she had to do was leave a minuscule portion of the mask exposed, and she would be able to take in oxygen without stress or impediment. The dirt and earth rolled off her body. She was another Ravenne operative, but not just some rogue operative who'd been left behind. This was Agent Triple Z, Zara Zimmermann.

"Drop the weapon," she called out from behind Stirling.

When he heard her feminine voice, Stirling had been double-checking for signs of life of one of the members of the fallen third team. He dropped the crossbow turned slowly to face her. She was pointing a Mossberg pump action riot shotgun with laser sighting directly at him.

"Dr. Stirling... a pleasure to finally meet you."

Stirling suspected who she was, but he wasn't sure.

"I don't believe we've met..."

"Let's just say that I'm a very close friend of Iris's."

He hadn't observed the way she emerged from the earth and grass at the end zone, but he was struck at how she was covered in an unusual amount of dirt. His eye shifted over to the open mound of muck and mire behind her, and he connected the dots.

"Very clever hiding space," he said.

Zara was coy in her response, flirtatiously shrugging her shoulders. "I was warned about you, Doctor. You're not a man to be taken lightly, and by the look of things..." She gave a slight nod at the carnage of her fallen fellow agents. "...you clearly know how to take care of yourself."

Stirling, staring down the barrel of that Mossberg pistol grip shotgun, meticulously studied her eyes and body language. "What do you want?" he asked.

She stood directly in front of him, pointing her weapon at his head, with the transparent glass booth right behind her.

"It's what we want, Doctor... Your absolute and final extermination. For years, you've been an obstacle to the progress of both the Sandbox and Ravenne Industries. But I'm here to tell you without even the slightest degree of uncertainty... those days are over."

She pumped the shotgun, but Stirling wasn't even remotely fazed. He didn't flinch or move a muscle.

"Hands above your head," said Zara.

Stirling listened. He wasn't about to be combative or clever with a woman pointing a shotgun at his cranium.

"Any last words before I remove you from the face of the planet, Doctor?"

Stirling didn't react, let alone respond to her question.

"Very well… In that case, let me enlighten you to a fact of which I'm sure you're not even slightly aware… I actually owe you a debt of gratitude."

Stirling furrowed his brow as if her words puzzled him. Zara noticed his reaction.

"You see, thanks to you, I was gifted with the greatest rapture of my life provided by your beautiful friend, Tyler."

Stirling's eyes closed as he became silently enraged. The image of Tyler's sincere wide-open smile raced through his subconscious mind even as Zara held him at gunpoint. She could see she got a rise out of him, and it boosted her arrogance even more.

"You cared about him, didn't you… You loved him… almost as if he were a son."

She could see Stirling's steadily rising fury on his face, his eyes narrowing, the rage making his lips tremble. And he used that to his advantage, because it diverted attention from his thumb, which he moved surreptitiously to firmly press the winding button of his watch, unnoticed by his opponent.

"The bond between parents and children… It's a powerful thing," said Zara.

Stirling sneered, "It certainly is."

The glass booth behind Zara began to emit a discordant hum, as if it were revving itself up like a car engine. The lights inside it became brighter, and suddenly the images of two older people, a man and a woman both dressed in elegant evening wear, who had been huddled in the corner enshrouded in a pocket of darkness, now became crystal clear. Stirling shifted his eyeline as he looked directly over Zara's shoulder. The curiosity of what Stirling was looking at consumed her, and she glanced back to see what it was all about. Her eyes connected with the two people inside the booth. She gasped and suddenly turned pale, so emotionally shattered was she by the sheer terror of what she saw.

"Mama... Papa..."

The two older people extended their hands and tried to speak, but their voices were muted. Their mouths were moving, and by the way the words were forming as they spoke, the mother seemed to be saying, "Zara," while the father kept repeating, "We love you." A glass door opened. Zara couldn't contain herself—she rushed inside. The door quickly shut and sealed tight. Zara tried to touch them her loved ones, but there was a barrier between them, and she still could not hear their spoken words. She turned, completely livid, to face her nemesis, Stirling.

"What have you done my parents?? You bastard!! Why can't I hear them?"

Stirling said nothing. He slowly stepped back and retreated. As he moved away, Zara pointed the shotgun and fired at him. The booth didn't shatter—only shallow surface cracks appeared on the inside; the glass was inches thick, bulletproof, and the encasement merely cracked. She dropped the shotgun and ran to her parents as all three continued to pound on the glass, attempting to break through and connect. Out of sheer anger mixed with desperation,

Zara was unable to keep her tears from flowing. She pounded incessantly against the glass. Her parents felt her pain and cried as well, continuing to mouth her name and telling her how much they loved her.

At the same time, down below, Damon was getting close. With his remaining vestiges of physical strength, he was finally able to grab the dangling pipe from the ceiling above. Thankfully, it came loose without unleashing more debris upon him. Once in his hands, he reached out for the shoulder strap of the Mp5, hooked it, and pulled it towards him. Successfully reacquiring his weapon, he fired into the rubble that was weighing down on him. He kept his finger on the trigger until the magazine emptied and clicked. That was all he needed. Once there was enough of an opening below, he managed to slide out from beneath. He rolled out of the way just seconds before there was a creaking sound immediately followed by the remaining fragments of ceiling cascading down with a force that would surely have crushed him. His other rounds of ammunition had detached from his body during the initial blast, and there were no other weapons to be found. All he had was his sidearm, a 9mm Walther PDP with an extended silencer. He cocked and holstered it on his pant leg. Quickly, he dusted himself off and began to limp back towards the main field to see what had happened to his other team members.

As Zara's desperate struggle to shatter the glass barrier between herself and her parents became increasingly futile, she turned and raged at Stirling with tears streaming down her face. "You fucking parasite... Your precious Angela Miller... the cunt deserved to die!"

Once Stirling heard that, any remaining iota of mercy he felt towards Zara instantly disappeared. He coldly pressed the wind button of his watch one more time. Right away, there was a crackling sound inside the glass booth, as if something within was on the verge of short circuiting. Zara turned her attention back to her parents, and in that instant, the glass barrier dividing them dropped. But as she reached out towards her mother and father, they disappeared into thin air. The truth was made clear. They were holograms.

Seconds later, Damon appeared at the opposite side of the field, running towards Zara, trying to warn her, but the doctor's next move unveiled itself all at once like a house of falling cards as Damon screamed, too late, "Zara, noooooo!!!"

In a fit of unparalleled fury, Zara pulled out her Glock 18 machine pistol and fired at the glass, trying to kill Stirling. Instead, she lit the fuse. She went up in smoke as the glass booth exploded like a powder keg, sending shards of glass and steel all over the field. The shock wave of the blast sent Damon reeling backwards as a shower of glass fragments descended all over him. Stunned, he looked across the field and saw Stirling approaching him. The mounting rage coursed through Damon as he screamed, "Stirling!!!"

Stirling stopped in his tracks, and the steely eyed gaze of the killer he could easily become glared right back at Damon.

"Come and get me," said Damon in a hushed, assertive tone.

Stirling heard him, and gladly obliged. Damon got up and began to run across the field, towards the exit and out into the street. Stirling had a keen sense of focus and knew there was only one place where Damon could run and hide. As he trotted after him, he unholstered his custom made Beretta 92SB, which had recently been modified by Bernie Llewelyn. Exiting the stadium, Stirling gave chase as he saw Damon head to the only place where he could take refuge.

Damon was now in the parking lot of the Outdoor Universe multi-level department store across the street from the abandoned football stadium. He sprinted quickly towards the loading and receiving area. There were three store employees standing by the service truck. The leader of the group spun around and motioned for Damon to slow down. Damon, barreling towards them, drew his pistol. Three quickly administered shots to their heads and all three store employees fell to the ground, dead. The service door was ajar. Damon quickly made a beeline for the massive store inside.

Stirling was close behind him. He slowed down to check on the three employees. Immediately noticing the headshots, he knew that, sadly, they had all been ruthlessly killed by Damon. He exhaled and walked purposefully towards the door. This was the moment that he and Damon had been waiting for... their final confrontation.

As he entered, Stirling held his weapon tightly with both hands. He was awed by the sheer size and scale of the store; in all his travels, he had never seen anything like it.

The most interesting factor of the brightly lit store was that even after hours, it was illuminated by primary-colored neon strobes and Mondrian lights placed perfectly along the corners of each floor. This highlighted some of their top selling items to maximum effect. There was also a conventional elevator as well as an escalator at the center of the store leading up to the second and third floors. The escalator was in motion, and the radio was playing a selection of songs at a high volume. Currently playing was the classic Jefferson Airplane song, "White Rabbit."

Stirling noticed all the various camping gear, ski equipment, tennis gear, volleyball paraphernalia, and countless other items. The store was stocked to the nines with absolutely everything relating to sports and the great outdoors. He walked towards the escalator and made his way up to the second floor. This was where the children's gear and clothing for sports such as surfing, skiing, and water polo were displayed. After a quick but thorough scan of the second floor perimeter, he stepped back onto the escalator and made his way up to the third and final floor. Still, there was no sign of Damon Chambers.

Stirling kept his Beretta drawn and tightly held in both hands as he swept each corner. He was meticulous and exacting because he knew he was up against a deadly adversary. "White Rabbit" continued to echo throughout the cavernous store. He now stood by the railing at the center of the third floor, overlooking the floors below. The top of the extra-wide elevator was stationed on the second floor just beneath where he stood. Stirling suddenly shifted his attention to a series of mannequins, dressed in tennis gear for both men and women. The primary sports focus here on the third floor was apparel and equipment for tennis, volleyball, and soccer.

He moved catlike across the aisles, scanning each row and end cap with military precision, Beretta drawn and at the ready. Swiftly, he turned and realized that each floor had been searched and visually dissected with no sign at all of Damon Chambers. Stirling thought to himself that he may have disappeared, but there was no indicator that he would run and hide. He stood back at the railing overlooking the other floors, noticing the mannequins dressed and posed elegantly below, and instinctively, something told him to turn around. And in that instant...

Like a banshee, Damon hurled himself from behind one of the tennis-garbed mannequins where he had been hiding all along. He tackled Stirling full-force, and they both smashed against the railing. The impact of that initial blow knocked the Beretta 92SB out of Stirling's hand, and it fell all the way down to the ground level below. Stirling instantly struck back with a firm elbow to the face followed by a side swung Karate chop to the chest which pushed Damon back. It was a well-delivered combination. As Stirling pivoted his body backwards, Damon turned and arched himself forward grabbing Stirling's arms and flipping him across the floor, sending him crashing against the standing case of tennis gear including rackets, cans of balls and packages of wristbands, all of which came crashing down on him.

Damon was excellent, a supremely trained fighter with speed, stealth, and precision. His coordination was superb, and his anticipation of the next move was exceptional. As Stirling got back to his feet, Damon stood across the way facing him in fighting position, legs somewhat apart and fists clenched at his sides. Stirling was standing next to the enormous cage display housing all of the volleyballs and soccer balls. His hand was on the lever of the release which opened the caged box. They stared each other down like the primed combatants that they were, prepared for whatever came next.

"So, Doctor... I've been waiting for this moment for a long time... You ready for this?" hissed Damon.

Stirling gave him a slight smile, saying, "Only one way to find out."

As Damon took a few steps forward, Stirling dropped the lever of the ball cage. Instantly, the balls cascaded out of the cage like a furiously triggered avalanche. Hundreds of multi-colored soccer balls and volleyballs slid across the third floor as Stirling bashed, kicked and maneuvered his way through to meet Damon in the middle, where he knew they would ultimately clash and continue their fierce battle. Damon kicked his way through and delivered a thundering roundhouse kick which spun Stirling around violently, sending him back with the force of a sledge hammer as he fell on the ground next to a few of the mannequins. Damon charged forward, but Stirling saw his rage leading his technique, so he raised his leg, grabbed both of Damon's arms and flipped him backwards. The perfectly delivered defensive maneuver sent Damon crashing up against a volleyball net in which he got momentarily tangled. Still a bit dazed by the rock-hard kick Damon had laid across him, Stirling took the offensive by grabbing Damon off the floor and landing a firm fist to his midsection. But Damon was quick, even better than Stirling had anticipated. As he crouched, Damon planted his feet firmly on the ground, and in a single, sweeping move, tore through the mesh of the volleyball net and threw a hard closed side fist to Stirling's face, which knocked him back even further.

The extended version of "White Rabbit finally ended. There was a small gap of dead air, and the song changed to Nilsson's timeless classic "Jump Into the Fire." Damon rose from the ground, charging Stirling, who had made his way back near the railing of the third floor just above the elevator ceiling parked on the second floor. Sensing Damon's furious thrust forward, Stirling smoothly rotated his body to the side and delivered a full top-kick to Damon's midsection which connected perfectly, causing Damon to wince in pain and grab his stomach. Enraged by the mere notion of Stirling gaining the upper hand, Damon took no notice of the railing behind Stirling, and like a bull in a China shop, he tackled him, sending them both over the railing. Their bodies landed on the extra-wide elevator ceiling which was the epitome of white, clean, and neat. It was spaced out almost like a large wading pool because the elevator was capable of housing twenty people comfortably. With the width and expanse of a freight elevator, it doubled perfectly as a fighting floor. Stirling and Damon both shook off the impact of the drop, and as soon as they scrambled to their feet and faced off, they began to strike.

Both men were equally adept and skilled at full-throttle street brawling, and fists were connecting with flesh and bone in a major way. Hard rights to the face and solid lefts to the side and gut. It was a coarse pummeling, and they eventually grabbed one another again and flew off the elevator ceiling, landing on the case of baseball gear below on the second floor. The case was loaded with baseball equipment including aluminum bats, mitts, balls and catcher's gear.

Fast as lightning, Damon spun off the table, grabbing an aluminum bat at the same time as he landed feet first, ready to strike. Stirling, equally adept at shifting maneuvers, tucked and rolled across the floor and stood right next to the section for horseback riding and equestrian-related items. He immediately noticed the extra-large pairs of horseshoes hanging on a display bar, connected by a short section of chain, long enough to be spun and used almost like the chain-and-sickle weapon of the Ninjas. Stirling noticed how Damon was brandishing the aluminum bat, and it was clear that whatever found objects could be used and transformed into lethal weapons was the order of the day. They both paused momentarily and looked up at the top of the store where the speakers were placed and from which Nilsson's "Jump Into the Fire" was projecting. The acoustics in the store were superb; it sounded like a concert performance.

Stirling tilted his head as they faced off, ready for their next round, but taking a moment to listen to Nilsson's marvelous song, seemingly in approval.

Damon noticed, and echoed Stirling's sentiment. "Great track," he said.

Stirling nodded his agreement. Then it was back to business.

They approached each other and began to strike. As the steel horseshoes clashed against the aluminum bat, it became clear that the blows were not connecting with flesh because both were so adept at using their bodies as defensive weapons. But a break in the action came when Damon spun across the floor kneeling and landed a firm swing against Stirling's side. And whether by impulse or sheer brute force, Stirling took a massive side swing with the chain and the pair of horseshoes connected firmly with the side of Damon's face, cutting the skin and shattering his cheekbone. A stream of blood followed, spraying the wall like a water gun. Damon fell backward and hit the clothing rack of baseball uniforms, spilling the assortment of outfits all across the floor. In a gesture of frustration, he grabbed a baseball jersey and wiped the blood off his face. As he threw the garment across the room, Stirling spun the chain and carefully encircled him.

Frantically, Damon's eyes darted across the room as well as the downstairs section of the first floor. Squinting slightly to focus on something that captured his attention, he quickly dropped the bat and ran to the stairwell making a stealthy beeline for the first floor. Keeping an eye on his maneuvering through the store, Stirling saw what was directly in front of and below him on the first floor, so he doubled down and, grabbing the railing with one hand while holding the chain and horseshoe in the other, jumped over the railing. He landed below on a well-stacked row of cushioned sleeping bags, which he knew would catch him.

Instantly, a sharp, stinging blade lashed across Stirling's forearm. As Stirling he rolled to his feet and turned to face

Damon, he noticed the weapon he was brandishing. They were in the section of the first floor devoted to samurai/ninja gear, where the walls were adorned with everything from katanas to shuriken to nunchaku and everything in-between. Stirling was definitely familiar with the sword being utilized by Damon. It was not the traditional Katana employed by the samurai but rather the shorter, straight blade known as the Chokuto. There was one other Chokuto mounted on the wall in half of an X formation from where Damon had clearly claimed his weapon. The Nilsson track "Jump Into the Fire" ended. A small space of empty air, and it was immediately followed by the indelible 80s song by Laura Branigan entitled "Self-Control."

Stirling snatched the other Chokuto from the wall. He and Damon began to circle one another, very much in the traditional style of the Shinobi Ninja. They stood across from each other, weapons extended, while Laura Branigan seductively sung her evocative lyrics. Each man raised his sword to his face. Stirling could feel blood droplets fall to the floor from his forearm, but it was a flesh wound; he wasn't internally injured. After staring one another down a few final seconds, they struck at each other. The whooshing sounds of steel blades hissed through the air like two serpents lashing out, immediately followed by the furious clanging and clashing of dueling Chokutos.

As swordsmen, there was no doubt that Damon and Stirling were equally matched. Neither could connect and neither one landed a damaging blow save for the slash Damon administered to Stirling's forearm. They seemed to duel for an eternity, but in fact, a scant minute was all that passed. Growing increasingly impatient, Damon swung back and took a large swing attempting to decapitate Stirling. In stealth mode, Stirling dodged the perilous strike by rotating his entire body to the opposite side while raising his sword and striking forward at the same time. Damon was prepared and deflected the blow, but it allowed Stirling enough weight and momentum to push forward. Now their blades were connected and crossed as they stood face to face. The sharp steel was mere inches from their faces, and Stirling, employing the maximum force of upper body strength he could muster, pushed slightly and the edge of the Chokuto sliced down the side of Damon's face, causing him to emit a cry of pain and disconnect from their crossed sword formation as he lunged back. Stirling stepped back as well, never losing eye contact with Damon while moving backward slowly but defensively.

Damon began to display some circus-like tricks with the sword, spinning and twisting it furiously at a heightened, almost dizzying speed. Stirling merely stood and watched. He had neither the patience nor interest in showing off with ostentatious parlor tricks to intimidate his rival. In a lightning quick motion, Damon lunged the sword at Stirling, hoping to possibly impale him against the wall. But Stirling was too fast—he dodged it perfectly, allowing the Chokuto to simply penetrate the wall and become stuck there. Damon was now unarmed, and Sterling wanted this to be a fair fight. He dropped his sword and waited for Damon to make his next move. They stared each other down like a pair of sleek cats. Damon stood next to a mannequin dressed in Ninja gear. He ripped off one of its arm with the idea of using the limb as a bludgeon. Stirling took a glance at the mannequin beside him, which was dressed in western apparel. He also tore off its arm and removed the fragment of garment stuck to the fingers of the hand.

They approached the center of the open floor on the first level. There was ample space here to fight capably and completely. Both were clearly wearing down, their energy reserves becoming depleted.

There were a few seconds of stillness as they stood across from each other, then Stirling lunged, Damon countered, and the battle continued anew. As a blunt instrument of brute force, the mannequin arms were surprisingly effective in how they so savagely mimicked Billy clubs or nunchakus. Stirling and Damon were both adept in their use of these weaponized limbs. They struck fast and hit hard, with each man connecting brutally to the bodies and face. Bloodied and battered, they fell against the displays of clothing and equipment as they struck at each other with everything they had.

Eventually, Stirling began to gain the upper hand. He swung and delivered a full-force clobbering to Damon's jaw, breaking it and sending a few of his teeth airborne. The hit sent Damon hurtling back, and his body cascaded against a display case full of clearance items, including sporting gear and apparel of all shapes and sizes. As Damon shook his head and regained his senses, he brushed. the rogue items away from his body and looked sharply to his right. Instantly, his eyes caught the shining glint of the weapon Stirling's Beretta 92SB. He smiled, spun around and quickly retrieved the weapon, aiming it directly at Stirling's head. Stirling froze and dropped the mannequin limb immediately. There was approximately a dozen feet of space between them.

"Just like that, Doctor..." panted Damon, satisfied. "And as you can see, I'm not just going to shoot you... I'm going to kill you with your own fucking gun!"

Stirling stared coldly at Damon without moving a muscle or saying a word.

In that instant, the Laura Branigan tune of "Self-Control" ended, and there was a prominent clicking sound that followed. The music playlist had concluded.

"Perfect timing...," gloated Damon. "Sounds like the concert's over. And now, Dr. Stirling... so are you."

Damon pulled the trigger and nothing happened. He pulled it again, and it clicked empty. One last time, and it still did nothing. In a fit of frustration, Damon tried to throw the weapon at Stirling's face, but it wasn't going anywhere. The Beretta was grafted to his hand. Damon's eyes widened in unknowing fear. Stirling winked at him. He desperately tried to rip the gun from his palm with his other hand, but it didn't work. Suddenly, a series of beeps emanated loudly from the gun. Damon trembled with a mixture of fear and hatred.

Stirling winked at him.

At the top of his lungs, Damon yelled, "Motherfucker!!!"

"Boom" replied Stirling very quietly.

Instantly, the Beretta ignited like a hand-grenade in Damon's hand, setting off a precise, calculated explosion designed to destroy only the brandisher of the weapon. His head instantly burst with a lemon-sized hole through the forehead and he fell back, hitting the ground like a stone. Damon Chambers was dead. Stirling approached him and looked down at his freshly transformed corpse.

"You're right, Mr. Chambers... It is over."

Bernie had programmed Stirling's Beretta with print recognition sensors so that only he could fire it. Although that technology had been used and implemented before, Bernie added the one additional caveat that the unwanted user of the gun would also lose their head if they attempted to fire it. As he caught his breath, Stirling looked toward the exit noticed a sign next to a gray access door with a crash bar—trash and disposal. Seeing the gave him an idea of how to dispose of Damon's dead body. But before any cleaning was undertaken in regard to the late Mr. Chambers and his crew, he needed to fix himself. He went to the camping gear section, grabbed an emergency first aid kit, headed to the men's room.

* * *

After his forearm was firmly mended and bandaged, Stirling strolled away from the Outdoor Universe store to the nearby parking lot where he had left the 1981 Lamborghini Countach. Once inside the car, he felt a soothing familiarity. He passionately treasured the vehicle, another of Bernie's many gifts he'd received over the years. He turned over the engine and cruised out of the parking lot.

On his way back to the city he mentally replayed and reviewed everything that had just transpired, the small battle from which he had emerged the victor. And as he looked out at the New Orleans skyline, he could think only about the single loose end that remained.

"And then there was one," he said quietly to himself. Then he shifted the Countach into third and sped into the unknown mysteries of the night.

25

Just east of the French Quarter, Marigny was a well-known local spot for live music and a more authentic experience than Bourbon Street. It was equally scenic and lively as the Garden District, but with a greater degree of seclusion from the hustle and bustle of the core sections of the Quarter. This was where Stirling resided while in New Orleans. His place was on the upper level of a very popular business situated just below the architecturally ornate structure housing them both. It was a restaurant/market called Menagerie, very popular on all nights of the week, but Stirling never minded the music or the bustling activity. It enhanced the overall atmosphere.

On this particular evening, his place was dimly lit as he came through the front door with renewed purpose. He tossed the keys on the foyer table and flicked on the switch which lit the entire interior of his home.

The knife flew through the air with deadly pinpoint accuracy, expertly thrown at him from across the length of his dwelling. The blade penetrated his right shoulder, stunning him and causing him to stumble backwards. When he looked up to see his assailant, he was not the least bit surprised to see her standing there before him...

"Iris," said Stirling.

Iris Ravenne wore a floral patterned form-fitting sleeveless dress, slit quite elegantly at the inner thigh to reveal every bit of that glorious length of leg she so flagrantly loved to flaunt. By the look of her, it appeared she was there to seduce Stirling as much as she was to eliminate him. She spoke with the confidence of a cat toying with a mouse. "I wish I could say that I was happy to see you, Kent. But the moment I saw you approaching the building, I knew right away that you had done what I least expected... you obliterated my entire team... didn't you?"

"Every last one," he smirked.

Iris shook her head, not so much in disbelief as with a resigned acceptance. "In a way, I knew that when I sent them on their way to deal with you, there was a very good chance I would never see any of them again. That's the one thing about you that's never changed, Kent... You've always been so predictable."

Stirling shrugged as he held his shoulder tightly to compress the wound and lessen the bleeding. He did not remove the knife, fully aware that pulling it out would worsen the injury.

"I'm happy to disappoint you," said Stirling.

Iris raised an unusual weapon—a tri-barreled knife launcher, created by her tech expert at Ravenne Industries. She walked across the floor sideways, keeping her eyes and the shooter trained strictly on Stirling. She had him in her sights, and this time, she was not going to fail.

"I suppose it was time, though... In hindsight, my team needed to be... replenished," she said.

Stirling cringed at this woman's ruthlessness. To think he had once known and loved her as Irina Contreras was staggering to him. He shook his head in disbelief.

"But thinking back..." she continued, "...I suppose the only one I'll truly miss... is Zara. She was excellent. She was so very, very good... at everything."

Stirling arched his eyebrows. His scorn and contempt for her was readily apparent. "She killed a very close friend of mine," said Stirling.

Iris looked at him with a nonchalant sense of bemused irony.

"Kent, please... when it comes to the task of killing, you, my dear, have it down to more than just a science... For you, killing is a way of life. You've transformed the act of killing into nothing less... than an art form."

Stirling was disgusted hearing her analogies and interpretations. Killing was what Stirling detested more than anything in the world. But taking lives became necessary at times... such as when dealing with the Sandbox and all of its fringe-related organizations.

"And I'm sorry about your loss, Kent. Your truest loss..."

Stirling looked at her with piqued curiosity.

"Angie Miller. It was unfortunate, but sadly, she was an obstacle we no longer had the luxury of indulging with her indignant ways and obstinate manner. I needed the Rhodesia En Rouge to complete my task, but now that Miss Miller is gone, my organization has been eradicated, and you are soon to be joining all of them, I guess that only leaves one thing left for me to do... start over."

"Good luck with that."

Iris couldn't help but to snicker as she got closer to Stirling, keeping the hand-held blade launcher pointed at his skull.

"Kent, I just have one question for you. Angie... was she really that good?"

Stirling seethed, but remained still and didn't dignify the question with a response.

"I mean... a woman like that. You could hardly... begin to think that she compares... with a woman like me."

Stirling mustered all his inner strength to keep from lunging out and strangling her. She was in full toxic mode. And as Iris kept the weapon pointed precisely at Stirling's head, she began seductively licking the fingers of her other hand.

"How about it, Doctor? One last dance... for old time's sake?"

Slowly, she began to move her hand across the length of her dress slit, revealing her perfectly shaved landing strip. Even as she twiddled herself vigorously and moaned ecstatically, Stirling wasn't the least bit moved or aroused.

She fingered herself to climax and licked her fingers clean, never losing sight of Stirling as her target, ready to shoot him through the head with her unusual weapon. She was truly a sexual devourer and a destroyer of lives to boot.

Like any cat with any mouse, having had her fun, Iris was now becoming bored.

"Kent, I'm through with you... New beginnings also mean bringing closure to the remnants of the past. That includes... Operation Beech Grove."

Stirling was stunned to hear her mention it.

"That's right... You think our mutual benefactor, Max, is the only one in pursuit of absolute power...? Hardly. Of course, it stood to reason that as his prodigal son, he wanted you by his side, but now that he's in the wind and in pursuit of other scientific insanities, I am prepared to bring it to fruition once and for all... Bernie doesn't have the plans. We know that now... This means that the only one who could be in possession of them... is you."

"Am I?" asked Stirling.

Iris shifted her aim a few inches to the left and fired the knife launcher. The blade flashed by Stirling's ear, barely missing him, sticking into the wall with potent force.

"The next one is going through your forehead… I'm going to ask you one last time… Where are the plans… for Operation Beech Grove?"

Stirling exhaled, and dutifully acquiesced to her request. With a resigned sigh, he said, "Through that door. On the desk."

Iris quickly glanced behind her at the bedroom door to the right. She immediately shifted her focus back to Stirling as she carefully turned around and proceeded to walk backward in the direction of the door to which he had gestured.

"Put your hands above your head, Kent… I don't want you pushing any hidden buttons or lowering any secret levers… I know you all too well."

Stirling did as he was told, wincing in pain from the knife still protruding from his shoulder.

Iris now stood at the door with her left hand firmly holding the knob. She was about to turn it.

"Do I need a key?" asked Iris.

Stirling shook his head, and she opened the door. Quickly, she turned to look inside and was momentarily flabbergasted by the look of the room's interior…

It was completely green with plants and small trees everywhere. There were even ambient sounds of birds and waves emanating from the wall mounted speakers. The room had the look, sound, and feel of a little piece of the Audubon Zoo.

"Alright, Doctor, where is the desk?"

Iris turned back to face Stirling.

"It's a jungle in there," said Iris.

Stirling looked slightly above and over Iris's shoulder and Stirling gestured for Iris to look back inside. She did, and immediately the terror she felt so filled her soul that it tore the scream from her throat.

Lilia, Stirling's beloved Himalayan snow leopard, was right there. She saw that Stirling was injured and bleeding. She then shifted her intense gaze to Iris whose hand was trembling as she nervously emitted her final scream and fired the third and final blade from the knife launcher, missing Lilia by a foot. Lilia instinctively understood that Iris had hurt Stirling. That made her a threat. She leapt.

Lilia mauled Iris with furious strength and unparalleled wrath. This was vengeance for what she had done to Stirling. The leopard clawed at Iris's face and mercilessly bit her arms and midsection, tearing through and devouring whole pieces of flesh.

"Lilia!" shouted Sterling.

The big cat pulled away and went to Stirling's side, licking his hand as he reached out and affectionately petted her head.

Trailing blood as she crawled backwards towards the French doors leading to the balcony, Iris managed to pull her way back up to her feet to face Stirling. Her once beautiful face was now a scratched and shredded mess.

"You think this is over, Kent... You have no idea... what's coming for you... But I'll give Angie your regards when I see her... in hell."

Iris smiled wickedly, and Lilia's supreme intelligence told her instinctively that this woman was the enemy. Without receiving any signal from Stirling, she again pounced and attacked Iris at full strength, pushing her with all of her might. The blow sent Iris crashing through the French doors. Shattered glass rained across the balcony and onto the street below as Iris toppled over the ledge, screaming as she plummeted.

As fate would have it, a Sparkletts delivery truck was driving at modest speed just as Iris was descending and in mid-flight, the driver caught sight of her and slammed on his brakes, but he couldn't stop the truck from smashing into Iris's body, which sent her flying across the street. She exhaled her last breath impaled on the railings of the elegant patio of the 5-star restaurant known as Le Fin. It was a fitting demise for the woman Kent Stirling knew as Irina Contreras, but the rest of the world knew as Iris Ravenne, alias... the Raven.

The restaurant patrons screamed. Panic ensued, and the distant sounds of burning rubber and screeching tires echoed loudly across the vast New Orleans streets. The French Quarter was alive and bustling, but not in the way that was traditionally revered. Stirling peered furtively out the window and assessed the damage. He saw Iris's dead body and simply turned away, heading back inside.

Stirling spent the next hour mending his shoulder, carefully removing the knife, cleaning the wound, and sewing it closed with the necessary medical supplies he kept readily available in his own home. When he was finished, he poured himself a stiff drink and sat at his office desk. Picking up his phone, he scrolled through the contacts and made a call on speaker phone. The phone on the other end rang twice, and Bernie Llewelyn answered.

"Are you clear?" asked Bernie.

Stirling looked at Lilia, sitting next to him as he petted her softly on the head.

"We're clear here," replied Stirling.

"We?" asked Bernie.

Stirling smiled warmly as he looked over at Lilia. "Me and my girl."

There was a slight silence. "Of course... How is she doing?"

Stirling looked at her with great affection as he spoke. "Bernie... she saved me... Twice, now... this girl saved me."

Moved by Sterling's words, Bernie said softly, "No, Kent... You saved each other."

Stirling embraced her closely, and Lilia purred as she rested her head upon his shoulder.

"Son?"

"Yes?"

"Iris?"

There was an extended silence.

"Kent?"

Stirling heaved an exhausted sigh. "Finished... All of them. We won't be hearing anything else from Ravenne Industries... or The Raven."

In the distance, Stirling could hear the commotion outside his home, augmented now by the incoming sounds of wailing sirens.

"Bernie, on a related note... Get local cleaners over to my place here in the French Quarter ASAP. We need a total make-over and disposal unit. Lay down and smooth out all the details for our contacts in local law enforcement here. This doesn't need to make news headlines. And please do it quickly."

"Of course, as soon as we end this call," replied Bernie.

"Thank you... One more thing. Please make the necessary arrangements for Lilia and I to assume permanent residency where you and I previously discussed."

There was another momentary silence between them.

"Are you sure you're ready for this?" asked Bernie.

"Yes, Bernie... We're going home."

* * *

Known as The Garden Isle, Kauai was renowned for its spectacular natural beauty, featuring dense rainforests, winding rivers and dramatic geological formations. The island boasted stunning features like the Napali Coast with its towering sea cliffs and the majestic Waimea Canyon. From the emerald valleys and jagged cliffs of the interior to the white sand beaches, the scenery varied from the wet and lush to drier, more arid areas. However, the island had distinct microclimates, with the north shore being wetter and the south shore drier, resulting in varying scenery and weather patterns across the island.

Three months had passed, and it was safe to say that Stirling was settled in firmly and comfortably to this island paradise he now called home. The '81 Lamborghini Countach pulled up and parked in a massive lot situated somewhere between the north and south shores. This was a forest and jungle preservation society which resided over and provided solace and safe haven to special breeds of animals from around the world. It was a close neighbor and ally of the Kauai Animal Education Center, located in Kapa'a. The center was always trying to expand and refine its surroundings, and in doing so, they had perfected the creations of some wonderfully simulated environments which mirrored the indigenous regions form which some of their beautiful creatures originally came.

One of their happiest residents was Lilia. She was surrounded by a gorgeous natural setting that was the spitting image of the glorious Khangai Mountains where she was born. In fact, she was happier than ever here, for a few reasons. Not only was it a vivid and enriching memory of her native homeland, it also struck a delicate balance between primal enchantment and the bellowing sounds of the place she always knew as home. The tropical birds and even some neighboring feline companions were her close friends and doting companions. Lilia could not have felt safer or happier being here, but that happiness was always reinforced when she received a visit from her closest friend on two legs...

Stirling was standing across the way, watching her drink from the crystal blue lake just next to her cave dwelling where she slept. When their eyes connected, he smiled and waved to her. Immediately, her head rose from the water, and she ran to his side, climbing by the fence and railing which divided them. He was easily able to reach over and hug her close while she stood. She licked his face affectionately. Their reunions were always warm and loving.

"Looks like the two of you are doing better than ever," said the familiar male voice from behind.

Stirling turned and smiled from ear to ear when he saw his colleague and dear friend.

Bernie ambled up to him, and they embraced after a while of not being in touch with each other.

"Great to see you," said Stirling.

"Same here," replied Bernie. He looked over at Lilia and he petted her face affectionately. She knew Bernie, and was very fond of him. "Lilia seems happy here."

"You have no idea, Bern. This is her safe haven. Seeing her this way makes me feel... complete."

Bernie turned his attention back to Stirling. "You both seem happy. This was missing from your life, Kent. Now you're here, and..."

"I know what you mean. I'm finally feeling like this is where I'm meant to be. I'm actually putting together a new and improved cardiovascular wing at the Wilcox Medical Center, and for the first time in a long time… it feels like I'm… home."

"Listen, I've got a flight to catch. I'm actually in the process of completing a major rebuild and renovation at the place in Vail."

"Great to hear!"

"So as soon as it's done, I want you to come and visit." Bernie caught a glimpse of Lilia, who was listening, out the corner of his eye. "Both of you! You're both welcome." Bernie began to massage the bottom of her neck and rub the top of her head. "I think she understands me."

"Of course she does! She's amazing!" smiled Stirling.

"I mean it, Kent. Come see me."

"We'll be there," said Stirling, giving Bernie a warm hug. "Take care, and have a safe flight.

"See you soon," replied Bernie. He gave Stirling one last pat on the back before walking away.

Stirling turned back to Lilia and quickly looked down at his watch. He held her close and kissed the top of her head. "I have a meeting to get to at the hospital. But I'll be by to see you tomorrow."

Lilia kept her gaze on Stirling as he departed, turning back to give her a wave. When he was out of sight, the snow leopard casually strolled back to the clear blue lake of her paradise home to quench her thirst.

Stirling opted to take the slightly more scenic route out of the animal preservation park, looking at all of the neighboring exhibits and various makeshift homes of so many different animals from around the world. It warmed his heart to see all of this, and as he turned the corner, leaving the general park and exhibits, he walked a long outdoor corridor that vaguely resembled a hotel lobby. It was extremely wide and expansive as were the twelve foot bamboo pillars filled with stone and marble which gave them heft and strength to sustain the immense ceiling that preserved and protected tourists and locals from any rainfall during visiting hours. It was quiet, and there wasn't a tourist, employee, or local visitor in sight.

A text message came in on Stirling's cell phone, the sound of the notification echoing across the vast outdoor walkway. He looked down as he walked and began typing a response. One of the enormous bamboo pillars, imposing not only in their height but in their width, was just a few feet ahead of him. Stirling kept typing, and the moment he walked past the pillar, a powerful steel hand lowered by an unseen figure slammed him across the back of the head, knocking him out cold instantly.

* * *

Slowly but surely, Stirling came around. He was groggy and completely disoriented. His eyes opened, and he struggled to rack focus and get a clear view of his surroundings. The first thing he felt and noticed was that he was bound by metal contraptions hooked around his ankles and his hands. He was literally spread eagle, lying on his back across a large table. The surface of it was felt, akin to that of a billiard table, but this was a deep shade of scarlet, reminiscent of blood. It was round and mounted on a wall, and Stirling was affixed to it almost like a specimen in a butterfly collection. What he couldn't see was that there was a pair of twin daggers mounted on the scarlet table in a crossed sword X formation placed just above his head.

He tried to get a feel for this unfamiliar place. It was a cavernous room, similar to a ballroom one would find in a Viennese palace. The walls were divided and carved out with spaces for tall, rectangular windows and paintings alongside them. Elegant chandeliers hung from the ceiling. It was literally a window followed by a painting around the entire perimeter of the room, a decadent display of limitless wealth at its very peak of unchecked extravagance.

As his vision became clearer, he first took notice of the windows. It was unusual that he couldn't see anything above and beyond the clear blue sky, but there were long shafts of shadows which peered through some of the windows as well. This was a clear indicator that he was definitely somewhere high. An elevated place of some sort, but he had no idea where that could possibly be. Then he became attuned to the sounds. As he listened more closely, he could hear the distant sound of water and waves looming in the distance. There wasn't a preponderance of them, but the beckoning presence of water was definitely near the immediate vicinity. Beyond that, he was at a total loss, utterly clueless as to where he was, or how he may have gotten here.

A rolling sound began to echo throughout the room, like an elevator making its gradual ascent. Sterling looked straight ahead. It was hard to make out any semblance of a door but the noise was getting closer. Stirling's intuitive instincts did not fail him. As he continued to stare straight ahead, what looked like the beige colored wall opened to reveal an elevator interior.

Five figures walked out. Their silhouettes were the only thing Stirling could initially make out as they stepped out of the elevator in unison and proceeded to approach him. Their footsteps clicked across the hardwood floor, the sound of both dress shoes and heels. As they got closer, Stirling was gradually able to make shapes and bodies out of the shadowy forms. It took longer to discern their faces because the room's chandeliers weren't illuminated. There was only long shards of natural light streaming through the windows, further obscured by the shadows of whatever objects were on the outside.

There were two females and three males, dressed in tailor-made grey business suits and formal footwear. They looked like models who had just walked off the latest fashion runway. But as the figure in the middle moved a bit slower, the face began to take on form and features. In his heart, Stirling had a bad feeling this may have been the person behind his capture, and he was right... Max Thulin stood before him, focused squarely on Stirling with a grim and dour expression. Magnus, his constant bodyguard and driver, was another of the men. Stirling didn't recognize the other man or the two women. Slowly, they stopped beneath the stunning archway with dual statues of angels at each side. There was a five-step drop which Thulin walked down as he approached Stirling. God only knew how many years it had been, but the memories suddenly came rushing back. Stirling knew that often the worst memories were the most vivid.

"I suppose this day was inevitable," said Thulin. Stirling arched his eyebrows, surprised to hear the first thing out of Thulin's mouth. "You don't agree?"

"Max, you... always had a way with words. I've spent decades, quite frankly, trying to forget that you were ever a part of my life."

Thulin slowly nodded his head in disbelief. He always kept his true emotions close to the vest, never revealing anything like anger or pleasure. This is what made him the master manipulator he had always been. "Your apparent lack of gratitude comes as a shock. You are the prodigal son. You, Kent, possess a gift that could unlock the key to a new beginning."

Stirling looked at the others and then returned his focus to Thulin. They were face to face, separated by no more than a few feet.

"Why Angie?" asked Stirling.

Thulin's expression changed to one of curiosity. "Excuse me?"

"Angela... Denise... Miller... Why did she become... another one of your expendable assets?"

"Really, Kent, you can't possibly think that I sanctioned or had anything even remotely to do with Angela's unexpectedly tragic demise?"

"The thought had occurred to me."

A glimmer of disappointment, apparent even to Stirling, flashed across Thulin's face. Averting his gaze, he walked over to one of the tall, rectangular windows and focused on the view outside as he continued. "After raising you, putting you through the best medical school in the world, training you, preparing you for what would eventually become your life's work... you still don't really know me..."

"What's that supposed to mean?" asked Stirling.

"I loved that girl, Kent."

Stirling closed his eyes.

Thulin turned back around to look directly at Stirling as he continued. "I loved her as I did you. You were both... my children, and you were both blessed with the same uncanny gift that I have yet to encounter in anyone else. I wanted you both together, by my side, bringing this dream to fruition in a way that would have made humanity blossom like we never could have imagined. The world... surely would have been a better place. But the fact that Angela died as she did at the hands of the Raven... I suppose that, in a way... it was my fault."

The silent rage simmered once again deep inside Stirling. He exhaled and looked coldly at Max Thulin. "Elaborate," he said.

Thulin took a few steps forward, away from the window. His minions, including Magnus, remained still, watching and listening intently to both of them.

"Kent, one thing the Sandbox never did was encourage fraternization amongst our operatives. Especially the ones we were grooming for bigger and greater things..."

"That has absolutely nothing to do with Angie or Iris Ravenne." said Stirling.

Thulin actually raised his tone ever so slightly, saying, "It has everything to do with them!"

Puzzled by his remark, Sterling focused completely on what Thulin was saying.

"You asked me to elaborate, and that is precisely what I am trying to do," Thulin continued.

With an almost imperceptible nod, Stirling said, "Go on."

"Iris Ravenne was a street urchin when we found her. Eking out a miserable adolescent existence on the streets of Paris. She was ramshackle in her ways and demeanor, but she had a feeble glint of potential in her eyes. I saw it the day I first met her because she tried to pick my pocket, believe it or not."

Stirling couldn't believe what he was hearing, but he paid full attention.

"I offered her the opportunity of a future," Thulin continued. "One where she could take full advantage of her gifts, which we eventually discovered through trial and error. Where she could harness those gifts to create a better self. The best version of her. She had been orphaned. She knew her chances of survival on the streets were extremely slim. And she knew, instinctively, that we were more than just a way out... We were her shot at a second chance."

Thulin toke a few paces as he spoke. "We taught her. Trained her. She was a quick learner, and she moved up to the ranks of top operative sooner than expected. But in time, she met a gentleman named Philo Gabin, and I suppose you could say... that was the beginning of the end."

"I don't understand," said Stirling.

"Gabin was being groomed for international liaison duty, but he was also in the midst of a passionate affair with Iris. They were young and in love. But you see, Kent... when it comes to being deep undercover, that type of situation can only lead to failure, or worse. This is why we never encouraged or endorsed the idea of any of our agents getting involved with one another because it was always a recipe for imminent disaster, no matter what the circumstances."

As he took it all in, Stirling glanced for a moment at Magnus, who seemed distracted by the sound of the lapping water outside the window. Then he turned his attention back to Thulin, asking, "And what became of Gabin?"

Thulin came closer to Stirling, once again facing him eye to eye. "He was eliminated. Made to look like an accident, of course. But nevertheless, he became a liability we could no longer afford because... Iris was our priority."

"Why am I not surprised?"

"I'm afraid it didn't end there." "Iris—what happened to her?"

At first, Thulin couldn't answer.

"Max?" said Stirling a bit more forcefully.

"She was pregnant with Gabin's child... We allowed her to carry the child almost to full term, but again, an operative couldn't serve the global interests of the Sandbox while being a parent at the same time."

"What did you do to her?" asked Stirling.

"Inevitably, she realized what we had done to Gabin. It enraged her. Drove her mad, put her completely over the edge. And I would be damned if I was going to allow her to lose that child."

Stirling's heart sank like a stone. His eyes widened because he knew innately the extremes to which Thulin was capable of going in order to exercise total control.

"You didn't..." said Stirling.

Thulin nodded reluctantly in the affirmative. "Eight months along, we induced her, with a general anesthesia of course, and brought her child into the world safely and without problems via Caesarean section. A healthy, beautiful girl. No complications. We had watched over and taken very good care of Iris throughout the course of her pregnancy."

Stirling was quietly stunned. Shocked as he had never been before. "When we were together, and I knew her as... Irina, she had told me that she had had a child, but the child was lost at birth due to a series of complications. She conveyed the story to me with such conviction, she was beyond anguished just remembering the details and telling me the story. I trusted her with everything... Of course... I believed her."

"Don't blame yourself, Kent. Why wouldn't you? After all... the two of you were in love."

In that moment, Stirling knew that no matter how much veiled empathy Thulin seemed to have for his reminiscence of the history of Iris Ravenne, it was all a ruse.

"What became of Iris's daughter?" asked Stirling.

"She was adopted... by a wonderful family. People that would adore her. Look after her. And see to it that she would grow to realize... her full potential. They care about her, Kent."

Stirling was taking it all in, absorbing the tragedy behind the history of the woman he once knew and loved.

"And Iris?" asked Stirling.

"I'm afraid that's where I become... indirectly responsible for the woman she became," said Thulin.

"How?" asked Stirling.

"She became filled with hatred for everything she had believed in... the organization, her assignments, her contributions to the world as a whole... In doing so, she severed all ties with the Sandbox and with me. By that time, she'd moved to the Yucatan, where she met the Contreras family. They brought her into their home and eventually their lives. That was when you met her. And when she realized the priceless value you possessed to our greater plans within the Sandbox, she decided to leave you to pursue her own agenda away from all of us... That was the day Irina died... and the Raven was born."

"You fucking bastard," Stirling said quietly. Thulin raised his eyebrows, a bit stunned by Stirling's reaction. "Your calculated agendas to create your own little legion of super-soldiers. It was never at the benefit of those you brought into your precious inner sanctum... It was always just to feed and enhance the greater cause. Your madman's lust for power and a new... world order. Whatever humanity you may have once possessed was decimated a long time ago... And Angie... Iris... Myself... You never cared about any of us... It was always about molding us... so that we could serve you. All we were to you, Max... was your servants. Nothing more."

"Kent, that is where you are so wrong... I loved you as if you were my own. Above all others, and this is why I need you now. I don't want us to continue taking lives for the greater good. I want us to start saving lives together, side by side, in a world free of strife and conflict. A world our children would one day be happy to inherit and call their own... After all these years, understanding your own very fragile nature, please tell me that you understand and that you'll stand with me side by side... as it was meant to be."

Stirling's eyes met Thulin's, locking in with laser focus. "What do you want, Max?"

Thulin actually smiled like never before, grinning from ear to ear. He was convinced that Stirling was ready to acquiesce and join him in his quest for a new beginning and a replenished society. "It's simple, Kent... Just show me the way to realize Operation Beech Grove."

Stirling dropped his head in disappointment. The smile on Thulin's face slowly transformed into a frown of concern. "Kent, please... I can't do this without you. I finally have the plans. The blueprint after years of scientific research to bring Operation Beech Grove to fruition. Please don't say no, Kent... If you do, I promise... You will live to regret it."

And that was the line in the sand being drawn. Stirling knew then beyond a shadow of a doubt that Thulin wasn't merely deranged... He was evil personified. But if it all came down to making a choice, he was more than happy to sacrifice himself to make absolutely certain that Operation Beech Grove would never see the light of day. "Max... You'll have to kill me. I will never take part in anything having to do with your madman's scheme. The world will fend for itself. And when push comes to shove... Life will always find a way."

Thulin was now noticeably livid, fury was emanating from his eyes. "That's your final answer?"

Stirling nodded affirmatively. Thulin then looked at his watch and pressed a button on the side of it. "Then know this... I'm not going to kill you... Make no mistake, you are going to die. But it's going to be slowly, and it won't be at my hands... No, I'm leaving this rather unenviable task to someone you once valued very highly. One of your nearest and dearest. Someone who you actually saved... a long time ago."

A few moments of silence passed between them as Thulin and Stirling merely glared at one another. Suddenly, the silence was broken when a bell sounded in the distance by the north wall. The elevator doors opened, and from within emerged a lone figure. Even at a distance Stirling could see that he was a tall, extremely fit man. The heels clicked slowly. It was a man with a heavy step. A formidable person with tremendous physical presence and strength.

He came down the five steps and emerged from the darkness into the light. As Stirling saw who was standing before him, it literally sent a chill down his spine. This was impossible. It couldn't be. But there he was, as real as Thulin and his minions—the one person on the planet Stirling never imagined he would see again.

The man approached Stirling and turned slightly to acknowledge Thulin, revealing his slicked back hair tied in a ponytail, and a metal sensor grafted into the back of his neck, on which a green light blinked. It was like a remote homing beacon implanted into the flesh, the same device that was embedded in the neck of the unknown man who had absconded with the plans for Operation Beech Grove that were hidden on the yacht in Bermuda.

"Exactly as we discussed... Understood?" spoke Thulin, finality in his voice.

The man simply gave a silent nod, remaining silent. He then turned to face Stirling directly, standing inches away from his face. Now it was clearer than ever, no escaping or denying it. It was him. Stirling could not begin to fathom how or why he was there. Slowly, the man raised his arm above and behind Stirling's head and removed one of the daggers from the wall. The glint of the dagger reflected over Stirling's wide open eyes as the man lowered it. There were twin spiked protrusions rising from the centerpiece housing the slender blade, and the oak wood handle was outlined with gold and silver inlays. The man brought the blade millimeters from Stirling's eye, but as he looked behind Stirling very carefully at the panel on the wall where the daggers had been stocked, his finger moved ever so slightly towards one of the bronze protrusions just to the right of the blade itself. His index finger curved around it. Stirling's eyes widened. A sly smile formed across the other man's face, and all at once, Stirling's memories with this man flashed before his eyes. They had fought side by side in Belize. Stirling had saved him from certain death in the Yucatan. And almost as if he had risen from the ashes... he was back.

It was Ignacio.

NAME: Steven Kobrin

LOCATION: California

DISTINGUISHING CHARACTERISTICS:

Lover of espionage novels, thrillers,
action-adventure stories, and sci-fi —
and expert on spy films and TV..

OCCUPATION:
Author of action/adventure thrillers.

CURRENT MISSION:
Sins of the Raven

NEXT ASSIGNMENT:
The next adventure of Kent Stirling —

THE MAN FROM BELIZE 3:
SERVANT OF THE EARTH

MORE GREAT READS FROM HENRY GRAY!

THE LAST STAGE by Bruce Scivally

In his final days, lawman Wyatt Earp dreams of one last showdown—gold, gunmen and love with his devoted wife, Sadie.

VEIL OF SEDUCTION by Emily Dinova

In 1922, journalist Lorelei Alba infiltrates a gothic asylum for "troublesome" women—and falls into the orbit of a dark, mysterious doctor.

THE UNDERSTUDY by Charlie Peters

A kidnapping plot during a high-stakes merger quickly unravels, exposing every flaw in a "perfect crime."

THE DEVIL IN THE DIAMOND by Gregory Cioffi

First on a WWII battlefield and later on a baseball diamond, two soldiers, once enemies, find themselves bound by history, family, and the game they love.

THE MAN FROM BELIZE by Steven Kobrin

Dr. Kent Sterling's perfect life in paradise shatters when his past as a government hitman catches up—and the Viper comes calling.

SINS OF THE RAVEN by Steven Kobrin

Dr. Kent Stirling returns to face adversaries from his past, forcing him to confront buried secrets and fight for his life before the sins he thought forgotten consume him completely.

A PRAYER FOR THE DAMNED by Joe Cornet

Bounty hunter Cole faces a deranged preacher and seeks a lost Confederate treasure in a town on the brink of violence.

SHELBY'S VACATION by Nancy Beverly

Shelby runs from heartbreak into the arms of Carol, a woman carrying her own relationship scars. Together, they discover love worth risking.

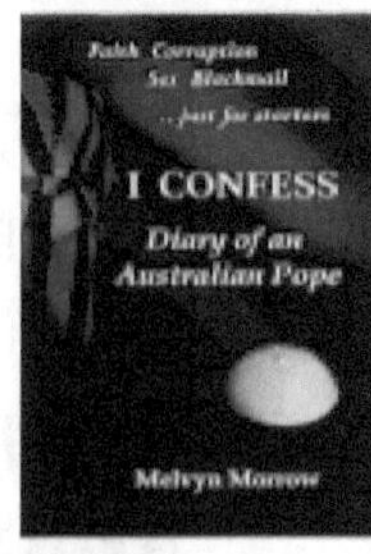

TOO MUCH IN THE SON by Charlie Peters

Mistaken identity plunges Leo Malone into a twisted web of lies, gangsters, and family deception.

I CONFESS: DIARY OF AN AUSTRALIAN POPE by Melvyn Morrow

An Australian pope battles corruption, blackmail, and betrayal as he tries to reform the Vatican from within.

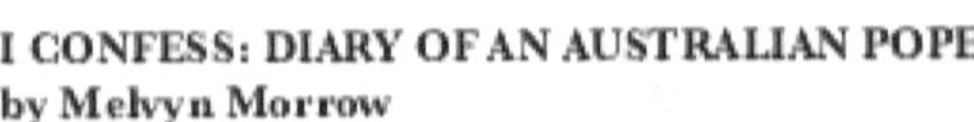

SEARCH FOR FUN WITH PAPA ROCK!

PAPA ROCK'S HORROR MOVIES WORD SEARCH
by Rock Scivally & Jeffrey Breslauer
150 puzzles based on horror films from *Frankenstein* to *Godzilla* equals 150 reasons to keep the lights on all night!

PAPA ROCK'S SON OF HORROR MOVIES WORD SEARCH by Rock Scivally & Jeffrey Breslauer
Looking for more Word Search chills? In this edition, monsters from the 1960s and 70s haunt every page!

PAPA ROCK'S REVENGE OF HORROR MOVIES WORD SEARCH by Rock Scivally & Jeffrey Breslauer
Looking for more monter Word Searches? Here you'll find the classic movie monsters from the 1980s and 90s!

PAPA ROCK'S ROMANCE MOVIES WORD SEARCH
by Rock Scivally & Jeffrey Breslauer
From *Casablanca* to *Titanic*, here's 150 Word Searches based on romance movies, so pick up a pen and turn on the love light!

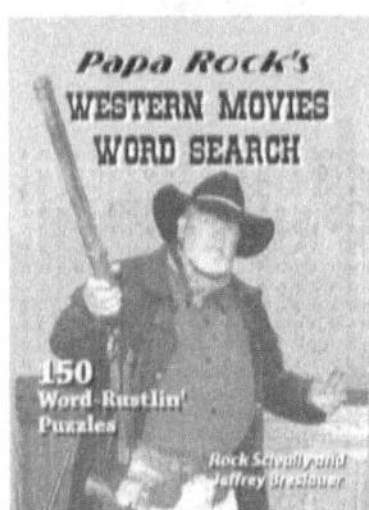

PAPA ROCK'S WESTERN MOVIES WORD SEARCH
by Rock Scivally & Jeffrey Breslauer
Hop into these 150 Word Searches and ride with John Wayne, Randolph Scott, Clint Eastwood, and cowboy favorites!

PAPA ROCK'S ANIMATED MUSICALS WORD SEARCH by Rock Scivally & Jeffrey Breslauer
You'll be humming along as you do 150 Word Searches on favorite animated musicals from *Snow White* to *Strawberry Shortcake!*

PAPA ROCK'S WAR MOVIES WORD SEARCH by Rock Scivally & Jeffrey Breslauer
Climb into your foxhole and challenge yourself with Word Searches based on classic war films from *Sergeant York* to *Saving Private Ryan*.

PAPA ROCK'S SCI-FI MOVIES WORD SEARCH by Rock Scivally & Jeffrey Breslauer
Relive science fiction's greatest hits with these Word Search puzzles covering classics from *Metropolis* to *Star Wars!*

PAPA ROCK'S DETECTIVE MOVIES WORD SEARCH by Rock Scivally & Jeffrey Beslauer
Solve 150 puzzles inspired by classic detective films, from Sherlock Holmes and Sam Spade to noir favorites.

PAPA ROCK'S MOVIE COMEDY TEAMS WORD SEARCH by Rock Scivally & Jeffrey Breslauer
From the Marx Brothers to Abbott & Costello to Martin & Lewis to Cheech & Chong, celebrate the greatest comedy teams with this laugh-out-loud puzzle collection!

Thank you for reading

SINS OF THE RAVEN

please leave a review on
the website of your
favorite bookseller

for more information, please visit

www.HenryGrayPublishing.com

Granada Hills, CA
"Select books for selective readers"